Broken Bow, M... ....
beginning to think of it as home.

Each day Clint Andrews put aside another piece of his Chicago persona. And more and more he liked the Montana farmer he was becoming. Until he thought about his career. He was now just a stone's throw away from a vice presidency at the prestigious firm of Garrity and Garr. Could he give it all up?

He recalled a conversation he'd had with Gail when he'd gone next door to see what he could do to help her parents on their farm. She'd asked if he was happy with his life.

"Pretty much," he'd replied.

"Which part? The farmer or the investment banker?"

"Both. A farming investment banker. It's what I always wanted to be when I was a little boy."

She laughed. "So, do you plan to stay here?"

Before he could reply, they'd been interrupted and Clint had been thankful. He still had three months here. And his kids were coming to spend time with him. Time he'd use to work through Justin's hostility and win Brad back over. And Megan—Clint smiled at the thought of his four-year-old daughter. She still thought her father was a knight in shining armor.

And of course, there was Gail....

ABOUT THE AUTHOR

Sherry Lewis's first Superromance novel, *Call Me Mom*, (January 1995) won her critical acclaim. "A fast-paced, action romance, with several wonderful characters" was one reviewer's opinion. Sherry's second, *This Montana Home*, proves again how talented this Utah author is. In addition to her success with Harlequin Superromance, Sherry has also published the first book in a new mystery series.

Although Sherry "can't remember a time she didn't want to be a novelist," she only began her writing career a few years ago. She enjoys traveling and always visualizes stories set in the places she visits. She loves long drives and often finds inspiration when she's behind the wheel. She also loves music, and of course, reading. Sherry is the mother of two daughters, Valerie and Vanessa.

Books by Sherry Lewis

HARLEQUIN SUPERROMANCE
628—CALL ME MOM

Sherry Lewis
THIS MONTANA HOME

Harlequin Books

TORONTO • NEW YORK • LONDON
AMSTERDAM • PARIS • SYDNEY • HAMBURG
STOCKHOLM • ATHENS • TOKYO • MILAN
MADRID • WARSAW • BUDAPEST • AUCKLAND

ISBN 0-373-70692-8

THIS MONTANA HOME

Copyright © 1996 by Sherry Lewis.

CHAPTER ONE

CLINT ANDREWS RUSHED from the barn into the bright June sunlight and stole a glance at his watch. Scanning the yard for his great-uncle Hal, he cursed under his breath and hurried toward Hal's truck. He was supposed to have met Hal half an hour ago, but he'd only now finished his morning tasks. Hal hated to be kept waiting.

Clint hated being late. After ten months in Broken Bow, Montana, he was getting faster every day, but he still took longer to finish than he should.

"I was just about to give up on you," Hal said as he climbed out of the cab of his truck.

"Sorry. I still can't keep up with you."

"You're doin' all right for a greenhorn." Hal grinned and leaned over a roll of barbed wire on the ground beside the battered old pickup Clint drove. "Grab that end and help me with this, would ya?"

After pulling on his work gloves, Clint lifted his end of the roll. He'd grown hard and tanned and lean over the past several months, and he finally looked the part of a Montana farmer, even if he couldn't match Hal job-for-job yet.

He gave the wire a shove, and the roll tumbled into the truck bed. "Did you get the tools in?"

Hal nodded. "Had to do somethin' while I was waitin'."

Tugging off his gloves, Clint tossed them through the open window into the cab of his pickup. "You want me to follow you, or are you riding with me?"

Hal made a face. "I rode in that rattletrap truck for ten years, I don't have to do it no more. Besides, it'll save time if you follow me. You can head straight over to Boone's place after we finish the fence."

Three days ago, Hal's longtime friend, Boone Knight, suffered a stroke that had laid him up completely, and his wife, Dorothy, hadn't left the hospital since. At Hal's suggestion, Clint had been making the ten-mile drive to the Knights' place every day and spending most of his workday there.

Before long, Clint had realized that Boone hadn't been managing well for some time. The place had a run-down look that only came with neglect. Clint hadn't discussed it with Hal yet, but the Knights needed more help than he could give them.

At least their daughter was coming home tonight, and Clint had agreed to pick her up at the airport in Billings. According to Hal and his wife, Phyllis, the daughter hadn't been home in several years; still, her being here should help.

As he reached for the truck's door handle, he heard the telephone ringing inside the house. He hoped it wasn't Leslie calling, then instantly felt guilty. But he needed today to run with as much precision as his days in Chicago always had. He wouldn't have time to stop until sundown.

He struggled with the Chevy's beat-up door and finally wrenched it free just as the back door of the house opened and Phyllis stepped onto the wide porch, shading her eyes with her hand.

"Clint? You've got a phone call. Long-distance."

Hal leaned out the window of his truck. "Who's that, your gal-friend?"

"Probably."

"Well, try not to take too long. The day's wastin'."

"I know. I'll be right back." Whether Hal disapproved or not, Clint had to talk to Leslie, but he'd have to cut it short and hope she'd understand.

Every day he put aside another piece of his Chicago-bred up-and-coming persona. And every day he liked this Montana farmer he was becoming a little better. Until he thought about his career. He'd spent half his life working toward this point, and now he was just a stone's throw from a vice presidency at Garrity & Garr. Duncan Morris was expected to retire within two years and, if all went well, Clint would have Morris's job.

If all went well. Two years ago, a stomach full of ulcers had perforated and landed Clint in intensive care. They'd put him back in the hospital again last summer so—on doctor's orders—he'd agreed to allow himself a year to heal. But he wouldn't sacrifice a day more. He wasn't about to lose the opportunity of a lifetime.

He started up the steps of the back porch, surprised that Phyllis had remained outside.

"It's not Leslie," she said quietly, as if she wanted to keep the other caller from hearing her.

That set him back half a step. "Who is it?"

Phyllis touched his arm tenderly. "I think it's Barbara."

Clint came to a complete stop and studied Phyllis's face. Her eyes were full of concern, proof she wasn't joking.

Even two years after the divorce, even with Leslie part of his life, Barbara's name sent a jolt of pain through him. "What does she want?"

"She didn't say."

He didn't want to talk to Barbara. Not right now. But she had custody of their three children, and she never called unless there was trouble. Praying none of them had been hurt, he hurried inside and snagged the receiver from the kitchen table where Phyllis had dropped it. "Hello?"

"Clint? God, you sound old. Is that what playing cowboy has done to you?"

"It's nice to hear your voice, too, Barbara. How are you?"

"Wonderful. Thank's for asking. I need a favor."

"And I'm dying to do you one." He dredged up his most sarcastic tone from the bottom of his soul. He hadn't had to use it much since the divorce and he'd kind of missed it.

"I'm sure you are." Barbara used her own sarcasm.

Clint took a deep breath and tried to bring his anger at his ex-wife under control. The marriage was over and done. She'd left him. She'd remarried and moved to St. Louis. She was ecstatically happy with Dave McAllister, and the kids were delighted with their new stepfather. Clint saw evidence of that every time they visited.

"What do you need?" he asked.

She hesitated, probably because she didn't believe he was abandoning the argument so easily. "It's the kids."

"Are they all right? Has one of them been hurt?"

"God, no." She laughed. "This isn't anything bad. The fact is, Dave's been given a wonderful new career opportunity."

"Great." Dave's career mattered less to Clint than the names of the seven dwarfs.

"He's going to South America."

Now, that perked Clint up a little.

"And he wants me to go with him."

Even better.

"So, of course, that's where you come in."

"How?"

"We need a place for the kids to stay while we're gone. I wouldn't ask this of you, except my parents have gone to Europe for the summer—"

"I'm their father, Barbara. This is where they should be."

"Of course." Said with real conviction.

"How long will you be gone?"

"At least a year."

"A year?" Clint's heart leaped, then immediately dropped. A year.

"I know it seems like a long time—"

Clint wanted nothing more than to have his kids with him, but he wanted a permanent arrangement. In a year, he'd get wrapped up in their lives once again, they'd pull him back under their spell and then Barbara would whisk them away again. Clint didn't think he could survive losing them a second time.

Barbara obviously sensed his apprehension. "Look, I wouldn't ask under any other circumstances—"

"When do you want them to come?" he interrupted.

"Next Tuesday?"

"Perfect." He didn't hesitate, even when he thought of Hal and Phyllis. They knew how much his enforced separation from the children hurt him. They'd jump at the chance to bring father and kids together.

"Really?" Barbara sounded surprised. "I can't tell you how much I appreciate this. They'll be so excited."

He didn't know whether he believed that—at least about Justin and Brad. When they'd visited at Christmas, Justin had been withdrawn and aloof. Brad had raved about Dave and Dave's new computer and Dave's new car until Clint had thought his heart would break.

But Megan... Clint smiled at the thought of his four-year-old daughter. Megan still thought he was a knight in shining armor.

He listened with half an ear while Barbara made promises to call with the kids' flight information. He made all the appropriate responses, gave her the shipping address so she could send the bulk of their things ahead and hung up.

But the entire time, his heart demanded that his head explain why it had put him in this position. He'd vowed never to leave himself open to hurt again. Now, the first time Barbara offered him significant time with the kids, he ran after pain open-armed.

He wondered what they'd think of him now—so changed from how he'd been when they last visited. Had the past few months made any difference in the way the boys felt about him? Had Megan joined her brothers in adoring Dave?

Pushing worry aside, he concentrated on his mounting excitement. A year would give him time to work through Justin's barriers and win back Brad.

And in twelve months with Megan, he'd probably never know a dull moment.

For the first time since Barbara sent him away, he felt a ray of hope. He might be able to salvage his relationship with his children, after all.

GAIL WHEELER FOLLOWED the stream of passengers down the boarding ramp and scanned the waiting crowd for her mother's face. Since Dorothy's frantic telephone call three days earlier, Gail hadn't been able to concentrate on anything. Sleep had eluded her, her appetite had dwindled and she hadn't been able to work.

So far, she'd been able to get only sketchy information about her father's stroke. Each time she'd phoned the hospital, her mother had been unwilling to tell her anything except that Boone was strong and healthy and that he'd recover quickly.

She wanted to believe it. Her father had never been sick a day in his life—had never even had a sniffle that Gail could remember—but the lack of detail bothered her and she suspected that her mother wasn't telling her the whole truth. Finally, she'd abandoned her efforts to deal with the crisis from San Mateo, California, and had booked a seat on the next flight to Billings.

She planned to use the drive to the hospital to draw a few more details from her mother. Face-to-face, Dorothy would have to be more forthcoming.

Passengers brushed past Gail and hurried away to meet connecting flights. A small family group huddled on one side of the concourse. A beaming young woman with a baby leaned into the walkway and searched the crowd. Across the wide passageway, a tall blond man wearing a straw cowboy hat over his medium-length hair leaned against a wall, one booted foot crossed over the other. Gail turned to look down the concourse, but couldn't see her mother anywhere.

The cowboy across the hallway uncrossed his boots and pushed himself upright, rising to an even greater height. In three strides, he stood beside her. "Gail Knight?" His voice—deep, bass and warm—did something strange to her insides.

She looked up and met his eyes, clear blue, the color of a Montana sky. "Wheeler," she corrected automatically, then hesitated. "Who—"

"Clint Andrews. I'm Hal Taylor's nephew."

Hal's nephew? Gail had known Hal all her life. As her parents' dearest friends, Hal and Phyllis had played a big part in her life. They had no children of their own, but they'd often had relatives staying on their place. If Clint Andrews had been one of the Taylors' summer visitors, Gail would have met him. And if she'd ever met him, she would remember him now.

He smiled down at her. "Actually, Hal's my great-uncle."

She flushed, embarrassed that her confusion had been so obvious. "That explains it, then."

"Your mother asked me to meet you."

Her face froze. "Why? Is Daddy worse?"

He touched her arm as if to ward off her concern. "No. His condition hasn't changed. She just didn't want to leave him alone at the hospital. I thought she'd told you."

"No." Gail tried to force away the sudden ache his words caused and the resentment that he knew more about her father's condition than she did.

"Did you check any baggage?" he asked.

She forced herself to speak. "Yes. Two suitcases."

"Then I guess we'd better claim them." He touched her elbow to escort her down the concourse. She was vividly aware of his hand, and felt warmth rush to her cheeks.

She walked quickly, tottering slightly in her low heels as she struggled to keep up with his long strides. Even when he noticed and tried to adjust his pace to hers, she had trouble matching his gait, and she wished she'd worn jeans and flats rather than this narrow skirt and heels.

Her head only reached the top of his shoulder, and she felt small beside him. Protected and comforted.

Her reaction surprised and disconcerted her. She'd been on her own since her divorce from Richard, and in those three years, she'd handled everything without help. She didn't want or need protection now.

At the baggage claim, Clint located her bags easily and retrieved them for her. He tucked the smaller bag under his arm and carried the larger one by the handle. Laying the flat of his other hand on the small of her back, he led her to the parking lot and a beat-up old truck.

Clint opened the truck's door for her, and while she climbed into her seat, he tossed her bags into the truck bed. The cab dipped and settled as he joined her inside and pulled his door shut. "I assume you want to go straight to the hospital?"

"Yes, please."

She glanced at his profile as he drove out of the parking lot and onto the road that led off the rim-rocks and down to Billings. His presence seemed even larger in this small space, and she was far more aware of him than she wanted to be.

Turning away, she gazed at the familiar rocks and twisted cedar trees on the bluff. Far below, the city stretched to the Yellowstone River, then gave way to the plains that welcomed her home. Again she experienced a strange sensation of protection and comfort. But Montana wasn't home any longer; she'd been gone too long and she'd changed too much to come back. And this stranger couldn't offer her comfort.

"Your mother will be glad to have you home," Clint said after several minutes. "She sounded tired when I spoke with her this morning."

Recognizing how inappropriate her resentment was, Gail tried not to let it show. "Did she?"

He nodded. "I don't think she's been home once since your dad got sick."

Gail didn't want to admit she didn't know that, so she made a noncommittal sound.

He stopped at a traffic light and glanced at her. "I've been giving your parents a hand while your dad's in the hospital." As if that gave him the right to intrude.

Again, Gail had to push aside her unreasonable irritation. "Thank you."

"It's no problem. How long will you be staying?"

In spite of her best efforts, Gail snapped, "Look, do you mind if we don't chat? I'm not in the mood for small talk right now."

He shrugged and turned his eyes back to the road. "We're almost there."

She looked away and tried to concentrate on the familiar landmarks, but guilt nagged at her conscience. He hadn't caused her father's stroke. He hadn't intended to hurt her. All he'd done was give her parents a hand, and she'd repaid him by offending him.

She drew a deep breath and tried to pull herself together. "I'm sorry," she said softly. "I didn't mean to sound rude."

To her surprise, he smiled at her. "You didn't."

But she knew she had. "It's just that I—"

"You didn't sound rude," he insisted. "You sounded hurt. There's a big difference. And you don't need to apologize for feeling hurt."

"But it's not your fault. I shouldn't take it out on you."

"It's nobody's fault," he said. "Besides, I've got broad shoulders."

He certainly did. Gail tried not to smile at his choice of expressions. An easier silence fell between them this time, and several blocks passed before she said, "I'll only be here a month."

Nodding as if he'd just asked the question, Clint maneuvered around a car in their lane. "That'll give you time for a good visit."

"But not enough to be much help."

"You'll probably help more than you know. Hal told me your father thinks the sun rises and sets on you. It'll do him a world of good just to have you home for a while."

This time when the sensation of comfort came, Gail didn't push it away. But she wondered how it was that someone she'd known less than half an hour could offer such consolation.

When they pulled into the hospital parking lot a few minutes later, the sensation evaporated and reality came rushing back at her. Except for one brief visit just after her divorce, she hadn't been home in three years. Her mother wanted to see her married and happy. Her father also wanted to see her settled and cared for. Neither believed that she'd found happiness alone, or that she could care for herself. To avoid dealing with the issue, she'd stayed away. And their obligations on the farm had prevented them from coming to her.

Clint switched off the engine and studied her. "Are you going to be okay?"

"Yes, of course." She tried to force her lips into a smile, but as she hurried into the hospital, her anxiety increased with every step.

Inside, Gail's footsteps echoed in the hushed corridor. Behind her, Clint's boots struck the linoleum heavily as he followed. Tugging the strap of her purse onto her shoulder, she paused at the information counter to ask for her father's room number. Clint waited with her, rode the elevator to the second floor and matched her pace as she hurried toward Boone's room. But suddenly, she wished he'd waited outside or in the reception area downstairs. She dreaded seeing her father ill, and she didn't want the company of a stranger when she did.

As if reading her thoughts, he touched her arm and halted her progress outside a small waiting room. "I'll be in here."

She tried not to show her relief. "Thank you."

"Just tell me when you're ready, and I'll drive you home." When she nodded, he turned and picked up a magazine from an end table then sat on the couch.

Strangely reluctant now, she crossed to her father's room, pushed open the half-closed door and peered inside. The curtains had been drawn against the fading sun, and the room's only light came from one dim lamp near the bed.

He lay there, eyes closed, face pale and drawn, arms stiff at his sides. He looked old and sick, thin and shriveled. Not like her father at all. When had this happened? He'd only had the stroke three days ago, not long enough for illness to ravage his body like this.

Her mother sat beside him with an open book on her lap, but she made no pretense of reading. Her eyes were dark-rimmed and bloodshot, her hair startlingly gray. Like Boone, she looked much older than Gail remembered.

Gail took a step toward her. "Mom?"

Dorothy focused on her slowly, then dropped the book to the floor and stood. "Gail, honey. You're here." She opened her arms and Gail rushed into them.

"How is he?"

"He's doing fine, sweetheart." Her mother released her and smiled down at Boone. "The doctor says we may be able to take him home tomorrow."

Gail looked at her father's inert figure. "Thank God." She watched him for a minute, but he didn't move. "Has he been asleep long?"

"Oh, he's not asleep, honey. He's wide-awake. Let him know you're here." When Gail took a hesitant step toward her father's bed, her mother scurried around to the other side. "Boone, look who's here. It's Gail."

Boone's eyelids flickered.

"Daddy?" Gail stepped closer and touched his hand. It felt like ice. "Daddy?"

His eyes opened slowly, but recognition dawned immediately. He smiled, but only one side of his mouth lifted; the other half of his face didn't move. He mumbled something Gail couldn't understand.

But Dorothy seemed to have no trouble. "Yes, Boone. It's Gail. Come and give your dad a kiss, sweetheart."

Boone mumbled again and Gail strained to hear, certain she'd missed something the first time. She stepped closer and tried to keep the tears from her eyes as she leaned toward him. He looked so helpless.

She pressed a kiss to his cheek and he closed his eyes in response. But when he opened them a second later, they'd filled with tears. He tried to speak again, but only a garbled sound emerged.

Gail glanced at her mother, but the horror of her father's illness seemed to have escaped Dorothy's notice.

"Doesn't he look good?" Dorothy beamed, her eyes too bright, her smile too broad. "He's going to be back on his feet in no time."

Gail stared down at her father, but his eyes closed again as if he was too weary to keep them open. He'd always been her rock. Her strength. He'd understood somehow without talking, what her unhappy marriage and the subsequent divorce had done to her. He'd known how deeply the pain of her failure as a stepmother had cut her, and he accepted without question her refusal to discuss it. Now, for the first time in her life, she had to face her father's mortality.

She blinked back tears and thanked God she'd come home. If she'd stayed in San Mateo, she might never have seen him again.

She pressed another trembling kiss to his cheek and his eyelids moved again, but he didn't open them.

Dorothy settled into her chair and picked up her book. "So, I guess Clint found you all right."

"Yes, he seems very nice." Gail had to force herself to speak around the lump in her throat.

Dorothy thumbed through her book, as if looking for her place in it. "He's been giving your dad a hand around the farm the past few days, did he tell you that?"

Gail nodded, then whispered. "Yes."

"Well, it's nice to have neighbors to help out in rough times, that's what I say. Your dad'll probably insist on going over to Hal's to help out when he's up and around. You know how he is."

"Where have you been staying, Mom?"

Dorothy looked surprised. "Why, right here."

"The whole time?"

"Of course."

"But you are coming home with me tonight..."

"It's silly for me to drive forty miles home just to turn around and come right back," Dorothy said. "You go on with Clint."

"If you're staying, so am I," Gail insisted.

"Honey, I'm fine, but I'm not leaving your father."

But she wasn't fine, Gail thought. She obviously needed rest and food. She needed to get out of this hospital, if even for one night.

"Mom—" Gail heard the pleading tone in her voice and tried to change it. "Have you been sleeping much?"

Dorothy shrugged. "What I can get while I'm sitting here. When we go home tomorrow, I'll catch up."

For the first time in several minutes, Boone's eyes opened again. He looked from Gail to Dorothy and back again, then made a strangled sound.

Dorothy patted the hand nearest her. "Yes, dear. Gail's here."

But this time, Gail thought she'd understood him. She leaned closer. "What did you say, Daddy?"

He focused on her and smiled his half smile again, then struggled to form the word, "Home."

CLINT FOLLOWED Dorothy Knight's station wagon down the narrow two-lane highway and wondered what Gail had done to pry Dorothy away from Boone's bedside. Hal had tried. Phyllis had pleaded. Clint had even put in a word himself. But Dorothy had refused to listen to any of them.

Well, whatever Gail had done had worked, thank God.

Dorothy's appearance tonight had been a shock to him. She'd grown old overnight, and she'd walked like an elderly woman when she and Gail came out of Boone's room. Instinctively, Clint had wanted to help her, but her eyes had snapped at him the second he took a step toward her, so he'd followed them out of the hospital, feeling useless.

By the glare of his headlights he could make out their silhouettes in the car. Dorothy in the passenger seat. Gail behind the wheel.

Gail was a beautiful woman. Certainly more beautiful than the picture Dorothy had shown him when she'd asked him to meet her. Her nearly black hair hung to the middle of her back and her eyes were deep and wide and darker than the night.

During the drive from the airport, he'd felt there was something fragile about her. But as soon as they'd arrived at the hospital, the fragility had disappeared, replaced by a backbone of steel. He had no doubt she could handle herself in almost any situation.

Still, dealing with her father's stroke wouldn't be easy on her. The farm and the house needed full-time attention, and she'd have her hands full trying to see that her mother got some rest.

Well, Clint could stay on a few days longer. He wouldn't mind. In fact, he enjoyed working Boone's farm on his own. He liked the challenge of evaluating new situations, deciding on a course of action and putting his decisions to the test. He'd been training for a position like this all these years, but he'd never imagined the opportunity would pop up in the middle of a cornfield.

When Clint's father approached him about spending the year helping Uncle Hal, Clint had balked at the idea. But now he was almost sorry that the year was drawing to a close and he'd be back in Chicago in a little over two months. Back at Garrity & Garr. Back with Leslie.

At the thought of Leslie, Clint drew his eyes away from Gail's silhouette. Clint had a solid relationship with Leslie. She was a fine woman, devoted to her career, devoted to him. She went to all the right places and knew all the right people. They'd talked often about marriage, and he'd made up his mind to propose when he went to Chicago in two weeks for the birthday party she'd been planning for him.

But Leslie had never made him feel the way Gail did. Leslie had never made him intuitively want to protect and comfort her. He laughed a little at the turn his thoughts had taken. Gail certainly didn't need his protection. And if she wanted comfort, she wouldn't turn to him for it.

Pushing his hat back on his head, he cranked the dial on the radio, and the melody of a George Strait song filled the cab of the truck. He rolled down his window the rest of the way and leaned his elbow on the door as he whistled along. Aware of the picture he made in his hat and jeans and driving an old pickup, he grinned. He wondered what Leslie would think if she could see him now.

mother had washed the floors in the kitchen corners thoroughly?

Another thing she noticed was the need for a cleaning crew of some sort, she had...

CHAPTER TWO

GAIL PULLED UP the blind and let the morning sun stream into her mother's big old-fashioned kitchen. Tying the belt of her robe securely, she poured coffee into her favorite mug. She pushed open the back-door screen, stepped through and closed it without a sound. She hadn't heard her mother stir yet, and she wanted to let Dorothy sleep as long as possible.

She walked to the edge of the porch and looked out over the yard. It had been years since she'd started a morning this way, but she felt as if it were just yesterday.

When she was a girl, her morning ritual had included bringing coffee to her dad—strong, hot and black. She'd wait for him here on the porch swing, and within minutes, he'd stride out of the barn and join her.

Thrusting away her memories, she tilted her face to the morning sun, letting it warm her. In a few hours, the summer heat would intensify, now it was pleasant and fairly cool. But she couldn't ignore the dusty yard and the condition of her parents' home.

Everything looked different somehow. Older, like her parents. Run-down. How long had it been since her dad had painted the barn? How long since he'd replaced the hinges on the front gate? When had her mother last weeded the flower beds or the vegetable garden?

Lowering herself onto the swing, she tried not to let a rising sense of panic overtake her. Maybe her mom was right. Maybe her dad was in better condition than he'd seemed. He might recover quickly once they brought him home. But the truth had stared at her through Boone's eyes in that hospital room. He had a long road to recovery.

From the porch, she could see all the way down the lane to the highway, and when a windshield in the distance reflected the sun from its surface, she followed its progress. To her surprise, the vehicle slowed and turned toward the house.

She'd forgotten how early in the morning people got started here. Since she didn't want their caller to wake Dorothy, she left her mug on the porch railing and crossed the yard. Pebbles jabbed her feet through the thin soles of her slippers, and she pulled the long terry-cloth robe tighter around her.

By the time she reached the front gate, she recognized Clint's truck and regretted rushing out to meet him in her robe and nightgown. But he was too close now for her to dash inside to dress. She chided herself for forgetting he'd be here this morning, and pulled the robe even tighter.

He drew to a stop several feet away, and dust swirled around the cab of the truck as he opened the door and jumped to the ground. " 'Morning.''

"Good morning.''

He started toward her, hesitated for half a beat, then continued. His eyes raked the length of her and she felt herself grow warm under his gaze.

"Pretty day,'' he said as he drew closer.

"Yes."

"I thought I'd stop by and see if there's anything special you need before I head out to the fields."

She shook her head and studied the yard again. "I don't think so."

He followed her gaze. "I've been looking after the corn, but I'd like to see what I can do around here, too. One side of the barn's missing boards, and both it and the house need new shingles. We got hit by a hailstorm a few weeks ago, and if we get another one, you'll have trouble. The fence needs attention, and there are dozens of little things..." His voice trailed off and he lifted his shoulders as if it was futile to go on.

And it probably was. "I appreciate your help. You're being very kind," she said.

When he smiled, his eyes caught the sun and sparkled. "It's no trouble."

Gail had to struggle to not let him affect her this morning. "When you have a few minutes, maybe you can show me what you've done and what's left, but I don't want to interfere with whatever Hal needs you to do."

To her surprise, he laughed. "Hal's top priority is making sure your dad's place is taken care of. But I think it's only fair you know what you're getting if you take me up on my offer. I'm just a rookie on a farm."

He looked so much the part, his comment surprised her. "You're not from around here?"

"No. I'm from Chicago. I'm an investment banker."

"What are you doing *here?*"

"Doctor's orders. A year away from work if I want to stay alive."

She waited for him to elaborate. When he didn't, she asked, "Then you're not here permanently?"

"Just until the end of August, but Hal's hoping I like it enough to want to stay."

"Will you?"

He squinted into the sun and shook his head. "No. It's a nice life, but I've worked too hard to throw away my career now. A few more months and I'll be good as new."

This time, Gail lost the battle to temper her curiosity with manners. "What was wrong with you?"

"Ulcers. They damn near killed me." He paused, then grinned. "I guess my ex-wife was right. She always said I'd work myself to death, but I always assumed it was wishful thinking on her part."

Embarrassed at leading the conversation into such a personal area, Gail clamped a firm control over her curiosity and tried to steer the conversation to more neutral ground. "You must like what you do."

"Very much. And I can't see throwing away my career just because my stomach acts up a little now and then." He grinned again and shrugged. "I feel better every day, and I haven't had to take my medication in so long, I've forgotten where I put it."

Gail grinned back, but when Clint's eyes roamed over her again, she felt herself blush. She pulled the collar of her robe together and held it with one hand as she looked away, and caught a glimpse of her mother gazing down at them from her bedroom window.

Relieved that at least now she could dress, Gail waved, hoping they hadn't been responsible for waking her. "Do you want to come inside for a minute?

Maybe have a cup of coffee? Or is that against doctor's orders?''

Clint mocked outrage. ''I've learned there are two things you never mess with. One's a man's hat. The other's his coffee. I'd love some.''

She started toward the house, too conscious of him behind her. It had been a long time since she'd reacted to a man this way. Ever since her divorce, she'd known she wasn't ready for another serious relationship. She'd tried a couple of noncommittal ones, but dinners and movies inevitably led to expectations she wasn't ready to fulfill. Now, aware of Clint's scrutiny, she felt suddenly vulnerable, and she didn't like the feeling.

Grabbing her mug from the railing, she reached for the screen door just as Clint extended his hand to open it for her. Their fingers brushed, and Gail jerked her hand away, uncomfortably aware of his touch, but he gave no indication that he'd noticed anything.

Inside, she pulled a mug from the cupboard and poured his coffee, grateful for the excuse not to look at him. But when she handed it to him and met his gaze, he looked so clear-eyed and innocent she wondered if she'd imagined the interest she'd seen outside.

''Cream and sugar are on the table,'' she said, giving him a spoon. ''I'll be right back.'' And without waiting for his response, she ran from the kitchen and up the stairs to her bedroom to dress.

Clint watched the kitchen door swing on its hinges after Gail raced from the room. He knew he'd made her uncomfortable, but she and her bathrobe hadn't exactly left him unaffected. Even though the robe covered a lot more than the business suit she'd worn last night, it implied an intimacy that left him flushed.

When she rejoined him after less than ten minutes, she was wearing jeans and running shoes and a blue work shirt. She looked as if she belonged in this farmhouse kitchen with the sun streaming into it. Somehow, the room seemed even brighter with her in it.

She poured herself another cup of coffee and settled into a chair across from him. "Tell me the truth, Clint. Are things around here really as bad as they look?"

The question startled him a little, but he considered it for a second before answering. "Yes. I'd say so."

"How long have they been going downhill?"

"I don't know," he answered honestly. "But I don't think your dad's been keeping up for some time."

She looked at her hands and drew in a deep breath. "When did you say you'd be going back to Chicago?"

"At the end of August or first part of September. My kids are coming to spend a year with me, so I'll have to get them settled, find day care and get the boys registered for school."

"How many children do you have?"

"Three. Two boys and a girl. How about you?"

"No children."

Her face tightened noticeably, and Clint decided to let that subject drop and look for a less touchy one. "So, what do you do in San Francisco?"

"I'm a legal assistant at a law firm in San Mateo. Corporate reorganization, bankruptcy, and all the litigation that goes with it."

"You must like it."

She made a face. "I've been there for over ten years. Some days are good, some are bad. But the money's all right and it's steady work." The words sounded right, but there was no enthusiasm in her eyes.

He tried to lighten the mood with a laugh. "Sounds like a glowing recommendation for that kind of work."

She stared at him for one long minute before her lips curved in a smile. "Well, I didn't get into it by choice. It's the career my ex-husband picked out for me—he's an attorney."

"And you stayed after your divorce from habit? Or had you grown to love your job by then?"

"I guess it was habit." Her smile faded and her voice had an edge to it.

He opened his mouth to say something else just as the swinging door opened and Dorothy stepped into the kitchen. She looked a little better than she had last night. At least the dark circles beneath her eyes had faded a little and her cheeks held a hint of color.

"'Morning, Clint," she said before turning to Gail. "Are you ready?" she asked. "I don't want to be late to get your dad."

Gail's face softened. "Sure, Mom. Just give me another minute or two."

When she looked at him as if she was about to apologize, Clint drained his cup and stood quickly. "I'd better go. Thanks for the coffee." He turned to Dorothy. "I thought I'd check on the corn this morning. We'll need to thin the crop again soon, and I've been making sure it's irrigated on schedule. Then, I figured I could finish some of the things Boone must have been working on before he got sick."

Dorothy shook her head. "There's no need for you to go to all that trouble. Once Boone gets home, he'll take care of it."

Clint's eyes met Gail's over Dorothy's head, and he saw her concern. "It's no bother," he said. "Let Boone take all the time he needs to get back on his feet."

"You've been wonderful to help, Clint," Dorothy insisted, "but it won't be necessary any longer. Between the three of us, we'll get by. Now, come on, Gail. I don't want your dad to have to wait for us. Dr. Lethbridge is going to release him today."

As Gail gathered their cups and took them to the sink, she looked troubled. "For sure?"

"By ten o'clock," Dorothy insisted. She snapped off the coffeemaker and marched toward the door. "We'd better get moving."

Clint held open the screen as Dorothy stepped through. "I'd be glad to help get Boone home if you'd like."

She spared him a glance, but shook her head. "No, thanks. We'll be fine."

Gail followed her mother through the door. "I'm sure they'll have someone get him to the car in a wheelchair." She spoke to Clint, but her eyes followed her mother's progress across the yard, and her frown deepened as Dorothy settled into the passenger seat of the car.

Clint put on his hat and walked with her down the steps. "You're probably right, but I'll be here when you get back in case you need help getting him into the house."

She looked up at him and smiled, and warmth filled her eyes. "Thank you. We just might."

Dorothy tapped the horn and called out the window, "Come on, Gail."

"We'll probably be back around noon," Gail said softly, then hurried to the car.

Clint watched her drive off. He stared at the trail of dust she left all the way down the lane to the highway, and followed her with his eyes until the car disappeared from view. Only then could he make himself turn away.

CLINT WALKED behind Hal as the older man inspected the front gate and gave the barn a once-over. They didn't speak, but Hal's grunts of dismay convinced Clint he'd been right in his evaluation of the Knights' farm. Something had to be done, and Clint was in no position to give the kind of aid these people needed.

Hal led him out of the barn and pushed his hat back on his head. He lit a cigarette and smoked in silence for a minute. Finally, he exhaled heavily and flicked ash to the ground. "It's a damned shame, that's for sure. A man spends his whole life workin' the land, then his place falls apart once he gets a few years on him."

Watching the smoke drift from Hal's cigarette, Clint reflected that Boone was a few years younger than Hal. And he knew Hal's thoughts must be running along the same lines.

"I talked to Gail this morning," Clint said. "She asked me to bring her up-to-date. What should I tell her?"

Hal fixed him with his gaze. "The truth. They need help, and sugarcoating the facts ain't goin' to do no good. It's a lucky thing you're around."

"I can't give them what they need," Clint protested. "The kids are coming next week and I'm supposed to fly to Chicago the weekend after that—"

"The kids ain't a problem. But you might have to rethink the Chicago thing." Hal dragged deeply on his cigarette and scanned the yard again.

"But I'll only be gone three or four days—"

"Three or four days could put Boone and Dorothy completely under. If them shingles don't get put on, it won't make a lick of difference whether you get the corn in or not. One storm and them women will spend every minute tryin' to stop up the leaks in the house."

Clint opened his mouth to protest, then shut it again.

But Hal didn't miss it. "What?"

"Leslie's got a party planned for my birthday. I don't want to disappoint her."

"She'll understand if you explain it to her, won't she?"

Clint hesitated. Would she understand? Resolutely, he pushed aside his doubts. Of course she would. Leslie was a fine woman. And *very* understanding. So he pulled out his next argument. "I don't want the kids to be Phyllis's responsibility the whole time they're here," he said.

"I know that. But Phyllis don't mind. We already talked about it." Hal dragged on the cigarette again, then crushed it underfoot. "Thing is, Clint, out here, a man's got to be able to count on his neighbors."

"I'll only be here a couple more months."

"I know that, too. But you can buy 'em some time while they decide what they want to do. If they sell, they'll get a sight better price if the land's been worked regular and the property's kept up. If they stay, it's the only way they'll survive." Hal propped one foot on a rusted piece of equipment and looked Clint in the eye. "I think the best thing'll be if you and your boys help out here. I'll keep my place goin' and give you a hand here when I can."

"Justin and Brad?" Clint laughed. "Can you see either of them doing farm work?"

Hal's gaze narrowed. "As a matter of fact, I can."

Clint sobered. "They'll hate it."

"Maybe. At first. But as I recall, their daddy wasn't too good at it in the beginning, either."

"Their daddy still isn't."

"You're doin' fine, son. And so will they. Get 'em workin' a couple hours every day. It'll do 'em a world of good." He patted Clint on the back and started across the yard to his truck. "You want to break through to them boys this time, don't you?" he called back over his shoulder.

"You know I do."

"Then treat 'em how you like to be treated and quit handling 'em with kid gloves like you did at Christmas." Hal climbed into the cab of the truck and gunned the engine. "I ain't goin' to try and force you. If you don't want to disappoint your lady friend, I'll do what I can on my own while you're gone. It's up to you." And without giving Clint a chance to answer, he backed up in a wide semicircle and pulled out of the yard.

Clint had no idea what his answer would have been if Hal had waited for one. He started across the yard toward his own truck, and the image of Gail in her robe filled his mind. How could he turn his back on her? Or on Dorothy and Boone? How could he expect Hal at his age to do the work of two men? But how could he give the Knights what they needed?

Justin and Brad were boys—fourteen and ten. Certainly not old enough to work a farm. The most physically challenging thing either of them had ever done was to ride a dirt bike.

And he couldn't forget about Leslie. He disappointed her enough just by being here. He knew he'd never find a woman better suited to his position at Garrity & Garr or one more compatible with his lifestyle.

Driving along the unpaved road into the fields, he tried to push away his frustrations, but he couldn't find an acceptable solution. The party meant a lot more to both of them than just his thirty-sixth birthday celebration. Leslie planned to invite A. J. Garrity and his two closest advisers so Clint could make an unofficial bid for Duncan Morris's job, and they'd talked about buying an engagement ring when he came home for the party. If he didn't go home, Leslie would read more into his decision than an obligation to Hal's neighbors, and he'd miss a golden career opportunity.

How could Hal ask that of him, especially when this responsibility wasn't even his? He straightened in the hot sun and looked back at the house. On the other hand, how could he leave Hal to work both farms himself? Dammit, why didn't some other neighbor step in and offer a permanent solution?

Clint agonized all morning, pushing himself to the limit but finding only minor relief in the physical activity. By midmorning, sweat poured down his forehead and soaked his shirt, but he pushed harder, worked faster and wished he knew what to do.

When he noticed a trail of dust leading down the lane toward the house just after noon, he realized Gail and Dorothy must be back with Boone, and he'd almost missed them.

Abandoning his task, he drove through the fields quickly and arrived in the yard a few minutes after they did. Gail had already propped open the back door and the two women were struggling to pull Boone from the car.

Clint shut off the truck's engine and jogged across the yard. "Here, let me help."

Dorothy didn't budge, but Gail looked up, relief evident in her dark eyes. "I thought we could do this." She stepped aside and gently guided Dorothy out of his way.

Leaning into the car, Clint saw Boone for the first time since his stroke. The older man's appearance startled him, but even in this weakened condition he was obviously too much for Gail and Dorothy to manage alone—especially since Boone himself could offer little assistance.

Clint wrapped one arm around Boone's back. "Can you slide toward the door, Mr. Knight?"

Boone didn't speak, but his eyes shifted in Clint's direction and determination flickered across his face. Clint muttered words of encouragement and slowly helped him inch toward the door. He could easily have picked Boone up and carried him into the house, but something in the man's watery blue eyes warned him not to try. Clearly, Boone's pride was at stake.

After several tries, Clint helped Boone stand, and together they shuffled toward the house. It took them nearly twenty minutes to go from the car to the ground-floor guest bedroom, and Boone's face betrayed his exhaustion less than halfway to their goal. But his determination never wavered, so Clint continued to guide and support him.

When they finally reached the bedroom, Clint helped Boone lie down before Dorothy covered him with a sheet and a light quilt. Boone's eyes closed in weariness, his breath came in short gasps, and Clint knew there was only one decision he could make.

He only hoped Leslie would eventually forgive him.

CLINT WRAPPED a towel around his waist as he stepped out of the shower, and ran for the phone in his bedroom. With water still dripping down his neck, he grabbed the receiver before it could ring again.

"Clint!" Leslie's voice floated over the line, "I was afraid I'd missed you."

"Just getting out of the shower," he explained, and grabbed a clean shirt to mop his face.

"Oh. Sorry. Should I call back?"

"No, this is fine."

"You sound tired. How are you?"

"Fine. But I *am* tired."

"I don't know why you're doing this to yourself. How can working so hard be better for you than doing what you love—what you're so good at?"

"Physical exertion isn't my problem. Stress is."

"Yes, I know." She paused, then said, "Look, I didn't call to talk about that. I have something wonderful to tell you. Guess what I did."

"What?"

"I rented the O'Connor Mansion for your party. Isn't that great?"

No, it wasn't great. Not if he couldn't be there. "You've already done it?"

"Well, yes. Of course. You know how hard that place is to get. I was lucky enough to find out about a cancellation, so I snatched it up! Won't that be perfect?"

Clint sat on the foot of his bed and buried his forehead in the now-damp shirt. "I wish you'd called me first."

"Why? What's wrong?"

"I don't think I'm going to be able to come home for the party."

"You're joking." It wasn't a question.

"You remember when I told you about the neighbor who had a stroke?"

She hesitated. "I guess so. What about him?"

"He's in bad shape, Les. There's no way he can work his farm, and if they don't get the crop in, they'll go under. I've got to stay here and help him out."

"You're not serious."

"He's in bad shape," he repeated.

"Whose idea was this?"

"Nobody's idea, Les. It's just the way things are done out here. People help each other—"

"Fine, but can't somebody else help him? You've got responsibilities here. At *home*."

He heard the hurt in her voice and it made his own tighten. "I've got to stay."

"Clint, you're being ridiculous. I've rented the *O'Connor Mansion*. What do you expect me to do about that?"

"Can't we cancel?"

"Oh, yes. We can cancel." She sighed heavily, as if struggling for control. "But they'll keep my deposit. And what about the caterers?"

"I'll pay for everything."

"What about A.J.? How are you ever going to make up for losing this chance?"

"I'll figure something out."

"No. I'm not going to let you do this to me. It's all planned. I've been working on this for *three months*. The invitations should go out tomorrow, at the latest."

Clint drew in a deep breath and let it out slowly. He hated listening to proof of her unhappiness, and he hated being the cause of it. "I'm sorry, Leslie."

"Don't, Clint." Her voice broke and for several seconds silence burned between them. When she spoke again, she seemed to have regained some control. "Let's not talk about it right now. I've had a rough week and I just can't deal with this." Another lengthy pause. "So, tell me what else is new."

Clint dropped the shirt to the floor and changed the receiver to his other hand. "My kids are coming."

"Oh, Clint, that's wonderful! When?"

"Next week." Just the thought made him smile.

"How long will Barbara let them stay?"

"Dave's been reassigned out of the country for a year and she's going with him, so the kids will stay with me."

"For the whole year?"

"The whole year. As soon as we get home, I'll have to check out day care, get the boys registered in school—and, of course, buy school clothes."

"You're going to have them the whole *year?*"

Something in her voice made him pull back on his enthusiasm. "Yes."

"Sweetheart, how can you juggle three kids when you get back to work? You'll already be a year behind—"

"I can do it."

"You'll have to put in fourteen-hour days, as it is, just to catch up. And Megan's what—three?"

"She's four."

"Four. Well, *that* makes a big difference."

"Leslie—"

"I know how much you want the kids, but this just seems like such a bad time."

"If I had my way, the kids would be with me all the time." He stood and paced toward the window, stretching the telephone cord as far as it would reach.

"With your schedule? It would never work." When he didn't respond, she softened her tone and went on. "Look, sweetheart, I'm sorry. Of course you're right. Like I said, it's been a bad week and it just keeps going. I've had nonstop meetings, three new clients we're trying to sign and a new assistant who, I swear, is only in this business to collect a paycheck. And I'm supposed to be down at McGillicutty's right now. So why don't we forget all this and I'll talk to you again on Friday. Okay?"

He tried to match her warmth. "That'll be fine. But let me call you. I don't know what time I'll get through at the Knights' place and back here."

"Okay," she agreed, then paused. "Clint?"

"What?"

"I love you."

"Me, too," he said. But the words felt flat. He replaced the receiver slowly, but guilt gnawed at him as he dug through his dresser for a clean pair of briefs. He knew she must have felt his restraint. Besides being hurt over the party, she'd wonder why he'd sounded so withdrawn. And he'd have to think of some way to make it up to her.

CHAPTER THREE

GAIL CLIMBED the attic stairs behind her mother's slow, measured steps. Neither of them had slept well last night, and they both showed signs of it this morning. Gail hoped their restlessness had been because it was her dad's first night home and that they'd soon settle into a healthier routine.

She didn't know whether her mother's idea of reading aloud from her father's old journals would help him, but her mother had been so insistent, Gail had agreed to try, if only to make Dorothy feel better.

Coming to an abrupt stop at the top of the stairs, she studied the clutter. She hadn't been up here in years. The attic she remembered as orderly and neat had succumbed to the same confusion as the rest of her parents' property. Boxes leaned in stacks against the walls, an old rocking horse, a set of chairs, an antiquated sewing machine and a hundred things Gail couldn't name lay in patchwork pattern across the floor. Her parents' entire history must have been shoved into this attic.

Dorothy gestured toward a pile of containers below a narrow window. "Why don't we start over there?"

Gail had to turn sideways to maneuver through the clutter, and the dust made her sneeze three times before she reached the window. A thick piece of wire snagged the denim of her jeans and tore a hole just above her knee. It was more than cluttered up here, it was dangerous. "Maybe you could check those cartons over there," she said, pointing toward a stack near the stairway.

"Don't be ridiculous. I'm not helpless." Her mother stepped over the first set of obstacles easily.

"I didn't mean that, Mom."

"Your father might be ill, but that doesn't mean you have to treat me like a fragile old lady."

"I'm sorry."

Dorothy hmmphed as she took the second stack with ease, and met Gail's eyes triumphantly. She held that pose for an instant, then her face softened. "Oh, Gail, I'm sorry. Let's not snipe at each other. We're going to need each other more than ever, with your dad sick."

Gail smiled softly. "I know, Mom. It's okay."

Dorothy propped her hip against some boxes and wiped her eyes with her fingertips. "This is going to be hard on both of us, but it would be so much easier for you if you weren't alone."

Gail's smile chilled on her face.

But her mother didn't seem to notice. "Honey, I don't know how you manage on your own. I don't know how I'd have survived all these years without your father, and you don't even have *us* nearby... I wish you lived closer so we could help more until you find someone—"

Determined not to let the conversation go where her mother seemed to want to take it, Gail lifted the lid of the top box. "When was the last time you cleaned up here?"

Dorothy fluttered her hand in a gesture of dismissal. "Heavens, I don't know. Years ago." She stood upright and crossed another hurdle. "But I don't worry about this attic, I worry about you. And we haven't had a chance to really talk in far too long. How *are* you, sweetheart? Are you seeing anyone?"

"No."

"Aren't there any single attorneys at that firm you work for?"

"Mom, I don't *want* anyone."

Dorothy blinked rapidly, as if Gail's words were incomprehensible. "Don't be silly. Of course you want someone."

Gail turned her back. "I'm not going to discuss this."

"Is it because of Richard?"

Gail shuffled a couple of crates without answering.

But her mother didn't let that discourage her. "Have you heard from Richard lately?"

Richard had severed all ties so completely, Gail didn't even have a current address. She'd worked hard to exorcise the pain caused by her failure as a wife and stepmother, and she refused to let it slip back into her life. She lifted several books from the top of the box and placed them on the floor. "I guess Daddy wouldn't put his journals under these, would he?"

"Gail—"

"I'll bet he keeps them in a separate box somewhere..." Hands on hips, Gail surveyed the attic again.

Dorothy touched Gail's shoulders. "Why won't you talk to me about Richard, honey? It's not good for you to keep everything locked away inside."

"Or maybe he didn't bring them up here at all." She refused to meet her mother's eyes.

"Of course he did. Where else would he keep them?" Then, as if suddenly remembering where she'd left off, she said, "Oh, sweetheart, I can't stand to see you this way."

Gail gently pulled away from her mother and worked her way to the other side of the attic. "Will you recognize the journals if we *do* find them?"

This time, Dorothy refused to be diverted. "You can't let what happened between you and Richard ruin your life."

"It hasn't ruined my life."

"It'll help if you talk about it," Dorothy insisted.

"It's over, Mom. I refuse to keep dwelling on it. Now, can we please drop it?" As Gail dug into another box, she heard her mother cross the attic to stand behind her. She heard the silence of her waiting. But she would *not* talk about Richard. Or about his children. Talking about them would only open the wound again.

Finally, Dorothy sighed softly. "When you're ready to talk, I'll be waiting. And don't worry about Daddy's journals. We can look for them another time."

Gail didn't respond, but kept herself rigid as her mother patted her shoulder and then descended the stairs. Even when Gail knew she was alone, she didn't soften.

To keep her mind busy, she worked through several containers. She found a picture of herself with Randy Russell at the senior ball, and one with her best friend, Bette, all dressed up and ready to pick up their dates for the girls'-choice dance. And when she found her high school yearbooks, she took a minute to thumb through them and read the inscriptions. But she didn't find her father's journals anywhere.

In the last box she opened, she found a collection of squares she'd cut from her father's old shirts years ago. She'd had the idea of making a quilt for him and she'd spent hours that summer measuring and cutting. That fall, she'd met Richard and abandoned the quilt. Her mother must have saved the pieces.

She remembered Richard's first visit to this house and how he'd walked through it with his lips curled in disdain. Richard had always been more concerned with appearances than with facts. That's why he'd insisted on her taking a job that looked good rather than one she'd enjoy. And she'd been stuck in it ever since.

She'd had a dream of building a life with Richard like the one her parents had. A partnership between two equals. But she'd never felt equal to Richard. She didn't have the education to match him on an intellectual level, she didn't have the background to match him on a social one. And she couldn't work up enough enthusiasm in the complexities of the legal system to match him in the only conversation he seemed interested in having. Gradually, she'd come to see her parents' marriage as the exception rather than the rule, but she didn't want to settle for a relationship of any other kind.

In one way, her mother was right. It *would* be difficult for her to go through her father's illness alone. But it would have been worse if she'd still been married to Richard. He would have refused to come with her, and would have resented her coming alone. It would have taken months to put this visit behind them.

Hunkering down beside the box, Gail sorted through the quilt squares. Each piece brought back a memory. She could picture her father as he'd been then: strong and vital, his muscles stretching the shirt fabric as he worked.

This time when tears threatened, she couldn't stop them. Holding a handful of the squares to her face, she let them soak up her pain. She hugged them to her, as if this remnant of her father's strength could somehow underwrite her own. And she prayed silently for the strength she'd need to get through the next few weeks.

HOPING TO FIND Gail outside, Clint brought the pickup to a stop and scanned the yard. He wanted to offer his help when Dorothy wasn't around to turn him down. But it didn't look as if he'd be able to. The yard was empty.

Boone had been home since yesterday, but Dorothy still refused to admit how seriously ill he was. Less than an hour ago, she'd been on the phone with Phyllis, insisting that Boone would be up and around in no time. But Clint knew it would be a long time before Boone could fend for himself again. If ever.

After knocking on the back door, Clint stuffed his hands into his pockets to wait. A few seconds later, he lifted his hand to knock again, when the door opened. Gail stood before him, her eyes puffy as if she'd been crying. "Clint? Is anything wrong?"

Her distress left him feeling awkward and words escaped him, but he had to say something. "I wondered how your dad's doing."

"The same." She hesitated, then pushed open the screen. "Would you like to come in?"

"Actually, I wanted to talk to you for a minute. Alone. Would you mind coming out?"

She checked behind her as if making sure Dorothy hadn't heard, then she stepped onto the porch and pulled the door shut behind her. "What is it?"

"Walk with me?"

She studied him through narrowed eyes, and he suddenly felt like a schoolboy in pursuit of the prettiest girl in class. But she finally nodded, and he led her across the yard and out the front gate without speaking.

Her head barely reached his shoulder, and again he had that urge to comfort and protect her. But today he understood why. After seeing Boone, he understood her need for comfort.

She didn't look at him, but kept her eyes trained on the fields, as if she wanted to avoid meeting his gaze.

"I've been doing a lot of thinking since I saw your dad yesterday," he began. "He's in rough shape."

"Yes, he is."

"Worse than your mother thinks."

"Much worse."

"I know she doesn't want my help, but I'd like to stay on a while."

She slowed her step and looked up at him, squinting into the sun so he still couldn't see her eyes. "For how long?"

"As long as I'm here."

"Do you know how much work is involved?"

He nodded once. "I think so. And if I don't, I'll find out soon enough."

To his surprise, she smiled. "That's true." Her smile slipped a little. "Why are you doing this?"

He thought of all the reasons he shouldn't, then said, "Because I want to."

She looked away and started walking again. "You know my mom's sure Dad'll be on his feet soon. I don't know how to convince her how ill he really is. Part of me thinks they should sell the place and move to California near me. But the other part knows that leaving here would break their hearts."

He matched his step to hers and followed her gaze across the fields. "And your coming back here isn't an option?"

She sighed. "What's that old saying? You can't go home again? I grew up here, but I never learned how to work the land. It didn't interest me. I love it, don't get me wrong, but I never wanted to be a farmer."

"There's no law that says you have to be. What did you want to do?"

In the distance, a meadowlark's song broke the silence, then faded, leaving only the sound of their footsteps on the gravel. She smiled wistfully. "I wanted to be an artist."

"Why didn't you do it?"

She shrugged. "Richard—my ex-husband—wanted me to do something...presentable. He didn't think an artist could command the kind of respect he deserved."

"That's stupid," Clint said, then immediately regretted the impulsiveness of his answer.

But to his surprise, she laughed. "Do you really think so?"

"Absolutely."

"He always wanted me to go to law school. A secretary—even a legal assistant—still wasn't respectable enough for him. But no matter how hard I've tried, cold logic and sterile facts never appealed to me. And

I couldn't make myself take on a career that demands that kind of thinking."

"Sounds to me like you have, anyway."

She didn't respond to that, and again he regretted his choice of words. But after a pause, she said, "Yes, I have, haven't I?"

"Well, it's never too late to make a change. You still want to be an artist?"

"Of course, but—"

"Go for it."

She stopped walking and faced him. "Just like that?"

"Seems to me now's the perfect time to make a change. Your mom and dad need you here, and you don't like what you're doing."

"You make it sound easy. I could quit my job tomorrow, but where would the money come from to support me? To support *them?*"

"Lease the farm. Stay in the house so your parents can be with you. Use the money you get from the farm to set yourself up."

She shook her head. "It'll never happen."

"How old are you, Gail?"

A ghost of a smile flickered across her lips. "That's an awfully rude question."

"What? Twenty-seven? Twenty-eight?"

"Thirty-one."

He pretended to be shocked. "Maybe you're right. That's far too old to try something new."

Her lips twitched. "See? I told you."

"Forget I ever said a word."

"Now you're making sense," she said, but her eyes danced as she tried to hold back a smile.

He liked seeing her this way. Giving a low whistle, he pushed his hat back on his head and studied her. "Thirty-*one*? And still getting around on your own. You're an amazing woman."

"They're doing a feature story about me on the news."

"I should think so. You'll be an inspiration to millions."

She laughed, and it sounded like the meadowlark's call. "So what about you? Are you doing exactly what you've always wanted?"

"Pretty much."

"Which part? The farmer or the investment banker?"

"Both. A farming investment banker. It's what I always wanted to be when I was a little boy."

She laughed again. "So many little boys do. But if you're so happy with it, how'd you get your ulcers?"

"Stress."

"Oh. Well, that's a shock. I would have thought they came from an overdose of contentment."

He grinned at her. "My ex-wife said I was a workaholic. She didn't like it much. Said I needed to spend more time with her and the kids. Then one day she stopped saying it. She lost a few pounds, bought some new clothes and found a new boyfriend. I started suspecting something was wrong about the time she stopped complaining, but I didn't confront her with it. I don't know, maybe I didn't want to know the truth."

"So how did you find out?"

"Well, I carried my suspicions around inside of me for a while. One night, I was at the office late, and the ulcers perforated. The paramedics rushed me to the emergency room and because the doctors didn't think I'd make it through the night, the police sent a car to tell Barbara. But they couldn't find her. The kids didn't know where she was. The sitter didn't know where she was. She didn't get home until after three in the morning, and she didn't come to the hospital until late that afternoon.''

Gail's eyes widened and the smile slid from her face. ''Oh, Clint. That's terrible.''

''At least she didn't serve me with the divorce papers until I got out of intensive care.''

''She served you with the papers while you were in the *hospital?* What did you do?''

''I cried,'' he said automatically, then felt himself flush. He'd never admitted that before. Not to anyone except his father who'd been at his bedside when the papers came. But when he looked into Gail's eyes, his embarrassment faded.

''I'm sorry,'' she whispered.

''Nothing to be sorry for. I brought it all on myself.''

''How long have you been divorced?''

''Two years,'' he said. ''How about you?''

''Three.''

''Any men in your life?''

Her smile disappeared completely. ''No.'' Then a ghost of it reappeared. ''And you? Any special women?''

For some reason, he hesitated for a second before he answered. ''Yes.''

''Here? Or in Chicago?''

''Leslie's in Chicago.''

''Oh.'' She kicked at some loose gravel.

The next natural step would be to tell her about Leslie. But for some reason, he remained silent.

"Do your kids like her?" Gail asked after a long silence.

"They've never met her," he admitted.

"Oh," she said again, then looked over her shoulder toward the house. "I need to get back. I've probably been gone too long already." She smiled a little. "I hate having to take help from anyone, but I really don't know what else to do. I'd be grateful for anything you want to do, and I appreciate your offer. Thanks." And without another word, she ran back to the house.

He watched her, confused by his reactions, puzzled by his difficulty in telling her about Leslie and amazed that he'd enjoyed talking with her so much he'd almost forgotten why he'd stopped by in the first place.

GAIL SNIPPED a length of thread from the spool and worked it through the needle, knotting one end. She picked up two squares of fabric and matched their right sides.

On the bed, her father lay still.

"I found some old quilt squares in the attic yesterday, Daddy," she said. "I think I'll leave them in your room so I can piece them together while we talk."

Boone didn't move.

"Hal's nephew came by. You know, Clint Andrews? He seems like a nice guy. Pleasant. Easy to talk to. Do you know him very well?"

He opened his eyes a little.

"He seems nice," she repeated. She lowered the quilt squares and took a sip of the iced tea she'd brought with her. "He's offered to help out for a few days. I didn't think you'd mind, so I said yes."

Boone blinked and struggled to speak.

"You *don't* mind, do you?"

He lowered his eyelids.

"I'm glad." Gail worked a few stitches. A memory of her father wearing one of the shirts filled her mind, but a picture of Clint smiling down at her from the center of the sun blotted it out. She pushed away Clint's image and took another swallow of tea. "I talked to Dr. Lethbridge this morning. He said we should be ready to start some therapy next week. That's good news, don't you think?"

Boone nodded weakly and made another sound. His attempts to communicate broke Gail's heart. But at the same time, they gave her hope.

She finished the seam and knotted the thread as if she'd done this only yesterday. Choosing another two squares, she began the process again. "You know, when we drove through Broken Bow yesterday, I was kind of surprised to see the town all done up for the stampede. I'd forgotten it's always the last week of June. I guess it's been a while since I was here for it. A long time since I've seen a rodeo *anywhere,* for that matter. Or gone to a street carnival. Or marched in a parade." She lowered her needlework and let old memories play. But after a second, she shook herself and picked up her work once more. "I guess you get out of the habit."

Boone struggled to smile his lopsided smile. "Go," he said.

Gail shook her head. "No. Not this year."

"Go."

Lowering the squares, Gail met her father's eyes. "We'll see." She couldn't make any firmer commitment than that.

"Go." Boone turned his head away as if he'd settled something.

Gail had no intention of spending a day at the stampede when her father was so ill. But she knew that further argument would be futile. She stitched in silence for several minutes, convinced that he'd never know whether she'd actually obeyed him.

Through the open window, a sound caught her attention. Footsteps, strong and sure and masculine. A familiar sound, but the man who usually made them lay on the bed unable even to sit up by himself. She lowered her needlework to the floor and crossed the room to look outside.

Standing back from the window, she watched Clint cross the yard. His broad shoulders swayed as he walked, and his long legs ate up the distance quickly. She tried to imagine him in Chicago wearing a three-piece suit, but the picture wouldn't form. That had been Richard's world; Clint seemed more at home here.

It took only a minute for him to go from the front gate to the barn. The instant he disappeared, she wondered why she'd hidden from him. Every time he came near, his presence comforted her. Somehow he always managed to put her at ease. But that reaction frightened her because it left her vulnerable.

She went back to her seat and picked up her sewing, but several times during the long afternoon she caught herself straining to hear some evidence of Clint's being near. And every time, she laughed at her foolishness. She didn't know why she reacted to him this way. Even if she'd been interested in a relationship—which she wasn't—he had someone waiting for him in Chicago.

When her mother took Gail's place at Boone's bedside, late in the afternoon, Gail slipped out the back door. She spent the rest of the daylight hours weeding and picking spinach and peas where Clint couldn't see her, and she could avoid watching him. But in spite of her precautions, she remained acutely aware of his proximity.

By the time the sun started to slip below the horizon, every muscle in Gail's torso ached. She'd forgotten how backbreaking gardening could be, but she remembered that harvesting the vegetables was only the beginning. Tomorrow, she'd have to sweat over a hot stove while she blanched and then froze everything she'd picked today.

Lugging a bucket of spinach to the garden's edge, she heard Clint's truck start. She thought of half a dozen reasons she needed to see him, but she'd manufactured them all, so she forced herself to stay behind the house.

As she watched the dust settle on the lane behind him, she battled the disappointment she felt at not having given herself another chance to talk with him. Somehow, she knew he would have lightened her mood.

CLINT STACKED suitcases in the trunk of his Mercedes and checked Megan's seat belt three times before he pulled out of the airport parking lot. Beside him, Justin sat in sullen silence. In the back seat, Brad had the headset from his stepfather's latest present firmly clamped over his ears. Megan strained to see out her window, but she wasn't tall enough yet.

"Daddy?"

"What, Megan?"

"Are we almost there?"

"Not yet, sweetie."

In his rearview mirror he saw her stretching upward, craning to see. "Are there Indians here?"

"Yes, lots of Native Americans."

"On horses? With bows and arrows?"

"No, in cars."

"With bows and arrows?"

"No, Megan. With jeans and hats, or suits and ties."

"Oh."

Clint changed lanes and flicked his gaze over his eldest child. Justin had barely spared him a greeting inside the airport, and he hadn't moved since they reached the car. "So, tell me what's new with you, son," Clint said.

Justin shrugged. "Nothin'."

"He's got a girlfriend," Megan said.

"I do not," Justin snarled.

"Girlfriend, girlfriend," Megan chanted.

Clint stopped at a red light and looked into the back seat. "Megan, that's enough."

Immediately distracted by something new, she strained to look out the window again, and when the driver of the car behind him tooted his horn, Clint pulled his attention back to the road and drove on.

"I want to hear," she cried.

From Brad's distressed shout, Clint knew she must be tugging at her brother's precious earphones. "Don't break Brad's radio, Megan," he said.

"But I want to *hear.*"

"Brad will let you hear later, okay?"

"Okay." Distracted again, Megan lapsed into silence.

Justin turned to look out his window.

"So, what do you think?" Clint asked, but he knew his voice sounded too hearty—forced.

Justin sent him a sideways glance. "I can't believe you wear stuff like that."

"I guess you never thought you'd see me in jeans and cowboy boots."

Justin shrugged as if it made no difference to him. "Why did you bring *this* car?"

"It's the only one I own. Besides, you wouldn't fit into my pickup."

"*You* drive a *truck?*" Justin snorted a laugh. "That I've got to see."

"You will, tomorrow."

But Justin must have had his fill of conversation, because he turned back to the window.

"Did you have dinner on the plane, or would you like to stop for something?"

"I want to stop!" Megan cried, anxious for adventure, as always.

"We ate already," Justin said.

Brad didn't respond.

Abandoning that idea, Clint followed Exhibition Drive through town and onto the highway. Within a few minutes, Megan drifted off to sleep. Brad had turned up the music loud enough for Clint to hear its tinny sounds leaking out from around the headphones, but Justin looked bored.

"Hey, Brad," Clint called. "Will you turn that down for a second? I want to talk to you about a special project I've got for you this summer."

The music in the back seat faded, and Justin flicked a glance at him.

"Uncle Hal and Aunt Phyllis have a neighbor who's real sick. He can't take care of his farm himself, so I've been helping out, but there's an awful lot to do, and I was thinking maybe you guys could give me a hand while you're here."

Brad leaned forward. "Doing what?"

"Painting and mending fences—"

"Boring," Justin said.

"And oiling machinery and putting new shingles on the house and the barn—"

"Double boring," Justin said.

"Real farmer work?" At least Brad sounded interested.

"Yeah," Clint said. "The real thing."

"Are you going to pay us?"

Justin looked interested at that. "*Are* you?"

"Well, I don't know—"

Justin looked away again. "Probably not."

"Depends on whether you're worth it," Clint asserted.

Brad pulled himself into view by tugging on Clint's seat back. "What do we have to do to be worth it?"

"Just give me an honest day's work."

Justin sneered. "The whole day?"

"No, but a couple of hours each morning before it gets too hot. What do you say?"

"How much?" Brad asked.

When Clint named a figure, Brad bounced back into his seat, obviously pleased with the potential for wealth. Soon, the sounds of his Walkman floated up from the back seat again.

But Justin made a face. "I'll bet Mom doesn't know you're planning to make us work." He folded his arms across his chest and stared out his window.

"Look, I won't force you to do it," Clint said. "But I could sure use your help."

Justin shrugged, but refused to look at him. "Yeah. Sure. Whatever."

Clenching the steering wheel, Clint prayed for patience. With Megan asleep and Brad content with his Walkman, silence fell heavily in the front seat. Minutes ticked past and miles flew by, but Justin showed no inclination to talk.

Well, what had he expected, a miracle? He knew how Justin felt about him—as if the divorce were Clint's sole responsibility. The only way he could clear his reputation would be to tell Justin the truth about Barbara and her affair with Dave. But no matter how much he disliked Barbara, no matter how much she'd hurt him, he wouldn't resort to degrading her in front of the kids.

So he turned on the radio softly and listened to Travis Tritt lamenting a lost love. And he assured himself that things would get easier in time.

Nearly an hour later, he pulled into the yard and cut the engine. Immediately, the back door opened and Phyllis rushed outside to gather the children into her warm embrace. Hal followed more slowly, but his broad smile clearly showed how pleased he was to see them again.

Justin returned Phyllis's hug—at least he didn't act surly with her. Brad endured her kisses bravely, and in all the noise and confusion, Megan woke up again.

She stumbled sleepily from Phyllis to Hal, receiving kisses on her chubby cheeks and returning hugs.

Finally, Phyllis tried to cull some order from the chaos. "Boys, please help your father carry in your things," she said. "I've got your beds all ready, so take your bags to the big room you had at Christmas and put Megan's in the room next to mine."

Justin and Brad followed orders without even a murmur of dissent, and Megan ran after them. Clint picked up a load for himself and followed. They were good kids, and he was proud of them. He only wished the boys felt as kindly toward him.

Megan trailed her brothers through the kitchen and would probably have made it upstairs, but as she passed the kitchen table, she stopped and shrieked with joy. Diving between the table legs, she emerged with Phyllis's long-suffering house cat, Colonel Mustard, tucked under one arm. "I found the kitty!"

Phyllis chuckled, and bent to kiss the top of Megan's head. "He's been waiting for you to come back since Christmas. I think he missed you."

With one arm wrapped around the cat's middle, Megan used the other hand to gently pet the top of his head as she headed for the front room. Clint shifted the luggage in his hands and followed, grateful that Colonel Mustard had the patience of a saint. Matching Megan's pace, he'd almost reached the foot of the stairs, when the phone rang.

"Clint?" Phyllis called after him from the kitchen. "It's Leslie."

Overhead, Clint could hear running footsteps, then silence, then laughing and running again. Obviously, Justin and Brad had taken up the game they'd discovered when they'd been here, over the holidays—sliding up and down the long hardwood floor of the upstairs hall.

In the living room, Hal had settled into his favorite chair with the day's edition of the *Billings Gazette*. Megan started up the stairway, dragging Colonel Mustard with her.

"Clint? Did you hear me? It's Leslie," Phyllis called again.

Leslie. She had the worst timing of anyone Clint knew. He smiled in resignation, left the suitcases by the stairs and went back to the kitchen where he took the receiver from Phyllis. "Leslie?"

"Clint! How are you?"

"Fine. Busy. I just picked up the kids at the airport and we only walked in the door a few minutes ago."

"That's right. Today *is* the day. How are they?"

"Wonderful. Great."

"That's good," she said. "Listen, Clint, we need to talk about your birthday party—"

He could hear Phyllis asking Hal to carry the suit-cases Clint had abandoned. "Now's not a very good time," he objected.

"But, Clint—"

Something thudded overhead.

"Listen, Leslie, can we talk about this later? I really need to get the kids settled. I'll call you back, okay?"

She sighed heavily. "Tonight?"

He tried not to feel as exasperated as she sounded. "Okay. But it'll have to be late."

Silence. "Forget it, then. I've got an early break-fast meeting tomorrow, so I'm going to bed in a few minutes."

"I'll call tomorrow," he promised.

"Fine." Another brief pause. "Good night, then."

"Good night." Clint replaced the receiver slowly, very aware of the fact that for the first time in months, neither of them had said a word about love.

CHAPTER FOUR

"MEGAN, honey, where are your shoes?" Clint backed out from under Megan's bed and shook his head in amazement. She'd been here less than twelve hours and she'd already managed to lose one sock and both shoes.

When she started to wriggle under the bed, he snagged her ankle and tugged her gently backward. "Think, sweetheart. Where did you take them off last night?"

Her little face puckered in concentration for half a second. "I don't know."

"Was it here in your bedroom? Or did Aunt Phyllis help you get your jammies on?"

"Aunt Phyllis," she cried and jumped to her feet. "I'll go get 'em."

Clint watched her race from the room and waited for her to return, but a minute later he heard her delighted cry. Cat claws scrambled across the hardwood floor and Megan's excited footsteps followed.

Pushing to his feet, Clint looked into the hallway. "Megan—"

She stood at the entrance to Hal and Phyllis's bedroom with the morning sunlight spilling through her golden hair. "Kitty's in there, Daddy," she cried and disappeared inside.

"Look for your shoes," he called after her, but he didn't hold out much hope she'd remember. She could get sidetracked faster than any child he'd ever seen. The world delighted her and everything in it entranced her. She wanted to see, feel, hear and smell it all.

Her joy in life touched places in Clint he'd forgotten existed. Her curiosity sparked his own. And her child's eye helped him see beauty he'd long since learned to ignore.

He glanced at the one door in the hallway that was still closed and drew in a steadying breath. The challenges Justin and Brad presented didn't always feel so delightful, but if he could break through to his sons in the year ahead, he knew the results would be equally rewarding.

Knocking lightly, he waited for a response. He didn't get one.

He knocked again. "Hey, you two. Time to get up."

Furtive footsteps and hushed voices let him know they were awake, but they still didn't answer.

When he knocked the third time, he opened the door and looked inside. "Hey, guys—what's going on in here?"

Justin lay in bed with his hands locked behind his head and his gaze locked on the ceiling. "Can't we have a little privacy?"

Brad looked toward the open door but immediately returned his attention to his Walkman. After a second or two, he yanked off the earphones and tossed the whole thing onto his pillow. "This dumb thing doesn't even work. All I can get out here is static."

Clint struggled not to let disappointment turn into irritation. "I need both of you to get dressed and come downstairs for breakfast."

Justin groaned and rolled onto his side, but Brad jumped up and pulled his suitcase closer to his bed. Clint closed the distance between them and helped Brad settle the heavy bag in the middle of his mattress. Glancing at Justin, he asked, "Where's your suitcase, son?"

"I can get it myself."

"All right, then. But do it now. I have to get back to work." He'd spent a couple of hours at the Knights' place at first light, but he'd come home to fix breakfast for the kids and make his weekly phone call to A. J. Garrity at Garrity & Garr. And, taking Hal's advice, he was going to suggest the boys put in a little time at Boone's place in the relative cool of morning.

"I thought Mom said you *wouldn't* be working all the time we were here." Justin sounded like a recording of his mother.

Clint forced himself not to rise to the bait. "You'll need to wear jeans," he warned. "And good shoes with thick soles."

"I don't want to work on some dumb old farm," Justin said into the covers on his bed, and the sheets barely muffled the surliness in his voice.

Clint stared at his son's narrow shoulders and wondered how such a small frame could hold such anger. Sitting on the edge of the mattress, he touched Justin's back, but the boy jerked away.

"Mr. Knight's a very sick man," Clint explained again. "He needs us."

"He doesn't need *me*."

"He needs all of us. Everything you boys can do to help will be a godsend to these people."

Brad found a T-shirt and a clean pair of jeans in his suitcase and tugged the shirt over his head. "I'm going, Justin."

"So?"

"So come with me. Please?"

Justin didn't answer, but at least he didn't refuse.

"It'll be fun," Brad insisted.

Justin sent his brother a withering glance over one shoulder. "Fun? You're crazy."

"No. Really," Brad said. "We can be like cowboys..."

Justin let his head fall back onto the bed. "Real cowboys ride horses and rope cattle. They don't fix up some dumb old farm."

"Actually, real cowboys do both," Clint said.

Rolling his eyes, Justin turned back into his bedclothes.

But Brad persisted. "And we can pretend we're in a rodeo."

"It wouldn't be real," Justin snapped. "And I'm too old to play stupid little-kid games like that."

Justin had apparently scored a hit and Brad's eyes lost a little of their spark.

Clint bit back the sharp words that rose to his lips. He drew a deep breath and spoke carefully. "There's a real rodeo coming up in a few days—are you boys interested in going?"

The spark leaped back into Brad's eyes, and even Justin peeked out from under his arm.

Clint pretended not to notice his oldest son's interest. "It's the Broken Bow Stampede. There's a street carnival, a parade and a rodeo every night for three or four days. There are signs all over town advertising it."

Brad stepped closer. "For real?"

Justin opened his eye a little wider, and Clint worked even harder not to react.

"I'll be glad to get tickets—"

Brad threw his arms around Clint's waist. "Can you really, Dad?"

Justin rolled onto his back and tried to look unimpressed. "I guess it'd be okay if Brad wants to go so bad."

Clint kept his expression impassive in the face of this tiny victory. "All right," he said. "I'll work it out."

Brad grinned and gave Clint another hug. "This is almost as cool as the Bears game Dave took us to. Come on, Justin. Get dressed. I'm *starving*."

Clint deliberately ignored the mention of Dave's name. "I'll see you both downstairs in a minute." Crossing the room, he pulled the door shut behind him.

He had a long way to go, but he had time and determination, and more love to offer than Dave McAllister could ever give his sons. No matter what it took, he'd find a way to break down Justin's walls and win back Brad's devotion.

Just then, Megan padded across the landing lugging Colonel Mustard under one arm. Her bare feet slapped gently on the hardwood floor; she'd already lost the other sock.

In spite of himself, his lips curved in a smile. "Megan, honey. Where are your shoes?"

CLINT PULLED four glasses from the cupboard and filled each with orange juice. Downing his in a few gulps, he faced his children. "Any votes for breakfast?"

Justin narrowed his eyes. "I thought Aunt Phyllis would cook for us."

"Aunt Phyllis has a meeting this morning, so I thought I'd help her by cooking breakfast."

"Great." Sarcasm dripped from the word.

Clint did his best to ignore it. "So, what do you want?"

"Bacon and eggs," Justin demanded.

Brad grabbed his glass, took a sip and said, "Cereal."

Bouncing in her chair, Megan cast her own vote. "I want ice cream."

With his morning already half over, ice cream sounded good to Clint, too. But he leaned against the refrigerator and smiled. "Let's make this easy, okay? One thing at a time. How about bacon and eggs today, cereal tomorrow and—" He broke off and cocked an eyebrow at his daughter.

She started to giggle.

"And ice cream for dessert after dinner tonight." He chucked her under the chin and she grinned impishly at him.

Justin shrugged, but Brad nodded. "Okay by me."

"Great. Now, who wants to set the table?"

Nobody answered.

"All right," he tried again. "Who *will* set the table, even if they don't want to?"

Megan raised her hand and bounced higher.

"Justin, will you help her? You remember where everything is, don't you?"

The boy shrugged again, but crossed to the cupboard that held the plates. Clint opened the refrigerator and scoured the shelves for bacon, butter and milk. Just as he reached for a carton of eggs, a terrified scream pierced the morning calm. Shoving everything onto the table, Clint raced through the living room as a second scream sounded.

He'd grabbed the banister and started up the stairs when Colonel Mustard shot past, a blur of wet orange fur. A second later, Phyllis appeared on the upstairs landing, trembling.

Taking the stairs two at a time, he reached her as the kids skidded to a stop at the foot of the stairs. "What happened? Are you all right?" he asked.

Phyllis nodded, but she looked far from calm.

"What happened?"

Shaking her head to indicate she couldn't speak yet, Phyllis held one hand to her breast as if that would slow her heart rate.

"Was it the cat?" Clint demanded. "Did he scare you?"

"The cat." She nodded and pointed one shaking finger down the hall behind her. "The cat."

"What happened?"

"In the toilet!" Phyllis snapped.

Clint drew back and stared at her. "The *toilet?*"

Phyllis nodded, looking stronger now. "He was in the bowl."

"Doing what? Getting a drink?"

"I don't think so. All I know is that when I lifted the lid he came flying out at me and nearly scared me to death."

Clint looked down at the faces of his children. Justin and Brad were grinning. Megan was not. She'd managed to pull the dripping Colonel Mustard from his hiding place and was holding him under one arm.

"Kitty wanted to go swimming," she said proudly.

Justin and Brad burst out laughing and slapped each other on the back. Clint smiled at the look on his daughter's face.

Phyllis spoke again. "I'm glad you all find that so funny. I could have died of a heart attack."

Megan's lip began to tremble. She stepped closer to her father and held Colonel Mustard a little higher. His waterlogged tail dripped steadily on Phyllis's carpet. "Kitty wanted to go swimming," she insisted.

Clint put an arm around Phyllis's shoulder. "I'm sorry. I had no idea she'd done that."

"I could have died of a heart attack," she repeated. "Or the poor cat could have drowned."

Clint looked down at Megan. "You can't let kitty go swimming in the bathroom, sweetie. He might get hurt."

Her eyes widened. "I just wanted him to have fun."

Phyllis started down the stairs. She stopped beside Megan and hugged the little girl tenderly. "I know you didn't intend to hurt the cat, sweetheart, but swimming's not a good idea."

Megan nodded solemnly, patted the cat's head and planted a kiss between his ears.

Phyllis straightened her shoulders and beamed at the boys. "*Now*, what does everybody want for breakfast?"

"Bacon and eggs."

"Cereal."

Megan hitched Colonel Mustard onto her hip and said, "I want ice cream."

Clint gladly abandoned his ideas about fixing breakfast and watched the kids trail Phyllis into the kitchen. He was still smiling as he followed them.

Whatever the coming year had in store for them, one thing could be counted on. Life was not going to be dull.

GAIL SAT in the front-porch swing and waited for Clint to come back. He'd mentioned the roof on the house again yesterday and had urged her to decide whether or not to replace it. Sudden hailstorms could make June and July the most treacherous months of a Montana summer, and either option presented some risk. It was so frustrating—they might replace the roof now, only to have to do it again in a month. But they could suffer structural damage if a bad storm hit them now.

Her father's strength hadn't improved in the week she'd been here, but she didn't want to make this decision for him. His body might be sick, but his mind was still alert and she often sensed his frustration. He frequently grew agitated at bits of overheard conversation, and Gail didn't want to cause more aggravation by giving Clint the go-ahead on such a huge job.

She'd seen Clint drive out earlier, and she'd guessed he'd gone home to be with his children. But she'd timed her wait almost perfectly. Within ten minutes, she saw his truck turn into the driveway.

Pushing back the now-expected rush of anticipation, she walked out to the yard to meet him. Two young boys sat in the truck with him. He'd brought his sons.

She waited to speak until Clint had dropped to the ground beside her. Long and lean and muscled, he sent her heart racing, but she kept her voice firmly under control and vowed not to let him see the admiration in her eyes. "You were here awfully early this morning."

He frowned slightly. "Did I wake you when I came in?"

"No. I was up. It was my turn to sit with Dad."

The boys climbed out of the cab and inspected her.

"Good morning," she said.

"Guys, this is Gail Wheeler. Gail, these are my sons. Brad—" he nodded toward the smaller boy then turned to older one "—and Justin."

Brad grinned at her, but Justin curled his lip and grunted to acknowledge the introduction.

"They've come to help out," Clint said.

Justin glared at him and muttered something under his breath.

She tried not to read too much into the boy's reaction. "It's nice of you to come," she said.

"Yeah. Right. Like we had any choice." Justin grumbled. His expression reminded Gail vividly of the way Richard's daughter Shelly had looked at her, and the memory left her uncomfortable.

Clint didn't seem to notice. "What did the doctor say yesterday?"

"He showed Mom some exercises to keep Dad's muscles from atrophying, but he said Dad's made no progress."

"Did Dr. Lethbridge sound at all hopeful?"

Gail shook her head. "No. Not particularly. But he's not full of doom, either. He's got a wait-and-see attitude. Once we've done everything we can, we'll know how much recovery to expect down the road."

Clint's eyes clouded. "I'm sorry. It's got to be rough."

"Yes, it is," she admitted and felt a lump start to grow in her throat. She tried to pull herself together. "Do you have another minute or two before you head back out?"

He shrugged at the boys and smiled at her. "Sure."

She led them across the yard slowly. "I wanted to talk with you about the roof."

"Good. What did you decide?"

"Nothing yet. I was hoping you'd be willing to discuss it with Dad."

"All right."

"He can't say much," she warned. "But he *can* communicate a little. I just don't feel right making decisions about his property as if he weren't here."

"I understand. You want me to talk to him now?"

"If you don't mind. I'll give you a cup of coffee afterward."

He grinned at the boys as he pulled off his hat and held open the back door for her. "She's learned my price already."

The younger boy smiled back. The older one looked as if he'd like to hit someone.

Gail tried to work her lips into a smile. "It wasn't very hard to figure out."

Clint gestured toward the table and asked, "Do you mind if the boys wait here?"

"Of course not." In fact, she'd prefer not having Justin and his attitude around, but she didn't admit it aloud. Instead, she busied herself fetching glasses and ice and a pitcher of lemonade from the fridge. "I hope you both like lemonade." Brad nodded, but Justin didn't answer, so she poured two servings and left the pitcher on the table.

When Clint opened the door into the living room, Gail gratefully escaped Justin's hostility and led him toward the guest bedroom.

After knocking softly, Gail pushed the door open the rest of the way. Her mother sat beside Boone's bed with her eyes closed, but she looked up when the door creaked.

"Honey? What on earth?" She halted when she saw Clint and concern filled her eyes. "What's the matter?"

"Nothing's wrong, Mom. We need to make a decision about replacing the roof, and I thought Clint ought to talk to Dad about it."

Her dad's eyelids flickered open and Gail was sure she saw a spark of interest. But her mother hesitated for a full minute before she nodded grudgingly.

Urging Clint to step forward with her, Gail approached the side of Boone's bed. "Daddy? Clint needs to talk to you."

Clint looked at Boone as if the man were hale and hearty, not lying flat on his back. As he explained the dilemma, respect lined his voice, and Gail thanked him silently for it.

Her father moved his head and tried to speak.

"I'll do most of the work myself," Clint said, "but—"

Boone made a strangled sound deep in his throat and struggled to lift his head from the pillow.

Clint flicked a questioning glance at Gail, but she'd seen her father react the same way several times over the last few days, so she nodded for Clint to continue.

Her mother patted her father's hand. "Don't let it worry you, honey. We don't have to decide right now."

Gail leaned a little closer. "But we do have to decide right away, Mom. Once the corn is ready to harvest, Clint won't have time to replace the roof."

"If you'd rather take a chance against the weather," Clint began.

Boone interrupted with another unintelligible sound. He tried to lift his hand from the bed, but dropped it back to his side uselessly.

Dorothy smoothed her hand across his forehead. "I don't think we should discuss this now, Clint."

Gail leaned forward and whispered, "Mom, please—"

"Not *now*," Dorothy insisted.

Boone's agitation increased. He thrashed against his pillow again and gurgled low in his throat.

Dorothy's eyes snapped with anger. "Clint, I want you to leave. *Now*. Look what you're doing to him."

Tears burned Gail's eyes. "Mom, I think Dad's trying to talk to Clint. I think he wants to say something."

Boone made another garbled sound and tried to lunge toward Clint, and Dorothy whirled to face her daughter. "That's enough. Both of you get out of here. Right now." Turning back to Boone, she pressed him onto the bed with gentle hands and spoke softly.

Blinking back her tears, Gail rushed out and she could hear Clint following her. In the living room, she drew a ragged breath and faced him. "I'm so sorry. I had no idea Mom would react that way. And I don't think we did Dad any favor."

"It's not your fault, and I sure can't blame her. Or him. It must be hell to be trapped inside a body that doesn't work."

"I really thought asking his opinion would help him feel useful."

"I know. So did I." He fell silent for a minute, then tried to paste on a smile. "Come on. Let's walk outside for a minute. Maybe the fresh air will help."

His determination to console her touched something deep inside, but she really didn't need him to see her through this. She glanced at the kitchen door. "Your boys are waiting."

Lifting a finger in a silent signal to wait, he slipped into the kitchen, then rejoined her after less than a minute. "They're going to wait for me on the back porch. They'll be all right there for a few minutes. It's you I'm worried about."

"You don't need to be."

He lifted both hands as if to ward off an attack. "Hey, I'm a friend, remember?"

She hadn't meant to sound hostile, so she smiled grudgingly.

Touching the small of her back, he led her out the front door and across the yard toward the lane. In spite of her misgivings, she responded to his lead and she had to admit she was grateful for his company.

He didn't speak until they'd put some distance behind them. When he did, his voice sounded rough-edged. Worried. "Your mother's not facing reality."

"No, she's not."

He looked away and stuffed his hands into his pockets. "She doesn't want my help."

"No."

"Look, I don't want to push in where I'm not wanted, but there's too much to be done around here, and I don't think you can do it alone." His eyes looked dark with anxiety and that brought tears to her own, but she said nothing. "Is there any way your parents can meet their obligations if they lose this year's crop?"

"No. They *need* the money. Especially now, with all the medical bills—" This time, she couldn't force the tears away, and she tried to turn her head before he could see them.

But he'd noticed. He took her by both arms and turned her gently to face him. "Oh, Gail." And before she knew what he intended, he pulled her into an embrace so warm and comforting she wanted to stay there forever.

She wrapped her arms around his waist and held on. He cradled her against him while she cried for her father, for her mother, and for herself.

But gradually as the tears subsided, she recognized a new sensation growing out of the solid comfort she'd felt. Sheltered there against the solid rock of his chest, she took in his masculine scent and let it surround her. She felt his heartbeat quicken and knew her own matched it, and a new fear began to bud.

When he touched his lips to her hair, she didn't pull away. And she knew it wouldn't take any effort at all to lift her face to meet his and to kiss his lips. To let him hold her, to draw temporary strength from the physical contact. But she wouldn't allow herself the luxury. She'd worked too hard to protect her heart, to let this man make her vulnerable.

She pulled out of his embrace and used her fingertips to wipe away the last of her tears. But the open desire in his eyes warned her she'd have to be careful around him in the future. She'd learned to anticipate the advances men usually made and to deflect them in order to avoid attachments and commitment. But this man was already proving dangerous. She couldn't afford to let him get any closer, even if she could forget the girlfriend he had waiting in Chicago.

Clint watched Gail struggle to compose herself and used the few seconds to pull himself together. He'd held her without thinking, but the effect she'd had on him left him shaken. He hadn't expected to feel a surge of desire so strong he'd almost acted on it. Almost tilted her chin and met her lips with his own. Almost brushed her soft mouth—

He swore silently. What was wrong with him? How could he even *think* that way? What about Leslie?

He readjusted his hat and shoved his hands into his pockets as if they were offending creatures who'd betrayed him. And he tried to take up the conversation as if she'd just spoken. As if the ground hadn't just shifted beneath his feet.

"I'd like to help as long as I can. And the boys can give me a hand in the mornings . . ."

She nodded, but refused to meet his gaze. "Thank you. I'm going to need the help."

"What will your mother say?"

This time, she flicked a glance at him. "That we don't need help. That Dad'll be out of bed any day now and that he'll be able to do the work all himself. Oh, Clint, how can she be so blind?"

"She's seeing what she wants to see."

When Gail shook her head, her hair fell across her shoulder like chocolate silk. "I'm just going to have to convince her how much we need you around here."

"Do you think you can?"

She smiled bravely, but her eyes betrayed her uncertainty. "I *have* to. I have no choice." She looked back toward the house and a faint smile touched her lips. "I'll talk to her."

"Then I'll stay on."

"Thank you." Her smile grew a little. "I suppose you'll want that cup of coffee I promised you."

"I thought you'd forgotten."

"I wouldn't dare."

They turned back toward the house in silence. When every instinct urged Clint to touch her, he rammed his fists deeper into his pockets. When the sweet smell of her shampoo drifted up to meet him, he averted his head. And when she started up the porch stairs ahead of him and her feminine curves danced before his eyes, he ground his teeth and tried to concentrate on his list of chores. If he could just keep his mind off Gail.

Pausing midstep, he thought of Leslie. And with a welcome flash of insight, he realized why he'd reacted to Gail this way. Obviously, he missed Leslie.

He pulled his fists out of his pocket and straightened his shoulders. It had been far too long since he'd really talked to Leslie. Far too long since he'd held *her* in his arms. He'd call her tonight as promised, and by tomorrow he'd be back to normal.

Smiling now, he managed to follow Gail inside and ignore all her obvious charms. And he steadfastly refused to even think about kissing her again.

CHAPTER FIVE

CLINT CLOSED his bedroom door and pulled off his shirt as he sat on the foot of his bed. It had been an exhausting day, and a difficult dinner hour spent listening to Phyllis reciting a list of Megan's escapades. If Phyllis had been twenty years younger, Megan's zest for life might not have exacted such a toll, but she'd sounded tired already.

Tomorrow after breakfast, he'd talk with Megan again and remind her to slow down a little for Aunt Phyllis. And she'd remember for about an hour before curiosity and enthusiasm got the best of her. Tonight, he needed to talk with Leslie. With the kids settled, and Hal and Phyllis closeted in their bedroom, he finally had a few free minutes.

Leslie answered on the third ring, and her voice came through the wire cool and sharp, as if he'd interrupted something important. Had she forgotten he'd promised to call tonight?

"Leslie? It's Clint."

"Clint?" Her voice softened a little. "What a nice surprise. Nothing's wrong, is it?"

"No. Nothing's wrong." Unless he counted his unwitting reaction to holding Gail in his arms this afternoon. "We just haven't had a chance to really talk for a while."

She sighed softly. "I know. I miss you."

"I miss you, too."

"You know where to find me." Though the words might have offered an invitation, Clint didn't feel one in her tone.

"I sure do," he agreed. "And in another couple of months—"

She interrupted with an impatient sound. "I don't want to wait another couple of months, Clint. This has already been the longest year of my life."

"It's almost over," he promised, but his response felt inadequate.

Another pause, longer this time. He heard her pull in a deep breath. "I guess I'm still upset about the party. I can't pretend I'm not."

"I know, and I feel terrible—"

"If you did, you'd come home. You wouldn't have asked me to cancel everything I've worked so long to set up."

Clint's stomach tightened at the disappointment in her voice and knotted at the hurt he heard behind it, but he didn't want to get drawn into an old argument—especially when they were both right. Standing, he paced as far as the cord would allow. "I'm sorry, Leslie. I don't know what else I can say."

"Say you've changed your mind. Say you'll come home for your birthday. I can't get the O'Connor Mansion any longer, but we can be together."

He wanted to make her happy, but Boone's image flashed through his mind, and the memory of Gail's tear-streaked face and trembling body kept him from backing down. "I can't, Les. I might be able to spare a night but with connecting flights and travel schedules, I'd lose two full days."

"I see." Leslie waited so long to speak again he wondered whether she'd hung up. "Tell me, did their daughter show up?" she said at last.

"Gail? Yes, she's here."

"What's she like?"

"*Like?*" Clint hesitated. "She's nice."

"Is she any help? Or is everything still on your shoulders?"

"She's busy with the house, the garden and her parents. I'm doing the rest." But he didn't want to talk about Gail. Not even with Leslie. Or maybe *especially* not with Leslie. He wanted to get Gail, her thick dark hair and her wide black eyes out of his mind. "The boys are going to start helping me for a couple of hours every morning."

"The boys? What do they know about working on a farm?"

Clint chuckled. "Nothing yet. But they'll learn."

"Oh, sweetheart. You're killing yourself to help these people, and now you're going to slow yourself down by letting the boys go with you? That doesn't make any sense. Surely you can work faster if you don't have to teach them."

"Actually, I think it will be good for them."

"For *them,* maybe. But what about you?"

"This is going to give me a chance to rebuild my relationship with them, Les. My first real time alone with them since the divorce."

"That's wonderful," she said in a tone that suggested she felt otherwise. "But it's not as if you're going to stay in Montana forever, or even as if they're going to live with you for long—"

He'd never deluded himself into thinking this visit would last forever, but the callous way she'd reminded him stung as if she'd slapped him. "No, it's not."

"I just don't want to see you get hurt again when they go back to Barbara." This time, her voice sounded warmer than it had during their entire conversation.

A thousand responses rose to Clint's lips, but he didn't make any of them. He couldn't deny what he knew to be true, but he didn't know how to explain that forging this bond with his children and then letting go wouldn't hurt nearly as much as allowing his relationship with them to deteriorate.

When he didn't answer, Leslie said, "Just promise me you won't leave yourself open."

"These are my kids, Leslie. They're not going to hurt me."

"I never said they'd do it on purpose. But you're too vulnerable where they're concerned. I worry about you."

"Well, don't." His words came out sharper than he'd intended, so he softened his tone and tried to steer her onto a less touchy subject. "Tell me about the office. How did the meeting with that new client go the other day?"

When she hesitated, he wondered whether she'd follow his lead. But at last she said, "It went well. I think we'll cinch the contract, but their CEO's taking his time making a final decision. Of course, that means we're all putting in extra hours."

She tried to sound put-out, but Clint knew she loved her work, its frantic pace and its merciless demands on her time. Without Davis-Buehler, Leslie would be lost. His own career often demanded a ten- or twelve-hour day and extra hours in a crisis. But he didn't thrive on it the way Leslie did. "I'll be anxious to hear the minute he makes a decision."

"The *minute?* You have a fax machine in the middle of a cornfield?"

"Please, Les—"

But she interrupted him. "Of course I'll call, sweetheart. Just as soon as I know I can reach you."

"Great."

Heavy silence hummed between them before she spoke again. "If you change your mind about coming next weekend, call me on my cellular phone."

"I can't come home, Leslie."

"No, Clint, you *can* but you *won't.* There's a big difference."

He couldn't think of a suitable response, so he didn't make one.

She sighed. "Listen to us, we're starting to sound like an old married couple on the verge of divorce. What's happening to us?"

"We don't sound that bad, Les. It's just—" He broke off, unable to pinpoint exactly where the trouble lay.

"I've really got to go to bed," she said abruptly. "It's late and I have an early appointment—"

"Well, then, get some sleep. I'll talk to you again soon."

"Sunday would be good. And I'll call you next Saturday on your birthday. Will you be around?"

"Make it late."

"Of course. I'll give you time to get your chores done."

He didn't have the energy to fight her, so he let the sarcasm in her words hang there.

"Clint?"

"Yeah?"

"I love you."

Realizing he'd been about to hang up without saying those words to her, he tightened his hold on the receiver. "I love you, too."

When she broke their connection, he replaced the receiver and stared at his bedroom wall. He paced to the open window and replayed the conversation. He'd hurt her again, and she hadn't hesitated to let him know it. He'd give almost anything to find a way to keep her happy without abandoning Gail and her parents.

Shoving his hands into his pockets, he turned away from the cool night breeze. He sat on his bed and tugged off his boots. It never failed to amaze him how life could go along smoothly for months, then shift without warning and throw everything out of balance. It had happened to him when his ulcers had perforated and Barbara asked for the divorce. Again, when his doctor had insisted on this year's leave of absence from Garrity & Garr. And now...

He smiled to himself. At least this time the shift was a pleasant one. Or it *could* be. If he could make Leslie happy, contain Megan's zest for life when Phyllis was in charge and find a way to reach Justin and Brad.

Standing suddenly, he crossed the room and opened the door. Maybe a piece of Phyllis's leftover chicken and a glass of her iced tea would help him relax.

Once downstairs, he closed the kitchen door and switched on a light. He found a glass in the cupboard and pulled open the refrigerator. As he reached for the pitcher, a sudden movement on the shelf startled him. The glass slipped from his hand and hit the floor, shattering into a million pieces.

As if he did this every evening, Colonel Mustard leaped from the refrigerator's bottom shelf onto the floor. Clenching a half-eaten chicken leg in his mouth, the cat picked his way through the maze of broken glass and sauntered into the living room with a twitch of his tail.

Clint stared after the animal, unable to move until it disappeared. Then he turned back to the refrigerator and stared at the bowl of chicken with its ravaged foil cover and Colonel Mustard's rubber-mouse squeeze toy on the shelf beside it. Obviously, Megan had struck again. She'd probably decided the kitty might like a midnight snack and had left him where he could find one. Thankfully, the poor animal hadn't been locked inside long enough to suffocate, but Clint added it to his list of things to discuss with Megan in the morning.

He swept up the glass, pulled the cat's toy from the fridge, emptied the chicken into the garbage and washed the bowl. As he worked, he tried to figure out the best way to explain this to Phyllis. And he thanked his lucky stars *he'd* found the cat this time.

GAIL DRIED the last of the breakfast dishes and put them into the cupboard. She wanted to get the peas shelled and frozen and do something with those buckets of spinach before the kitchen grew too warm in the afternoon heat.

She let her gaze drift out the window to where Clint and his sons worked on the fence. The younger boy— Brad—looked eager. Justin looked angry.

She tore her eyes away from the picture they made and centered a vase of daisies on the table. Gail couldn't remember a time when she'd made a request of Shelly that hadn't provoked anger. The teenager had blamed Gail for Richard's divorce and her own pain. Looking back, Gail realized Shelly had been determined to make Gail suffer with her.

Maybe Gail would have done better if Richard hadn't been so much older. If his children had been younger. Her heart went out to Clint and his boys, but she didn't know what it would take to mend their relationships. And thank goodness, she didn't have to get involved.

With effort, she pulled her thoughts back to her morning tasks. Once she started the vegetables, they'd demand all her attention, so if she wanted to spend a few minutes with her father, she'd better do it first, she decided.

She hurried down the hall and looked inside the bedroom. Her father lay stretched out on the bed, and her mother occupied an easy chair, still pretending to read.

"Is everything okay in here?" Gail asked.

Dorothy looked up with a gentle smile. "We're fine, sweetheart. What are your plans this morning?"

Gail leaned against the doorframe. "I just did the dishes and I thought I'd work on the peas and spinach. Then maybe I'll finish piecing together the quilt top this afternoon."

Dorothy nodded but her mouth puckered. "Well, you *can,* I guess. But I'm sure there are strawberries in the garden, and you know how your dad likes frozen strawberry jam."

"Okay. I'll pick them this evening when it's a little cooler."

Her mother smiled. "Good. If you're going to finish that quilt this time, we'll need to borrow a quilting frame, I guess."

"Don't you still have yours?"

"Not anymore. I haven't quilted in so many years... I know, why don't you call Phyllis? I'm sure she'd love to loan hers to you."

"You don't think she's using it?"

"Heavens, no. She's so busy right now with those kids of Clint's—" Dorothy shot a glance toward the window, then looked back with a firm nod. "On second thought, let me call her. I need to see how she's managing."

"I'll stay with Dad while you do."

Propping open her book on the floor, Dorothy pushed to her feet. "He's looking much better today, isn't he?"

Gail couldn't respond. Her father's pale face and deeply shadowed eyes gave him such a gaunt look, she couldn't agree, and she didn't want to voice her disagreement where he could hear her.

When Dorothy left the room, Gail crossed to the chair. But just before she sat, she lifted the window shade and looked out at the yard again. Clint and his sons were lifting a long two-by-four into place, then the boys held the board steady while Clint hammered the nails.

Smiling, she watched for several minutes, then lowered the blind and turned back to her father's bed. This time, his eyes were open and she could tell he'd been watching her.

He blinked once, slowly, as if it cost him some effort, and his mouth worked for several seconds to speak. "Good man."

Gail's face flamed with embarrassment, and she dropped into the chair beside his bed. "Clint's a nice guy."

Her father lowered his eyelids again, then focused on her. "*Good* man."

Before Gail had to reply, her mother came back into the room. Dorothy wiped her hands on her pant legs and touched her fingers to Boone's forehead, but she spoke over her shoulder to Gail. "Phyllis sounds absolutely frazzled. She's trying to get that little girl of Clint's down for a morning nap, but you know how kids that age are..." She paused and shook her head solemnly. "Anyway, she'll be glad to loan you the frame. Just make sure Clint knows he's to bring it back with him after lunch in case she forgets."

"I'll go get it after I finish the peas. I'll probably be glad of a break, and Clint's got enough to do."

Dorothy looked exasperated, but held her peace. Boone kept his eyes on Gail and mumbled again. "Good man."

Looking concerned, Dorothy leaned toward him. "What did you say, honey?"

But Boone closed his eyes and lapsed into silence, as if his efforts to communicate with Gail had drained his reserves. And Gail hurried away before her mother could question her about her father's latest observation.

CLINT PULLED a nail from his pocket and positioned it on the two-by-four. "Hold that end steady, guys. Have you got it?"

Brad nodded. "I think so." But Justin didn't respond.

Because Clint knew his reactions to the boy's attitude only seemed to fuel the hostilities, he'd promised himself not to let Justin rile him this morning. But it was easier said than done. "What about you, Justin?"

"How much longer do you expect us to do this?"

"Until we finish. Another hour, maybe."

Rolling his eyes, Justin looked away. But when the board shifted slightly out of position, he sent Clint a look full of expectation and insolence, as if he expected the worst and intended to give it first.

With an effort, Clint kept all expression from his face and waited for the boys to reposition the board. Without speaking, he pounded in the nail and fished another from his pocket.

"We have to do this *whole* fence?" Justin demanded.

Clint nodded. "The whole thing. You can see what bad shape it's in."

Brad shifted his grip on the plank. "I think this is fun."

"You would, you little dweeb," Justin snarled.

Clint frowned. "Knock it off, Justin. Say what you want to me, but I won't tolerate you talking to your brother that way."

Justin flushed and his eyes glinted. "Fine. Do the stupid fence yourself." He pushed at the board and strode toward the house. But when he saw Gail standing in the doorway, he pivoted away and jogged down the lane.

Clint turned to Brad. "What's the matter with Justin? Was it something I said?"

Brad shrugged and stared after his brother. "He's mad at you."

"I know. Any idea why?"

"Nope. He doesn't tell me anything." Brad sounded convincing enough, but his gaze shifted.

Clint suspected the boy knew more than he was telling. But whether it was loyalty to his brother or fear of hurting his father's feelings that kept Brad silent, Clint didn't think he wanted to know.

He lay down the hammer and put an arm around Brad's shoulder. "Maybe Justin has the right idea. What do you say we all take a break?"

"Okay."

"Want to come up to the house with me for a drink of something cold?"

Again Brad's expression shifted. He shook his head. "Maybe in a minute. Okay?"

"Okay."

Without another word, Brad ran down the lane after his brother. And Clint cursed himself under his breath. Justin had been looking for an excuse to get angry with him, and Clint had practically handed him one on a silver platter. Now Justin was angry, Brad had chosen his brother's side in the battle and Clint had come out the loser once more.

He turned toward the house, embarrassed that Gail had witnessed his latest disaster. He told himself he needed a glass of ice water. He tried to convince himself he only wanted a few minutes' break so he could sit in the shade of the porch and cool down a little. But when he saw that Gail had disappeared from the doorway and disappointment flashed through him, he had to admit what he really wanted was a few minutes of her company. He hoped she hadn't gone far.

As he neared the porch, she pushed open the screen with her hip and backed onto the porch holding two huge empty bowls and two cans of cola.

She smiled when she saw him. "Thirsty?"

In spite of his turbulent emotions, her smile pulled an answering one from him. "Very."

"I thought you might be. There's punch inside for the boys—or they can have soda if it's okay with you."

"Either. Both." He tried to laugh. "*If* they come back."

She stared up the lane at the receding figures of his sons. Brad had caught up with Justin and they were walking side by side toward the road. She handed Clint an icy can, then opened her own. "I'm sure they will. Give them time."

Clint opened his drink and shook his head. "Maybe I'm just asking for too much too soon."

"Probably."

He didn't know what he'd expected her to say, but it hadn't been that. Surprised, he laughed. "Don't beat around the bush, Gail. Tell me what you *really* think."

She smiled again, and her eyes darkened. "They've only been here a few days, Clint. And I'm sure they've been through a lot the past few years. First the divorce. Then their mother got remarried almost immediately and they had to get used to a new man in your place. That's not easy for kids. Your kids are lucky they like their stepdad." He snorted his response to that observation, but Gail didn't let it faze her. "And now she's left the country and dumped them with you as if she doesn't care about them."

"That's not true," he protested.

"Maybe it is, in their minds." She sat on one of the white patio chairs beside several buckets of peas, positioned one bowl between her knees and placed the other at her feet.

Clint studied her just long enough to comprehend the wisdom in her words. Leaning against the porch railing, he took another mouthful of cola. "You really think that's how they feel?"

"I've had a little experience with kids whose parents have been divorced, but *I* was the stepparent. In my case, they hated me. In your case, they hate you." She grinned at him to show she was teasing, then sobered and stared up the lane again. "Look, I know I'm not good with kids, but I think *I'd* feel that way... Wouldn't you?"

"I guess I would." He watched her scoop up another handful of peas. "Maybe you're right about Justin, but Brad doesn't care so much. He already thinks of Dave as his new father."

"Well, of course he does."

He stared at her. Something inside him wanted to take offense at her words, but her tone of voice stopped him. *"Of course?"*

She gave a little laugh. "That came out wrong, I guess. But Brad's what—ten? You've been divorced two years? So he was only eight when you left home."

Uncertain what point she was trying to make, Clint nodded.

"He's getting on with his life the only way he knows how. Just like you're doing. And like Justin's doing. My stepkids were older. They didn't adjust so well. In a way, Brad's lucky."

He digested that thought in silence for several minutes. He'd never considered the boys' reactions in that light before. Something in her words sounded exactly right, but he wasn't ready to admit it. Yet.

"So you're saying I shouldn't feel bad when my boys would rather be with their stepfather than with me?"

"That's just the point, Clint. They probably don't prefer Dave to you. But what choice do they have? He lives in their house, he's married to their mother... He's there every single day. You're not."

Standing quickly, he glared at her. "That's not by *my* choice."

"I never said it was. I'm not talking about you and your feelings right now. I'm talking about those two boys." She gestured with a handful of peas toward the tiny figures of his sons. "Right or wrong, good or bad—that's the way things are for them. They're confused, and you need to help them find their way. If they knew what to do, they wouldn't need parents."

He wanted to argue. To defend himself. To tell her how wrong she was. But she wasn't wrong. He just didn't know how to admit it.

When his silence went on for several seconds, she looked away. "I'm sorry. It's none of my business."

"You're right."

She flushed. "I won't interfere again."

He closed the distance between them and hunkered down in front of her. "No, I mean, you're *right*. And I'm really glad you interfered."

"I'll bet you are," she said, turning to him again. Her eyes still looked serious, but a humorous note had crept into her voice.

He chuckled. "How can I ever repay you?"

Her lips twitched and she pushed one of the bucketsful of peas in his direction. "Shell these."

Shaking his head, he backed up a step. "I don't know how."

She grinned at him. "Well, it *is* very difficult. And it takes special skill. Manual dexterity. I'm not sure you have what it takes."

"Neither am I. How about another task?"

Her face grew serious. "You're doing a wonderful job with the fence. I don't know what we'd do without your help."

"I'll start on the roof next. Any idea how long it's been since your dad replaced the shingles?"

She shrugged. "I don't know. Mom can't remember the last time he did it. We've had hailstones the size of golf balls in the past, and the storm last month could have ripped it up badly."

Clint sat on the chair beside hers and reached for a handful of peas. "Well, other than replacing the shingles, we don't have a lot of structural repairs to make yet." He watched her zip open a pod and push the peas into the bowl with her thumb. "What are you doing with these?"

"Mom wants me to freeze them. And the spinach." With a wry smile, she gestured toward another cluster of buckets. "And there are strawberries to turn into jam, the green beans need to be staked and the whole garden needs to be weeded . . ." She trailed off and shook her head.

"Really? I've never met a woman who actually knew how to do all this before."

She laughed at him. "Of course you have. Phyllis does her own canning every year."

He answered with an embarrassed smile. He'd been thinking of the young, beautiful women he knew, but he didn't explain. "You want me to have the boys give you a hand?"

Her smile slipped. "No."

"Really. They need things to do, and they may as well help you, too." She shook her head, but he didn't let her interrupt him. "Having something constructive to do will be good for them, and there are some things they can't help me with. The roof, for instance. I can't let them up there—it's too dangerous. But they *can* weed and stake beans..."

She stared at him for a long moment before she finally nodded. "All right."

He smiled. "Great. I'll feel better knowing they're doing something helpful."

She smiled in return, but some emotion hid behind her eyes.

"Listen," he said. "If it's not okay with you—"

"It's fine. I'll appreciate their help."

He studied her, trying to decide how she really felt.

She lifted her chin and met his gaze squarely and he saw the same grim determination he'd seen the first night they'd met. "So, are you going to shell those peas?"

He dropped the few he was holding. "I'd love to, but the fence is calling me."

To his relief, she laughed and whatever she'd been hiding disappeared from behind her eyes. "Just in time, too. Your assistants are coming back."

He glanced over his shoulder as Justin and Brad turned into the yard, relieved that they'd come back on their own. "You kids want some punch or a soda?"

"Do you have Dr. Pepper?" Brad shouted.

Clint looked to Gail for that answer, but she shook her head. "Sorry," he said. "Second choice?"

Brad stepped onto the porch with a shrug. "I don't care. I like Dr. Pepper because me and Dave always share, but I like other stuff, too."

Dave again. Clint had to struggle to keep his smile in place.

Gail looked up at the boys. "If you don't mind checking the fridge yourselves, you can help yourselves to whatever's in there." She zipped open another pea pod, but instead of dropping the peas into the bowl, she popped them into her mouth.

"Can I try some of those," Brad asked.

She dropped several pods into his hands and held some out to Justin. Justin accepted the offer and watched intently as she showed them what to do. Neither boy spared Clint a second glance.

"I'll get you something to drink," he said. Still forcing a smile, Clint turned away and stepped into the kitchen. Obviously, Justin's anger didn't extend to the whole world; he was only mad with his father. Clint couldn't decide whether that made him feel better... or worse.

CHAPTER SIX

HALFWAY TO Hal and Phyllis's, Gail turned on the radio and rolled down the window to let the warm summer breeze mix with the music. And for a few seconds, she felt seventeen again. As if she were driving to pick up her best friend, Bette Heywood. As if they were heading into Broken Bow to meet Tom and Randy. As if life were fresh and new and exciting, and each day promised an adventure.

She could almost forget her father's illness and her mother's self-delusion. She could almost put aside the pain she'd seen on Clint's face this morning when Justin turned surly and Brad mentioned their stepfather. Almost.

She let the wind tug a lock of her hair out the window and she cranked up the radio another notch. Farmland stretched away from the highway, gold and green and brown, like solid patchwork pieces. In the distance, she could see dust rising from a truck as someone drove into the fields.

A little closer to the highway, Rosalyn Marsh's sheets stretched across a clothesline and tossed in the breeze. For the first time in years, Gail found herself wanting to hang her own sheets on the line so she could sleep with the sunshine at night. She smiled at the thought and realized that even with her father so ill, she'd been smiling a lot more lately.

Reluctantly, she admitted Clint played a part in that. And that his friendship might be good for her. He had a commitment to someone else, which meant their friendship could never develop into something serious, which kept her safe. Maybe it *had* been good for her to come home.

At the turnoff to Hal and Phyllis's place, she slowed the car and turned onto the dusty half-mile driveway to their sprawling old farmhouse. She let the car crawl down the track and relished the tangy smell of sunflowers and the clear song of a meadowlark.

Just ahead, she caught sight of something bright red a few feet off the side. When it moved, she stopped the car and watched as a small girl in crimson overalls hoisted an orange cat to her shoulder and toddled back onto the driveway. The child couldn't be more than four or five years old. Too young to be alone this far from the house.

When the child saw the car, she stopped and waved one chubby hand. "Hello, person I don't know."

"Hello. Where are you going?"

"I'm taking a walk with the kitty."

"Should you be so close to the highway?"

The girl nodded. "I have to. I'm going to find Justin and Brad. They're my brothers, and Colonel Mustard misses them."

Gail shifted into Park and looked behind her at the highway. Remembering the speed she'd traveled on her way here, nausea welled in her stomach. "You can't take the kitty out there," she said. "It's dangerous."

The child looked stricken and tightened her hold on the cat. "But that's where Daddy taked my brothers, and we need to find them."

"You must be Megan."

The child nodded again.

"My name's Gail. Your daddy took your brothers over to my house, but it's a long way there, and you might get hurt."

The little girl shook her head. "No, I won't. Because I'm *very* careful. My mommy taught me to look both ways."

Gail climbed out of the car so she could put herself on a level with the child. "I'm very glad your mommy taught you that, but people driving on this road aren't expecting a little girl and a kitty to be walking along it. Even *I* don't take walks along that road."

The child studied her for a moment before tears sprang into her clear blue eyes. "But how can I see my brothers? And my daddy?"

"Your brothers will be back soon for lunch. Then they'll stay here with you all afternoon."

"That's too long to wait. Colonel Mustard needs them *now.*"

"It's not really so long—"

The girl shoved the cat farther onto her shoulder and nodded. "It's *very* long. Hours and hours. And my daddy won't come home until it's almost dark outside and I have to go to bed before that. So, I'm going to walk to your house and I'll be very careful. I promise. And I won't let kitty get hurt."

A pang of guilt stabbed Gail at her unwitting role in keeping the child from Clint, and a new concern arose. "Where's your aunt Phyllis? Does she know what you're doing?"

"She's taking a nap."

"So she doesn't know where you are?"

"Oh, no." The girl looked solemn. "She wanted me to take a nap, but I wasn't sleepy. But *she* was, and she fell asleep."

In spite of her concern, Gail couldn't help smiling. "I think maybe you and I had better go talk to Aunt Phyllis."

"But I want to go see my daddy and my brothers."

"I'll tell you what. If Aunt Phyllis says it's okay, I'll take you back home with me and you can see them. But only if you promise you won't try to walk over there again."

The girl considered the deal, then nodded. "Okay."

"Shall I give you a ride back to the house?"

The child shook her head. "My mommy says I'm never supposed to get in a car with a stranger."

"You have a smart mommy. I guess I am a stranger to you, aren't I? Well, you're right, Megan. You shouldn't have a ride with me unless Aunt Phyllis or your daddy says it's okay." Gail held out her hand. "Can I walk back to the house with you? I'll leave the car here for a few minutes."

Megan shook her head at Gail's outstretched hand. "I have to hold on to the kitty. *He* still wants to take a walk and Daddy says I have to take care of him."

As they followed the driveway toward the house, Gail matched her pace to Megan's. Every few feet, the child stopped to study a creature on the dusty path, and twice she darted into the field to chase something. Colonel Mustard rode stoically on Mcgan's small shoulder, jostled and bounced and wearing a look of long-suffering on his feline face.

When they reached the house, Gail stepped onto the porch and knocked on the wooden screen door. The sound echoed through Phyllis's kitchen, but earned no response.

Megan lifted her finger to her lips. "Shh. She's asleep."

"I know, but—"

Pulling open the door, Megan tiptoed into the kitchen. "Come on. But be *quiet*. I have to be nice to Aunt Phyllis."

Gail followed her inside and held the screen to keep it from banging shut.

"You can have some lemonade if you want."

"Would you like some?"

Megan nodded. "Yes, but I can't pour it by myself. I tried yesterday and I spilled it and all kinds of bad things happened—"

When the little girl pulled open the refrigerator and tried to lug out the heavy pitcher, Gail rushed to ease it from her grasp.

"I tried to clean it up, but Aunt Phyllis said I shouldn't use the tablecloth to mop the floor. But it was the only thing I could *find*—"

Gail placed the pitcher on the counter and bit back a smile at the girl's serious expression.

"And she said I shouldn't have let the kitty step in it, but he was trying to help me clean it up, and he wanted a drink. And I *told* him not to walk on the couch with sticky paws—" She broke off and shook her head. "Sometimes he's just impossible."

This time, Gail let her smile show. Megan was obviously quoting something she'd heard adults say about her. Probably quite often. Thankfully, the child didn't seem to have internalized the criticism. Gail certainly hoped the censure would never quash the child's delightful spirit.

Gail touched the girl's cheek with one finger. "Where does Aunt Phyllis keep the glasses?"

"Over there." Megan pointed at a cupboard and raced toward it. Before Gail could catch her, the child had planted one sneakered toe on the handle of a drawer and started to climb onto the counter.

Gail snagged her by the waist and swung her back to the floor. "I don't want you to fall."

"I won't. I do that all the time." All at once, the look on Megan's face shifted from stubborn to concerned, as if she'd just remembered something. "But Aunt Phyllis doesn't like me to. You won't tell her, will you?"

"If you promise you'll try to remember not to do it."

"I promise." She grinned up at Gail. "My daddy lets me climb as long as he's there to watch me."

"Your daddy must be awfully nice."

Megan nodded. "He is. Nicer than my other daddy." Her forehead puckered. "Brad says Dave's nicer than our real daddy because Dave buys us stuff all the time."

Gail's smile wilted. "Oh."

"And Justin says our real daddy is a jerk, but I don't think he is."

"I don't think he is, either."

"But Justin says he's a jerk because he left us and Mommy."

Gail helped Megan onto a chair and placed a glass of lemonade in front of her on the table, then poured some for herself and took a seat across from the girl.

"Sometimes mommies and daddies just can't live together," Gail said, "and it's nobody's fault. But the children can only live with one parent at a time—"

Just then, the kitchen door opened and Gail broke off at the sight of Phyllis, hair tousled from her nap, eyes frantic.

The older woman took in the scene before her and sagged against the doorframe. "Thank goodness. When did you get here, Gail?"

"Just a few minutes ago. I ran into Megan taking a walk."

Phyllis came into the room and sank onto a chair. "I woke up and found her gone. She must not have slept very long."

Gail didn't know how to answer that. Phyllis's obvious concern for the child warred with Gail's growing fear that the girl was too much for the older woman to handle.

She reined in her thoughts and told herself she was imagining trouble because she'd found the child unsupervised once. Besides, what options did Clint have? She couldn't tell him he was making a mistake leaving Megan in Phyllis's care when the reason he was doing so was a result of Gail's own needs.

Phyllis ruffled Megan's hair and kissed her forehead. "You worried me, Sweet Pea."

Megan's eyes clouded. "I didn't *mean* to."

"I'm sure you didn't, but you mustn't do it again." Phyllis glanced at Gail and managed a thin smile. "Did you come to pick up the quilt frame yourself?"

Gail pulled her concern back into line. She was overreacting. Phyllis obviously loved the child and cared deeply about her welfare. "I didn't want Clint to have to bring it . . ."

Phyllis shooed her words away with one hand. "Nonsense. He has to go over there, anyway." She paused for a moment, then said, "Gracious, it's wonderful to see you again. It's been so long! Stand up and let me take a look at you."

Gail flushed with embarrassment, but stood while Phyllis studied her.

"You look beautiful. You've filled out so nicely—all that dark hair, and your eyes—"

"You look wonderful, too, Phyllis."

Phyllis laughed. "I know exactly how *I* look, missie." She pushed Megan's lemonade glass away from the edge of the table. "I talked to your mother this morning. She says your dad's feeling much better."

Gail shook her head. "She wants him to feel better, but I don't see any improvement."

"No? Well, that's what Clint says, too." Phyllis looked away for a second and smiled again at Megan. "I hope Clint's been some help to you."

"He's been wonderful. I don't know what I'd do without him there."

Megan retrieved her glass and filled her mouth with lemonade until her cheeks bulged. With a loud swallow, she grinned. "She doesn't think my daddy's a jerk."

Phyllis frowned. "Your daddy's *not* a jerk." She turned to Gail. "Honestly, the things that woman must have told these children..."

But Gail didn't want Phyllis to compound the mistake by saying things about Megan's mother within the child's hearing. She stood quickly and hugged Phyllis. "I wish I could stay longer, but I ought to get back. I'll bring the car around so I can load the quilting frame."

"Of course." Phyllis's forehead puckered. "Now, let me think. Where did Hal tell me he'd put that frame?"

Taking another large swallow of lemonade, Megan scooted off her chair. "Aren't I going with you? You said maybe I could."

Phyllis sent Gail a confused glance.

"I told her I'd take her to see her daddy and brothers—if it's all right with you."

"You don't need to do that—"

"Please," Megan begged.

"It's all right," Gail said. "I'd enjoy having her visit for a couple of hours."

"Oh, please, *please.*" Megan jumped up and down, and her sunny hair bounced into her eyes with every hop.

Phyllis tried to look stern, but a smile tugged at the corners of her mouth. "Oh, all right," she said at last. "But *behave.*"

"I promise." Megan stopped bouncing and raced toward the back door. "Come on, Gail."

Phyllis watched her scamper outside and race down the stairs before she turned back to Gail. "She's a handful."

Gail laughed. "Yes, she is. It only took me a minute to realize that."

"You don't need to do this—"

"I really don't mind," Gail assured her. And the truth of her words surprised her.

"Well, all right. I can't pretend I won't be glad for an hour to myself." She led Gail to the door and opened the screen. "But if she's too much for you, or if she bothers your dad, you bring her right back."

"I will," Gail promised. "Now, where did you say the quilting frame was?"

"It must be in the shed. I'm sure it'll be covered in dust. Let me grab a rag so we can get the worst of it off and I'll meet you around back."

Gail walked back to the car and pulled it as close to the shed as she could. Together, she and Phyllis dug the frame from its resting place. Megan darted back and forth from the shed to the car, carrying one C-clamp at a time to deposit in the back seat before returning for another. And she chattered the entire time—about Clint, the kitty, her mother and Dave, and her brothers.

Megan was about as different from Shelly as night from day. As Gail walked behind the child, she couldn't help wondering what life with Richard and his kids would have been like if she'd married him when Shelly was this age instead of thirteen. Before she grew sullen and angry. And for a moment, Gail wondered if she could have been a competent stepmother, after all.

CLINT BROUGHT his truck to a stop at the edge of the dirt road and jumped from the cab. He'd almost finished checking the crop in the quarter of land closest to the house, and with luck he'd finish the entire south section before nightfall.

The summer sun had climbed high in the clear June sky, and now it beat down on his neck and shoulders as he walked. Pushing back his hat, he wiped his forehead and worried that the two hours he'd spent with the boys this morning had cut too far into his day.

Leslie's words from their conversation last night echoed through his mind, and for one split second he wondered whether she was right. *Was* he making a mistake by having the boys help him?

He cursed under his breath and forced the niggling doubt away. He'd just have to work harder. And faster. And somehow, he'd get everything done. He had no choice.

He rubbed the back of his arm across his forehead again and glanced toward the house as he started into the field. But the sight of figures moving around in the yard stopped him. Even at this distance he could make out Justin and Brad painting the fence, but it was Gail getting out of her mother's car that caught his eye and held his attention. He'd seen her drive away less than an hour ago, so he hadn't expected her back so soon.

She reached into the car and stood again, and this time she held something—someone—small and blond and wiggly. Megan? It couldn't be.

He squinted into the sunlight and tried to make out details. When the child slid from Gail's grasp and scampered across the yard to the boys, he knew for certain. It *was* Megan. But why was she here?

Abandoning his tasks without a second thought, he raced to the pickup and climbed into the cab. As he bounced along the rutted road to the house, he told himself there were a dozen possible reasons for Megan's being here. But only one would form into conscious thought: something must have happened to Phyllis.

Though he hadn't gone far from the house, the drive back seemed to take forever. So, by the time he reached the yard, his hands trembled on the steering wheel, his heart slammed in his chest and his stomach churned at the news he anticipated.

Expecting to see Gail's face solemn, he cut the engine and climbed out of the cab. But she looked relaxed and happy, and she sent him a smile that made his heart lurch for another reason altogether.

He told himself his reaction must be one of relief. He couldn't remember Barbara or Leslie making him feel quite this way.

When Megan saw him, she shrieked with delight and raced across the yard. She threw herself against his legs and embraced him so eagerly she nearly knocked him off-balance. "Oh, Daddy. Daddy, Daddy, Daddy."

Clint lifted her into his arms and snuggled her baby-soft cheek. But even as he did, he searched Gail's eyes for an explanation.

She obviously sensed his concern, because she hurried to offer one. "When I went to Hal and Phyllis's to borrow a quilting frame, I found Megan and the cat setting off to come and find you. I offered to bring her back with me for a little while. I hope you don't mind."

"Then Phyllis is all right?"

She hesitated just long enough to raise another doubt in Clint's mind. "She's fine."

But before he could follow up with a question, Megan leaned close to his ear and whispered, "Gail's nice, Daddy. Aunt Phyllis wouldn't let me bring Colonel Mustard, but Gail said I could meet her kitty while I'm here."

"Well, that *is* nice of her, isn't it?" He smiled at Megan, then turned to Gail. "I didn't intend for you to step in and take care of her."

When she smiled at him, all trace of her earlier hesitation seemed to have vanished, and he wondered whether he'd imagined it. "It makes me feel better about everything you're doing for us."

Her gaze, deep and dark and full of mystery, held his, and he couldn't have looked away if he'd wanted to. But when Megan squirmed in his arms and broke the moment, he stooped to lower her to the ground and tried to regain control of his senses. Gail was a beautiful woman, but something deeper reached out to him—energy radiated from her, intelligence burned in her eyes, and something soft and fragile beneath her strength touched him.

Megan immediately squatted in the dirt and began to gather pebbles, so Clint forced himself to look back at Gail and steel himself for his reaction.

If she sensed his turmoil, she gave no sign. "Look, since you've been forced into taking a break, anyway, why don't you come in and have a cup of coffee. Or lemonade? Or *something?*"

He should get back to work, but he didn't want to. And obligation quickly lost the battle with temptation. "That sounds good. I'll take you up on it."

"And the kids, too, of course." Something crept into her voice then—another slight hesitation, a little uncertainty. Her face betrayed nothing, and again Clint wondered whether he'd imagined it.

He looked back at Justin and Brad. "How about it, fellas? You want some lemonade?"

Without answering, Justin dropped his paintbrush and started toward the house.

Brad tossed his brush into the pan beside his brother's and shouted, "I'm *dying* of thirst." He ran toward Clint and tried to match his step as they crossed the yard. "What do you think of the fence, Dad?"

"I think it looks great. You're both doing a good job."

Brad grinned with delight and called to his brother's retreating back. "See, Justin? You were wrong. He *didn't* find anything wrong with it."

At his words, Clint's step faltered. Justin broke into a run and climbed the steps just behind Gail.

Clint watched his son and ached for the way things should have been. He held the screen for Megan, then followed her inside the kitchen. Brad raced to the table and dropped onto a chair beside it.

Megan knelt on a chair beside Brad and stretched toward a vase of daisies on the table. "I like flowers," she said. "Come smell, Daddy."

Still sullen, Justin leaned against the far wall and crossed his arms high on his narrow chest.

Sniffing flowers for Megan, Clint caught his son's eye. "Come and have a seat, Justin."

But Justin looked away quickly. "I'm fine right here."

Gail crossed to the refrigerator with an anxious expression and Clint half expected her to say something. Instead, she pulled out a pitcher of lemonade.

Disturbed by Justin's lack of manners but unwilling to cause a scene, Clint ignored the boy's hostility and spoke to Gail's back. "If you'll tell me where you want the quilt frame, I'll bring it in for you when we're through here."

She shook her head. "I can do it."

"It won't take more than five minutes—"

She locked her hands on the counter behind her and turned to face him. Her breasts strained against the white material of her T-shirt and a surge of desire raced through Clint. He glanced away, then back like a young boy who couldn't help looking.

When she noticed the direction of his gaze. She flushed and dropped her hands. "You can put it in the living room. Thank you." She turned away from him again, but the tilt of her head and the set of her shoulders told him he'd embarrassed her.

But no more than he'd embarrassed himself. When he let his eyes sweep the room, he realized Justin was watching him and his discomfort climbed a degree. He expected the boy to sneer at him, to look disgusted or to grow angry. Instead, Justin looked mildly interested and a little perplexed.

The boy pushed away from the wall and took two full glasses from Gail's hands. "I'll help you." He placed one glass in front of Brad and handed Clint the other. Though Justin didn't meet his gaze, he didn't work quite so hard to avoid it this time.

More confused by his older son than ever, Clint drained his glass and stood. "I'll bring in the frame now. Then I'd better get back to work."

"I'll help you," Gail said, and started toward the door.

"No. You wait here. I'll get it." His voice came out harsher than he wanted it to, but before he could correct it, Megan stood and leaned across the table, and her chair began to tilt out from under her.

Gail lunged and plucked the child away just as the chair crashed to the floor. "Please be careful, Megan. You almost got hurt."

Megan threw her arms around Gail's neck in a hug of gratitude that lasted all of three seconds before she wriggled away and tried to right the chair herself. Again, Gail stepped in to help her, and to Clint's amazement, not even the slightest expression of annoyance crossed Gail's features.

Her patience touched him deeply. He found Megan's exuberance delightful, but not everyone shared his opinion. Hal found her amusing but tiring. Phyllis loved her dearly, but wanted to curb a little of her enthusiasm. And Leslie would—

But he wouldn't even let that thought form. Leslie would be a *wonderful* stepmother to all three kids. Loving, caring, patient. He couldn't ask for a better woman to mother his children this year and during his weeks of visitation in the future. Why, within hours she'd probably convince Brad that Clint was a model father and zero in on the cause of Justin's resentment. She was intensely analytical and practical. Exactly the kind of woman he and the kids needed.

He tried to make Leslie's image form in his memory as he headed outside, but no matter what he did, Gail's face wouldn't disappear. Her smile floated just beyond his reach in the sunlight. Her eyes filled his imagination. And the memory of her soft floral scent rivaled that of the warm summer breeze. Groaning inwardly, he pulled pieces of the quilting frame out of the car and started back toward the house, steeling himself for the jolt he knew he'd get when he faced her again.

CHAPTER SEVEN

IN THE PREDAWN DARKNESS, Gail turned her head on her pillow and stared at the glowing digits on her alarm clock. Less than an hour from now, the buzzer would signal the start of her day. But for the third day in a row, a strange sense of anticipation had brought her fully alert long before sunrise.

She rolled to her side and tried to understand why she'd suddenly grown so restless. When her eyes had popped open the first day, she'd stayed in bed and listened to Clint moving around outside.

Yesterday, she'd risen and watched him from her bedroom window; a long, lean silhouette moving against the shadows of the barn in the pale moonlight. He'd looked lonely. Vulnerable, somehow. And she'd had to fight the urge to go outside and keep him company.

And now, obviously, she'd started waking *before* he arrived. She didn't want to feel this way about him, so she closed her eyes and tried to make sleep return, as if sheer willpower could force him from her mind. But his image seemed to creep through her eyelids and refused to let her relax.

Flopping onto her back, she stared at the pattern of the moonlight on the ceiling. Clint would arrive in another fifteen minutes—an ungodly hour for anyone to work alone outside, especially on Sunday. Even in the middle of summer, the early-morning hours carried a deep chill, and her years of city living had tainted the early dawn with an eeriness she hadn't been able to shake since she'd come home.

With a sigh, she sat on the edge of her bed. She might as well admit it, she'd never sleep as long as Clint was out there by himself. She pulled on her robe and stepped into her slippers, then tiptoed past her mother's bedroom and down the stairs. Taking care not to disturb her father as she passed the guest room, she slipped into the kitchen.

Moonlight spilled over the half curtains at the window and painted the room in silver and shadows. Letting the door close softly behind her, she turned on the dim bulb over the stove and pulled the coffee canister toward her.

By the time the headlights from Clint's truck showed on the lane outside, she had a fresh pot of coffee ready. She poured two mugsful and stepped onto the porch. As he turned into the yard, her sense of anticipation increased until her heart slammed against her chest. Standing here in her robe in the early-morning hours, she felt as if she was stepping across a line into some new area she wasn't sure she should explore.

Before she could change her mind, his headlights played across the porch and framed her in their spotlight. He braked and jumped from the cab. In only a few strides, he'd reached her. "Gail? What's wrong?"

She shouldn't have done this, she decided. She'd worried him for nothing. "Everything's fine. I just couldn't sleep."

"Your dad's all right?"

"There's no change."

Before he could say another word, she handed him the mug. "It's chilly out. I thought maybe you'd like some coffee before you start working."

He accepted it, sipped and let his eyes slowly travel the length of her. "Thanks."

His gaze warmed her, but she pulled her robe a little tighter and sat on the porch swing as she lifted her own mug to drink.

To her surprise, Clint took the seat beside her and they rocked gently for several long seconds before he spoke again. "I want to thank you again for bringing Megan over here yesterday. She had the time of her life."

Gail smiled. "She's a sweet little girl."

"She's a handful, that's for sure—"

"Oh, Clint, she's delightful," Gail interrupted. "All I could think of yesterday was how sad it would be if that incredible spirit of hers were ever confined in some way."

He lowered his cup and stared at her. His eyes were buried in the shadows from the porch light, but the intensity of his gaze seared her. "Yes, it would."

Unsure what to say next, Gail stared across the yard.

Clint pulled in a deep breath and leaned forward to prop his elbows on his knees. "Tell me what really happened when you found her yesterday."

Gail didn't want to cause trouble for Phyllis, so she tried to keep her tone light. "I went over to borrow the quilting frame and found Megan setting off on an adventure."

"Alone?" He sounded concerned.

"No, Colonel Mustard was with her."

He didn't laugh. "Where was Phyllis?"

"In the house."

He nodded and studied the yard in silence. "She was asleep, wasn't she?"

Loyalty to Phyllis warred with concern and honesty. Heartsick, Gail nodded. "But I'm sure she hadn't been asleep long."

"I'm starting to think I'm asking too much of her," he said miserably. "She's getting older and slowing down a little. Megan doesn't mean to get in trouble, but she demands *constant* supervision like most four-year-olds."

"Phyllis woke up a minute after I got there, and she was horrified to find Megan gone."

With a heavy sigh, he sat up and leaned one elbow on the swing's arm. "I'm not worried about yesterday. I'm worried about today and tomorrow. And the day after that. I'm afraid Phyllis will keep watching the kids for me because she loves us and knows we need help. She won't ever tell me it's too much for her, and I don't want to insult her by insinuating I think it is."

Gail agreed silently. She knew Phyllis would collapse before she'd admit weakness. "After yesterday, I'm sure she won't let herself fall asleep on duty again."

Clint managed a smile. Draining his cup, he stood and stretched to his full height as he adjusted his hat. "I'm not sure what to do. Like I said, I don't want to hurt Phyllis's feelings—"

Gail reached up and touched his arm lightly. "I know. I wish I knew what to suggest."

He moved away at her touch, and she drew her hand back quickly. She'd reached out without thinking. When he'd taken her into his arms the other day, she'd felt desire stirring and she'd had to battle her reaction ever since. Obviously, he hadn't. His response to her touch told her more than he'd ever say.

Determined not to show her embarrassment, Gail held out her hand for his mug. "I need to get busy— I've got a thousand things to do."

He gave her the cup slowly, appraised her silently and turned away without another word. She watched him descend the steps to the dusty yard, but dismay tightened her throat and warmed her face. She'd allowed her emotions to take over a little, and that had obviously been a mistake.

From now on, she'd fight her feelings when he came near. She'd ignore the almost electrical impulses that warned her when he was around. And she'd push him straight out of her mind. She had no intention of doing *anything* that would leave her open to hurt again.

BY THE TIME he reached the door to the barn, Clint could almost breathe normally again. Gail's touch had affected him like a lightning bolt. She'd intended the gesture as one of comfort. She'd done nothing more than press her fingers to his arm. But her warmth had raced straight to his heart as if he'd been zapped, and he'd jerked away without thinking.

He'd seen the look on her face, but he hadn't known how to explain his reaction to her. He certainly *couldn't* say his body responded the way it did because he'd been away from Leslie too long.

Thrusting a pitchfork into action, he tried to work away his confusion. He enjoyed Gail's company and he was definitely attracted to her. But Leslie was waiting for him in Chicago. In two months, he'd return to his life there and leave Gail behind. No way he was going to jeopardize his entire future for a passing schoolboy crush. No matter how attractive the woman. No matter how good he felt around her.

Swearing under his breath, he forked up a load of hay and flung it out of the empty stall farther than he'd intended. He told himself he wasn't a weak man. He'd never had to indulge every physical desire. He could ignore Gail's hair, her eyes, her smile. He could disregard the way she made him feel whenever he was around her.

Two months. He could hold on until then.

But for the life of him, he couldn't imagine why the thought of leaving Montana suddenly weighed heavily on his heart.

GAIL HELD the laundry basket against her hip as she crossed the backyard to the clothesline. High above her on the roof, Clint stopped hammering as she walked. She felt his eyes on her back, warmer than the morning sun. Still embarrassed after his reaction to her touch yesterday, she'd kept her contact with him to a minimum. So now she didn't turn around or look up, but her heart beat faster just knowing he was watching her.

A car swished past on the highway and someone's farm machinery hummed in the distance. Birdcalls and the smell of freshly mown grass, droning insects and the echo of Clint's hammer on the roof had combined to give the morning an easy quality that spoke straight to her heart—like a lazy childhood memory.

"Hey, Dad—" Brad's voice cut through her musings and made her whip around in surprise.

Clint knelt on the edge of the roof, haloed by the sunlight, and his boys stood on the ground beside the ladder, lugging a piece of the old roofing between them. "What, son?"

Gail lowered the laundry basket and pulled out a sheet as Brad gestured toward his older brother.

"Justin says he's not going to help me load the rest of this stuff in the truck," he said.

As if it were her own, she felt Clint's frustration. The sun hadn't even had a chance to burn away the morning dew and already Justin's attitude threatened trouble.

Clint lowered the hammer slowly before he spoke. "I need both of you to keep loading the truck. And please, no arguments."

Justin's shoulders tensed and his head tilted upward. Though she couldn't see his face, Gail knew he was glaring at his father. But he didn't say a word. At least not one that she could hear.

"See?" Brad jeered. "I *told* you."

"Don't egg him on, Brad," Clint warned. "Justin, there's only a little bit left. Please help your brother finish. After that, you can be through for the morning."

But Justin obviously didn't intend to make things easy on his father. "I don't want to load the stupid truck."

"Justin—" Clint's voice gave way to weariness.

"Why can't I do what *you're* doing?" Justin argued.

"You want to help me?"

Justin shrugged. "Beats doing this baby work."

Gail heard longing in the son's voice, surprise in the father's. And she willed Clint to agree. Justin had reached a difficult age—maybe he needed one-on-one time with his father.

She pulled herself up short and shook her head, surprised at herself for thinking she knew what a teenage boy needed. She lifted a sheet from the basket and snapped it open before pegging it to the line. But she couldn't tune out the scene across the yard, couldn't keep Brad's small voice from reaching her.

"But I can't load the truck all by myself," he protested. "This junk is heavy."

Clint swung around the ladder and started to climb down. "I'll help you finish loading. After that, Justin, I'll be glad to teach you how to roof."

"Fine by me." Justin's voice betrayed nothing. In fact, he might have been accepting a punishment rather than receiving his own way.

"What about me?" Brad cried. "What will I do?"

Gail watched Clint look around the yard, searching for a task to set his younger son to. And in spite of the internal warning that told her not to get involved, she stepped out from behind the sheet and closed the distance between them.

She knew the moment Clint registered her approach, felt him take in her appearance with one long look and felt the heat creep into her face. She wore only cutoff jeans and a T-shirt. Since she hadn't planned to leave the lawn, she hadn't put on shoes. She'd done nothing to style her hair and she had no makeup. And for the first time, she realized how simple she must look compared to Leslie's Chicago sophistication.

She smoothed her hair and smiled at him. "I have to run something over to Phyllis for Mom this morning, and I could give Brad a ride back home."

Clint looked relieved and grateful.

But Brad looked heartbroken. "What am I going to do there?"

"What do you usually do in the afternoons?" Clint asked.

"Nothing. There's nothing *to* do."

"Except listen to Aunt Phyllis tell Megan not to do stuff," Justin put in. "There's nothing to do anywhere around here."

"Are you kidding?" Gail cried. "There are lots of things to do. Why, the best fishing hole in the entire state is in that creek at the edge of our property."

Justin snorted. "Yeah. Right. Like Aunt Phyllis is going to take us fishing."

Brad nodded. "Yeah. Right."

Clint's lips twitched. "I've got to admit, I'm having trouble picturing that, myself."

Gail held his gaze. "I never suggested *Phyllis* should take them."

Clint's smile faded and uncertainty replaced it. "Well, of course, I'd take them if I had time—"

Justin made a noise of disbelief. "Sure he would. Besides, he doesn't even know how to fish."

"You don't know how to fish?" Gail asked.

Clint shook his head. "I...uh...never had the time to learn."

"Too busy working," Justin said, the sneer in his voice becoming more marked.

Clint flushed, but he didn't say a word in his own defense.

Determined not to let the moment slip into something ugly, Gail forced a laugh. "Yes, well, it looks as if somebody needs to teach all of you about the better life."

Clint studied her with hooded eyes. "And I suppose you think you're the one to teach us?" He looked serious, but she heard the catch of amusement in his voice.

"I might be." She tried to sound casual even though his expression sent her pulse racing. "We work hard up here, but we also know how to play."

"Just because I don't fish, that doesn't mean I don't play."

"Really? Okay, when was the last time you went into Broken Bow on a Friday night?"

He shook his head, but his lips twitched.

She laughed. "And you call yourself a Montana cowboy. Can't fish. Can't dance—"

"Now, just a minute," he protested. "You asked when was the last time I went into Broken Bow on a Friday night. You didn't ask whether I could dance."

"I'm talking about a good old-fashioned two-step," she warned.

"I can count." He scowled deeply when he spoke, and Gail knew he had no idea of how incredibly sexy he looked. Or of the rush of anticipation he sent up her spine. Or of making her hands so weak and clammy.

She managed to squeak out a nervous little laugh, which made Justin narrow his eyes and study her.

Brad looked confused by their digression. "So do I have to go back to Phyllis's or not?"

"You really don't want to?" Clint asked, and this time his voice sounded fatherly.

Brad shook his head. "She's going to make me stay with Megan while she goes to some dumb old meeting this afternoon, and if I go back now, she might leave early."

Clint looked surprised. "What meeting?"

"It's something about the rodeo, I think," Justin said.

Brad nodded. "So, do I have to go?"

Clint flicked a glance at Gail and she could see the confusion in his eyes.

"I have an idea," she said without giving herself time to think about it. "Brad and I can drive over to Phyllis's and bring Megan back with us. They can both stay here with me this afternoon."

"So I wouldn't have to baby-sit?" Relief lit the boy's face.

"Not if your dad says it's okay—"

Clint nodded vigorously. "It's okay with me."

"And will you teach me how to fish?" Brad demanded.

Gail smiled down into the boy's eager face. "Yes."

But Clint shook his head slowly. "I don't think I like the sound of that."

Brad's smile drooped. "But, Dad—"

Clint shook his head again, but this time a smile tugged at the corners of his mouth. "I won't let her teach you unless she promises to teach all of us."

"Really? *You* want to go?" Brad nearly jumped with excitement.

Justin rolled his eyes. "I can't wait to see that."

To Gail's delight, Clint didn't take offense at the boy's words. He let his smile widen and met the challenge. "And *I* can't wait to see which of us catches the biggest fish."

Gail laughed again. "Even I can't wait to see that."

Brad tugged at the hem of her T-shirt. "Can we go tonight?"

Clint shook his head. "We'll have to wait until I finish that roof—"

"I knew it," Justin muttered. "Work always comes first."

Gail stepped in again. "Your dad's right. If a storm hits before you finish the roof, we'll be in big trouble."

Justin didn't look impressed, but Brad pivoted away and sprinted toward the truck. "Then come on, you guys. Hurry."

Justin followed much more slowly, but Clint held back. When Gail took a step away, he touched her arm to stop her. "Thank you," he said softly. "I appreciate your help."

His gratitude made her smile. "No problem."

"You certainly have a way with children."

Her smile faded. "No, I don't."

"I saw you with Megan the other day. Brad thinks you're wonderful. Even Justin seems less hostile whenever you're around."

She pulled her arm away from his touch, but gently, not the way he'd jerked from her. "We'd better go help the kids."

He stared into her eyes as if he thought he could read her thoughts, then shook his head. "You finish what you were doing. I'll help the boys load the truck."

Tears stung her eyes as she watched him go. Clint and his kids had helped her start believing in herself again, and for that she'd always be grateful. But she couldn't allow herself to grow too attached to any of them.

The days were flying past. Soon, they'd part company forever, and she had to keep some defenses in place until then or she'd put her heart at risk.

CLINT BROKE his rhythm to readjust one of the shingles Justin had laid out for him. From the corner of his eye, he saw Justin notice, and caught the boy's anxious glance. But he made sure his face showed that having to reposition the shingle made no difference to him.

After working together for the past two mornings, the silence between them had finally become an easier one. Clint found himself enjoying the time spent with his son—even if they had nothing much to say to each other. But if Justin suspected his father was criticizing his efforts he'd probably pull away again, and Clint didn't want to chance it.

From the ground far below, a giggle caught Clint's attention. He glanced over his shoulder at Megan running full speed across the lawn. Gail caught her in two easy strides and swung her high off the ground. With arms extended like an airplane, Brad ran toward them and all three indulged in a mock dogfight.

While he and Justin worked together, Gail had taken Brad and Megan under her wing. Another of Phyllis's committee meetings this morning had prompted him to ask Gail for help again. He hated imposing, but he loved having the kids around, and he enjoyed watching her with them.

At the edge of the lawn, Brad somehow decided he'd shot down Megan, so Gail put her on the lawn. Megan laughed aloud and raced away again, daring Gail to chase her. And, of course, Gail did. Clint smiled, warmed by the picture the threesome made.

"You like her, don't you?" Justin's voice cut through his thoughts and wiped away his smile.

"Who? Gail?"

Justin rolled his eyes. "Who else?"

"She's a nice woman. A friend."

"Is that why you watch her so much?"

Clint stared at the boy and tried to judge the reason behind the question. An attack? Justin didn't look hostile, but he didn't look overly friendly, either. Curiosity? Clint couldn't tell. He asked honestly, "You think I look at her a lot?"

Justin shot him an exasperated look. "Yeah. All the time. So, do you like her, or what?"

With all his heart, Clint wished he knew what answer the boy wanted. He didn't want to say the wrong thing and put up another wall between them. "I think she's a beautiful woman and yes, I like her—as a friend."

"What about Mom? Did you used to stare at her like that?"

This was the hardest part of divorce to Clint—remembering the good times and removing the bitterness from his voice when he talked to the kids about their mother. "Your mother was the most beautiful woman I'd ever seen," he said with a tiny smile. "All that golden hair, and her eyes . . ." He trailed off and laughed. "Yes, I stared at your mother—a lot more than I stare at Gail."

"What about Leslie?" Justin asked. Still not an attack; more like curiosity.

Clint relaxed a little. "What do you want to know? Do I stare at her? Yes."

"Is *she* beautiful?"

"Yes, she is."

Justin looked away and followed Gail with his eyes for several seconds. "What's she like? Is she as nice as Gail?"

"They're very different, but yes, she's nice."

"Does she have kids?"

Clint shook his head. "No kids, but you'll like her. She's intelligent, witty, hardworking, tops in her field—"

"Oh, great. She's just like you. So, who are you planning for us to live with until Mom comes back?"

Battling stiff muscles, Clint sat on the roof, pulled off his hat and propped it on his knees. "With me until Leslie and I get married. Then we'll all probably move in to Leslie's condo. It's bigger than mine."

The boy's shoulders tensed, but he didn't say a word.

"Why?" Clint prodded. "Does something worry you?"

Justin snorted his answer and turned, so Clint couldn't see his face. "So is *she* going to take care of us? Or are you going to actually come home after work?"

"Is that why you're so angry with me? Because of the time and energy my career requires?"

Justin didn't answer.

"That's not fair, Justin. You don't understand what it takes to make it in my field. I'll never get *anywhere* on just forty hours a week."

At that, Justin pushed to his feet and started toward the ladder. "Why don't you save it for somebody who cares? I've heard it all before."

Clint drew in a steadying breath and watched him climb down the ladder. If he hadn't been walking on eggshells around the boy already, he might have gone after him and demanded that Justin stay and finish what he'd started. Instead, he bit his tongue and silently cursed himself for having immediately taken the defensive, just as he had every time Barbara had brought up his career. That line of defense hadn't worked then—he'd lost his wife, his home *and* his children to another man. So what made him think he could win points with a fourteen-year-old boy using it now?

Bending to his task again, he tried to let physical exertion work away his emotional frustration. But his thigh muscles already burned from the effort of holding himself on the steep roof and his arms and shoulders ached from the repeated hammering. And they hadn't even finished half the roof.

Although the work didn't ease his frustration, it helped shift it so Clint could think more clearly. After only a few minutes, he put down the hammer and gathered the tools together.

He started down the ladder and allowed himself a self-mocking smile. Before the divorce, he would never have let Justin's hurt feelings interrupt his workday. In fact, he'd never let any family emergency interrupt him at work. Barbara had hated his attitude. She'd been convinced he was a lousy husband and a rotten father, and it hadn't taken any effort at all on his part to prove her right.

Stepping to the ground from the bottom rung, he listened to Gail's voice floating toward him on the summer breeze. For some reason, she believed he was a wonderful father, and that made him want to prove her right.

With a wry smile, he wondered whether things might have turned out differently if Barbara had expected him to succeed instead of waiting for him to fail.

Following the sound of voices, he walked around the corner of the house. Gail sat on the front steps with Megan on her knee. Justin was on the step below her staring out over the yard. Brad rode the front-porch railing as if it were a bucking bronco. And once again, Clint's heart softened at the picture they made. His children—and Gail.

He slowed his step and studied them together. He might never have another chance with Barbara, but he *did* have one with his kids. Fate was being kind to allow it—he'd be smart enough this time to take it. And this time, he didn't intend to fail.

CHAPTER EIGHT

GAIL STEPPED ONTO a footstool and reached into the cupboard for two cans of fruit punch. "Are these what you want?"

With a brisk nod, her mother held out her hands for them. "They'll do. I imagine those kids'll like this all right."

"I'm sure they will. What time did Phyllis say she'd be back?"

Dorothy punched holes in each can, filled one glass and reached for another. "She wasn't sure. The stampede is getting so close, you know, and there's still so much to do. And now that your dad's laid up and she's having to fill in for me on the committee—" Dorothy broke off with a shake of her head. "Anyway, I told her to just let Clint and the kids stay to lunch. I guess it's as easy to cook for half a dozen as for two."

Gail smiled. "I'm sure Clint will appreciate it."

"It's not *him* I'm doing it for. It's Phyllis," Dorothy said over her shoulder. "That little girl of his is a handful—"

"Oh, Mom. Megan's a darling."

"She's a full-time job," Dorothy said with a growl. "How on earth he figured Phyllis could keep up with her all the time is beyond me."

"I don't think he had much choice. It's not his fault his ex-wife decided to leave the country at the same time Daddy got sick."

Dorothy hmmphed and pulled open the bread box. "Well, it's not *my* fault. I didn't ask him to spend all his time over here."

"No, you didn't. But thank God, he's done it, anyway."

"Oh, for heaven's sake." Dorothy snapped the bread box closed and whirled to glare at her. "It's not as if there's anything that needs looking after *that* badly. The way you two have been acting, you'd think the house was about to fall in. Your father will take care of things."

Pulling in a deep breath, Gail faced her mother squarely. "He won't be able to for a long time, Mom."

"You talk as if your father's at death's door. But he's not. He'll be fine." She wagged her finger at Gail and scowled. "Don't you take that negative attitude into his room with you."

With a sigh, Gail sank onto a chair. She'd tried on several occasions to discuss the future with her mother, but Dorothy absolutely refused to consider any plans if they included Boone out of commission.

In silence, Dorothy poured two cups of coffee, then sat across the table from Gail and sent her a tender smile. "You shouldn't worry about us so much."

"What are you, a mind reader?"

"Of course. I'm a mother." Dorothy put a hand on top of hers. "Sweetheart, we're going to be fine."

"I wish I could believe that."

"Your dad's getting better every day."

"Mom—"

"Honestly, sweetheart. Maybe you can't see it, but *I* can. After all, we've been married nearly forty years, and I know that man almost better than I know myself."

Gail struggled to find a tactful way to phrase her response. "He's not getting better fast enough for you to make it through this summer without help."

"Of course he is. Now, what kind of sandwiches should we make for Clint and those kids?"

But this time, Gail couldn't let her run away from the truth. Gently, she took her mother's hands. "No, he's not, Mom. And denying the truth won't change it. Dad's sick, and you've got your hands full taking care of him. You *can't* take care of the house and the land, too."

Dorothy pulled her hands away. "We're going to be just fine until your dad gets back on his feet."

"Dr. Lethbridge says—"

"Arnold Lethbridge is nothing but a pessimist," Dorothy argued. "Why, if I listened to him, I'd just give up. He talks as if your dad won't ever get back to normal."

"Maybe we should consider the possibility," Gail said softly.

Red-faced, Dorothy shot to her feet. "Absolutely not. Don't talk like that."

"Mom, I have to go home soon, and Clint's only here for another two months. Then what? You're going to have to face reality—no matter how hard it is."

Gail didn't expect the tears that suddenly filled her mother's eyes. Or the lengthy pause before Dorothy drew in a ragged breath. "I *am* facing reality. Your dad will get better. He *has* to."

The longing in her mother's voice wrenched Gail's heart, and if the stakes hadn't been so high she might have softened. "I hope he does, Mom. But it's going to take time, and we have to make plans for right now. I can't go home and leave you here with Dad flat on his back and the place needing so much work."

Dorothy stared at her for several seconds before she lifted her chin and asked, "What do you want me to do?"

"Cooperate with Clint, for one thing. Quit fighting him every step of the way."

"His help isn't necessary."

"It *is* necessary. Let him take charge of things. Let him include Dad in the decision-making process whenever he can. Don't stand guard against him."

Dorothy made a noise of derision and looked away.

"That's what you've been doing, Mom. Guarding Dad from Clint, guarding yourself from the truth..."

Dorothy's chin quivered a little, but she set her jaw and nodded. "All right. Fine." Though her voice suggested otherwise. "I'll just waltz in there and tell your dad he's never going to get out of that bed. That he'll never be a whole man again—is that what you want?"

"No, of course not."

"Well, it's what Arnold Lethbridge wants me to do." Dorothy's voice rose a notch. "He wants me to just give up. But I *won't.*"

Gail clutched her mother's shoulders and pulled her into an embrace. "That's not what I'm asking, Mom. I just want you to let Clint help while he's here."

"And when he leaves?"

The thought of Clint returning to Leslie and Chicago left her cold. But before she could answer her mother's question, rapid footsteps sounded on the porch outside and she realized Megan and Brad must be returning from their walk around the house. Justin called out to them, and Clint's deep voice drifted down from the rooftop, bringing all her senses alert.

Her mother narrowed her eyes and smiled a little. "You like him, don't you?"

"We're friends."

"I know friends, and I know when a man's interested in a woman. And the other way around, too."

Gail flushed. "Clint's not interested in me. He's planning to get engaged as soon as he goes home to Chicago."

Her mother shook her head and made a face as if she didn't believe it, but before she could speak, Megan threw open the door and rushed inside, lugging Dorothy's tabby cat with her. "Can your kitty come fishing with us?"

"You said maybe we could go today," Brad said as he followed his sister into the kitchen.

Gail hugged Megan quickly. "Kitty doesn't like the water, sweetheart." With a soft touch on Brad's shoulder, she added, "I said we'd go when your dad and Justin finish the roof. Have they finished?"

Brad shook his head and looked disappointed.

"Well, when they finish the whole thing, we'll go," she promised. "I always keep my word."

"Yes!" Brad raced back to the door and rushed outside. "Dad, we're going fishing when the roof's done, so hurry, okay?" The sound of his excited little voice faded as he raced down the steps and around to the back of the house.

When the door banged shut behind him, Dorothy sent Gail a pointed look. "I'm glad to see you putting some of *your* foolish ideas behind you. Those kids obviously like you and Clint seems pleased with the way you're taking care of them.''

''Clint doesn't have much choice.''

Her mother clicked her tongue and looked impatient. ''You accuse me of refusing to see the truth—when are *you* going to realize Richard didn't know what he was talking about?''

''This has nothing to do with Richard.''

''This has *everything* to do with him. For years, you've blamed yourself for the way those kids of his acted. And ever since the day you married him, he let you. But it wasn't your fault. You did your best with them. Better than most women would have done under the circumstances.'' Gail shook her head, but Dorothy didn't let that stop her. ''If Richard had been any kind of husband—''

''*I'm* the one Shelly hated,'' Gail insisted. ''*I'm* the one who drove Lisa and Matt away.''

''Nonsense. Lisa and Matt went back to live with their mother because they couldn't stand the tension in that house. But that wasn't all your fault. Shelly made your life miserable, and Richard didn't *once* make her treat you the way she should have.''

''Richard wasn't responsible for the way she acted.''

''No, but he *was* responsible for the way *he* acted,'' Dorothy said angrily. ''I tell you, the way he talked to you sometimes—'' Breaking off suddenly, she stared around the kitchen. ''Where's Megan?''

In horror, Gail followed her gaze. Megan had wandered away, and she'd been too busy arguing to notice. The outside door was still shut, so she must be somewhere in the house. But with her curious nature, she could be into anything—Dorothy's knickknacks,

Gail's scissors and quilting needles, the bathroom, Boone's medication—

At that thought, Gail raced out of the kitchen and down the hall. Even if Boone saw and registered a disaster, he couldn't communicate it when both she and her mother were in the other room.

She found Megan perched on the edge of Boone's bed holding a daisy from the vase on the nightstand. She touched its center with a gentle finger. "See? This part is yellow like sunshine. And when you smell it, it smells warm. Smell it and see."

Pushing the flower close to Boone, Megan held it there for the few seconds it took Gail to reach the side of the bed.

"Megan, you frightened me," she whispered. "I thought you were lost."

"Oh, no. I wasn't. The grandpa wanted to see the flowers."

Gail opened her mouth to protest, to explain in gentle terms her father's condition and his need for quiet rest, but the expression in his eyes stopped her.

"I wish you could see the red one," Megan said. "But it's got a pokey part that hurts my fingers, and my mommy won't let me pick them at home."

Boone stared straight at Gail as if instructing her to lift the rose for him to see. When she did, he shifted his eyes to it and drank in the sight.

"He wants to smell it," Megan said.

Gail lowered the rose to his pillow so the fragrance could reach him.

"He likes the flowers," Megan whispered.

"Yes, sweetheart, I think he does."

Megan leaned close to him. "Do you want me to tell you a story? I know lots of stories."

He looked at her with incredibly gentle eyes and struggled for several seconds to say, "Yes."

Gail had worried that his illness might frighten the child, but Megan just smiled and folded her hands on her lap. "Doesn't anybody ever read you a story?" Boone blinked slowly.

"Well," Megan said firmly. "I'll tell you a really good one, but it might be kind of scary."

Again Boone struggled to form a word, but this time he spoke to Gail. "Grandpa."

The word touched her deeply, and she had to look away quickly to hide the tears that sprang into her eyes.

"Once upon a time, there was a little girl who lived in the woods," Megan said. "And her mommy maked her a pretty red coat to scare away all the wolves."

When a noise in the doorway caught Gail's attention, she turned and saw her mother there, watching.

Afraid Dorothy would be angry with Megan and try to remove her from the room, Gail tiptoed to her mother, slipped an arm around her waist and nodded toward Megan and Boone. "Why didn't *we* ever think of telling him fairy tales?"

To Gail's surprise, her mother smiled. "Somehow, I don't think they'd have as much charm coming from you or me."

"Because the grandma lived very far away and it taked almost five whole minutes for Little Red Riding Hood to walk there—"

For an instant, a picture of Boone sitting tall in his easy chair with Megan on his lap formed in Gail's imagination. She could see him frowning with mock seriousness as he listened. Pressing a kiss to the girl's forehead. Feigning horror at some particularly frightening part. She heard his booming laugh.

As if he'd actually laughed aloud, she shot a glance at her mother and glimpsed a wistful expression on her face. And for a heartbeat, she wished things had been different; that she'd given them grandchildren; that her marriage to Richard had worked out; that Shelly, Matt and Lisa hadn't been so hostile and angry.

"Because you aren't 'posed to talk to strangers. So Little Red Riding Hood just sticked her nose up in the air like this and 'nored the wolf—"

No, that wasn't true, Gail realized. She didn't wish Richard or his children back into her life. Against all reason, she wished Megan and her brothers there. Somehow, these children had wormed their way into her heart. And now—

Now Gail had to return to her empty life in California, and the kids would go back to Chicago. Then back to their mother and Dave and weekend visits with Clint and Leslie.

If someone had stabbed her, the pain couldn't have been worse. She tried to blink away her tears, but she lost the battle. She tried to gulp air into her lungs, but they refused to work. Suddenly, her delusions that she could come out of this in one emotional piece vaporized.

Pivoting away, she rushed up the stairs to her bedroom. She had to pull herself together, to force her emotions back under control. She didn't want Clint to come in for lunch and see that she'd been crying. How could she ever explain? What could she possibly say to him that wouldn't make the situation worse?

GAIL CHECKED her watch and straightened from the strawberry patch with a groan. Just eight o'clock in the evening, and they still had enough daylight for a couple more hours' work. But she doubted she could find the energy to pick even one more berry.

She glanced at Brad playing with Megan on the lawn. They'd wandered away from the garden, but she could see them both, and Brad seemed to have a firm handle on Megan's activities.

Behind her on the roof, she could hear Clint and Justin gathering tools and making their way to the ladder. A few minutes earlier, they'd reached the roof's crest from the back of the house, so they'd obviously decided to quit for the day.

Wishing she could follow suit, Gail pulled the bucket after her with juice-stained fingers. The sweet smell of ripe berries filled the air and brought back vivid memories of long-ago summer evenings. She could almost smell her mother's pot roast and hear her dad whistling as he finished his chores.

Shaking her head, she dug into the cool leaves and searched for edible berries. Many had been left too long on the vines, but she hoped to salvage enough for at least a dozen jars of jam.

When she looked up a few minutes later to check on the kids, Clint stood at the edge of the garden watching her.

With her dirt-streaked legs, stained sneakers and muddy hands, she must look frightful. Forcing a laugh, she pushed her hair out of her eyes. "You've finished the back of the house, I see."

He nodded slowly without taking his eyes from hers, and the contact made her nerve endings tingle. "I wondered whether you'd mind letting the kids stay with you another few minutes while I check on the corn in the north section.''

''Of course not.'' She stooped and picked up her bucket, more to have something to do with her hands than because she needed the berries.

But he stepped forward immediately, one hand extended. ''I'll get that for you.'' His fingers brushed hers and sent heat spiraling up her arm. As if the cool metal bucket had suddenly turned white-hot, she relinquished her hold on it and waited for him to step away again. Instead, he used his other hand to take her elbow and guide her across the deeply rutted garden. Even when she'd stepped onto the lawn, he didn't release her, but kept her arm tucked against the solid muscle of his side. ''If you want, I'll ask Justin to help you pick the rest in the morning.''

She shook her head quickly. ''Oh, no. There aren't that many left, and I can be through in another hour. Besides, he wants to work with you. I'd hate to have you make him stop.''

A satisfied grin lifted the corners of Clint's mouth, and he glanced toward a corner of the porch where Justin was putting the tools and ladder out of the way until morning. ''I think he does like it.''

''Having him help you was a great idea. Obviously, you're doing the right thing.''

''I sure hope so.'' They walked in silence for several steps before he spoke again. ''I think we'll be able to finish the roof by Saturday.''

She studied the house, grateful for anything to look at or talk about that didn't border on something personal. ''It looks great.''

''Not bad for a couple of amateurs, huh?''

"After you finish that big old roof, nobody will be able to call you amateurs any longer."

He grinned and lifted one shoulder in a casual shrug. "I'd rather be called an amateur than some of the things I've been called in my life."

His expression won a laugh from her and her earlier discomfort faded. She liked the way he could put her at ease. In fact, she liked a great many things about him. The way he smiled. The way he listened as if every word she said had value. The way he looked at her as if she were endlessly fascinating. And she liked his strength of character—not showy or flamboyant, but calm and quiet.

Richard had prided himself on being a strong man, but his idea of proper womanly behavior had differed from hers. His concept of femininity had included a degree of incompetence. Clint, on the other hand, made her feel competent and capable, small and feminine, all at once. Beside him, she felt strong, resilient and powerful.

Smiling a little at the turn of her thoughts, she tried to match his stride. As if he sensed something different in her, he tightened his hold on her arm. This time when the warmth of his skin burned her flesh, she allowed herself to enjoy it. When his fingertips scorched her arm, she didn't pull away.

"I won't be gone long." His voice sounded low and deep in her ear and his tone felt strangely intimate despite his casual words.

With effort, Gail pulled herself back into the conversation. "Don't rush. We'll be fine."

"I know that." He met her gaze and held it. "I never worry when the kids are with you."

The tenderness in his voice seemed to heal something deep within her soul, the trust in his eyes wakened something long dormant within her. And this time she didn't fight it.

He released her arm and climbed the porch to leave the bucket near the back door. Strangely, the absence of his fingers on her arm affected her almost as powerfully as the touch itself.

She watched him tousle Brad's hair and swing Megan around, then plant a kiss on top of her head as he lowered her again. Lifting a hand, he waved to Justin. The boy returned a grudging one of his own, then sank onto the porch steps. With one last smile at Gail, Clint crossed the front yard and climbed into the cab of his truck.

Confused by her emotions, she stared after him until he'd disappeared out the front gate and turned down the lane. A shriek of laughter from Megan finally broke the spell, and she turned toward the house. Megan and Brad raced around the corner again and out of sight, but Justin still sat on the porch steps looking tired, lonely, dejected.

Some instinct urged her to join him, but she hesitated. Though he'd never directed any anger or hostility toward her, she still wasn't anxious to deal with either emotion. But she couldn't stand out here all night, and she couldn't ignore the boys obvious unhappiness. Cursing herself silently for being such a coward, she started toward him.

He must have heard her coming, because his head jerked up as she drew closer. Standing quickly, he folded his arms across his chest and watched her with narrowed eyes.

She reached his side in a few strides and worked up a smile. "You look tired. Ready to call it a day?"

He nodded. "I ache all over. That's hard work up there."

"I know. I used to have to help my dad and I remember how hot and tired we got." She dropped to the steps and leaned back on her elbows. "At least it cools down a little when the sun goes down."

Justin hesitated for a few seconds, then sat down beside her. "Yeah, it does—a little."

Gail stared out over the yard wondering what she should say to this young man. She pulled her bottom lip between her teeth for a few seconds. "What grade are you in?" she asked finally, and then wanted to kick herself, the question sounded so stupid.

Justin obviously thought so, too. He looked confused. "I'll be in ninth."

"Oh. That's a fun year."

"Yeah, I guess." He pulled back and studied her in a gesture so like his father's it touched her. "So, do you like my dad or what?"

Caught off guard, her face flamed. "He's a friend."

Justin ticked his tongue against the roof of his mouth. "That's what he says, too."

"That's because it's true."

He shook his head. "He smiles all the time when you're around, and I've never seen him act like that before—even with my mom. So, *do* you?"

"Your father's a great guy and a good friend. Yes, I like him."

Justin scowled. "I just want to know whether he's getting ready to bail out on Leslie, too."

"Of course he's not."

He rolled his eyes. "I know what he's like. He did it to my mom and us. Now he's going to do it to Leslie."

His words reinforced her earlier suspicion that Justin didn't know about Barbara's affair with Dave. And Gail certainly had no business bringing it up. But she hated hearing Justin blame his father for something he hadn't done. "I don't think that's what your dad's doing," she said.

He snorted and looked away. "Yeah, right. Just watch him—he'll leave you, too, if you're not careful. He *always* leaves."

Though she'd never met Justin's mother, Gail disliked her intensely at this moment. "Have you talked to your dad about how you feel?"

"He won't talk to me."

"You might be surprised. And you might find out a few things you don't already know."

Justin looked wary. "Why? What did he tell you?"

"What he's told me isn't important, Justin. What you believe—what you're angry with him about—is. But I can't clear it up for you." She smiled gently. "You're old enough to have an honest conversation with your dad, but you're not going to solve anything until you're willing to sit down and listen to what he has to say."

Countless emotions flashed across the boy's face. Finally, after a long silence, he said, "You really think he'll talk to me?"

"Of course he will."

"What if he won't?"

"Believe me, your dad's anxious to clear things up with you. Just give him a chance."

Justin didn't respond, but at least he didn't refuse, and Gail supposed she couldn't ask for anything more. Just then, Brad and Megan raced around the house again, and when Megan saw Justin, she shrieked with delight and ran to him with Brad close on her heels.

Justin's face melted into a smile that softened Gail's heart. Catching Megan just before she hit him, he swept her off the ground and the joy on her small face broadened Gail's smile.

"Make me fly way up in the sky like an airplane, okay?" Megan cried.

Justin complied, and Brad scowled in the direction of the fields. "Isn't Dad back yet?"

"Not yet," Gail said.

"I was hoping we could go fishing. It's not even dark yet."

Gail looped an arm across Brad's shoulders. He certainly was persistent. "We will when the roof's finished, Brad. Not before. Now, why don't we all go inside and I'll fix root beer floats while we wait for your dad."

When Justin lowered Megan to the ground, she dashed up the stairs and hopped excitedly. "Yummy! Come on, guys."

Neither Brad nor Justin needed to be prodded twice. Brad raced for the back door and even Justin looked interested as he jumped onto the porch and took Megan's hand. Once inside, he helped Megan onto a chair while Brad opened the freezer.

"Where's the ice cream?" Brad called over his shoulder. "Do you want me to get it for you?"

Gail pulled four glasses from the cupboard. "Sure. I know I saw some vanilla in there yesterday."

He retrieved the carton, then whirled to face his brother and sister. "Hey, do you think Aunt Phyllis will buy some ice cream for Dad's birthday?"

"Sure, she will." Justin dropped onto a chair and drummed his fingers on the edge of the table.

"And a bir'fday cake?" Megan asked.

Gail pulled four spoons from the drawer and tore paper towels from the roller. "When is your dad's birthday?"

"Saturday," Justin said without looking up.

"*This* Saturday?"

Brad nodded.

"The day after tomorrow?"

"Yeah," Justin said. "Why?"

"Nothing. Just that he never even mentioned it." She spooned ice cream into one tall glass, then looked at the kids. "What are you going to do for him?"

"I'm going to give him a kiss," Megan said.

But Justin shrugged and took on that defensive look he usually wore. "Probably nothing."

Dropping to his knees on a chair by the table, Brad nodded. "We never do anything because we don't have any money."

"There are lots of things you can do that don't need money," Gail said.

Brad shook his head. "Nothing good."

"Besides," Justin said, "he wasn't even going to be around. He was *supposed* to go back to Chicago. Leslie was going to throw him some big party. But now he's not going."

Gail abandoned the spoon in the ice-cream carton. "He's not? Why?"

Justin didn't answer, but the look on his face spoke volumes.

"Because of us?" she asked.

"I don't know. Maybe." He tried to sound casual, but Gail suddenly understood the boy's earlier comments. He believed Clint had decided to stay because of her.

She turned back to the ice cream, scooping another glassful as she thought. If she left it up to Clint, Saturday would drift past like any other day. But she didn't want that to happen, and his birthday seemed like the perfect time to thank him for his help. "Is Phyllis going to bake him a cake?"

Brad shrugged one shoulder. "Who knows? She's so busy doing all that stuff for the stampede, she's never home."

"But Daddy *has* to have a party," Megan protested and her bottom lip began to tremble.

Gail touched the little girl's cheek and smiled. "You know what, sweetheart? You're absolutely right. What do you guys say? How about if *we* give him a party?"

Justin stared as if she'd lost her mind. "Where?"

"Right here."

Brad jumped up. "Yeah. A *surprise* party. That'll be fun."

"Can we play games?" Megan asked.

Justin leaned back in his chair and shook his head. "He won't like it."

But Gail refused to let him dampen the others' excitement or her own. "You never know. He might. It's worth a try." She pulled out a chair and joined them at the table. "We could sneak into town tomorrow and pick up a few decorations. I'll call Bowman's and order a cake—"

Megan clapped her hands in delight. "And we can have balloons and play Pin the Tail on the Donkey."

"And a *piñata*," Brad said. "I've always wanted to have one."

Gail smiled. "All right. We'll see what we can find in town tomorrow. Dad's probably got some chicken wire in the barn, and we can throw together some kind of *piñata*. It might not be very fancy—"

"I don't care," Brad insisted.

Justin actually looked a little disappointed. "I can't go to town tomorrow. I have to work on the roof."

"You're right," Gail said. "We'll have to go without you, and I'm sorry about that. I'd love to have you go with us. Tell me what you want for the party and I'll get it."

Justin tried to appear nonchalant, but Gail thought she saw a glimmer of excitement in his eyes. "Decorations. Streamers and stuff. And those dumb-looking hats."

Brad laughed. "Can you see Dad wearing one of those?"

"He'll never do it," Justin predicted, but his lips twitched.

Gail reached for the junk drawer and pulled out a sheet of notepaper so she could start a list. "What's his favorite kind of cake?"

Brad looked blank.

But Justin gave it a few seconds' thought. "Chocolate, I think. The light kind."

Gail made a note. "Ice cream?"

Megan cried, " 'Trawberry."

Justin shrugged. "Probably not, but—"

"Yes, it is," Megan insisted. " 'Cause he always wants a lick of mine. It's 'trawberry."

"Okay, strawberry." Gail added it to her list. "Now, how are we going to surprise him?"

"Somebody has to keep him busy and then bring him inside when we're ready," Brad suggested.

Gail nodded. "Justin's the most logical person to take charge of that."

Justin shook his head. "Not me."

"All you have to do is get him to drive you out to look at the corn," Gail said. "Pretend you're suddenly fascinated by how to tell when it's ripe, or something."

Brad bounced out of his chair. "Yeah. You can do that."

"And we'll decorate the living room and get everything ready while you're out there." Gail made a few more notes on her list, then caught Megan's eye. "Now, Megan, this is a big surprise. You can't tell your daddy anything about it, okay?"

The little girl nodded solemnly. "I promise."

"Neither can you guys." She winked at each in turn and they grinned back at her. "Anybody have ideas for presents?"

Brad's face fell. "I told you, I don't have any money."

"I don't mean *expensive* presents. Think of what you'd like to get him—within reason, of course. I'll take care of it when we're in town tomorrow."

Suddenly, Megan raced to the kitchen window and a second later, Gail heard the sound of Clint's truck pulling into the yard.

"Here he comes, here he comes," Megan cried. "Be quiet, everybody."

Gail stashed the list in the junk drawer and busied herself with the ice cream and scoop while Justin grabbed Megan away from the window. A few seconds later, Clint's footsteps sounded on the porch and

Gail's pulse quickened. When he pushed open the back door, her heart jumped.

He stood framed in the doorway, highlighted by the setting sun, and studied their expressionless faces. "What's going on in here?"

Brad's eyes widened as if he'd been caught, but Gail held up a glass and spoon to divert Clint's attention. "We're making root-beer floats. Want one?"

Clint's eyes lit. "Are you kidding? I haven't had one of those in years. I'll take you up on it." Yanking off his hat, he found a place at the table and settled in to watch her work.

She filled the rest of the glasses and slowly added root beer, only too aware that he hadn't yet taken his eyes off her. Indulging in fantasy for a moment, she let herself enjoy the picture they made—a family sharing a relaxing moment together. And she liked the way it felt.

She'd expected to find this with Richard and his children, but she never had. And now that she had found it, she didn't belong. Her place belonged to someone else.

Pushing aside a sudden shaft of pain, she stole a glance at Clint. His eyes narrowed slightly as if she'd confused him. She tried to smile, but her lips felt stiff. She tried to drag her gaze away, but he held it without blinking.

Her pulse raced and her mouth grew dry. She willed him to smile, to break the tension of the moment, but he didn't. She silently begged him to look away since she didn't have the strength to do it herself.

For the space of a heartbeat, time stood still. And in that moment, the truth became even harder to bear.

Her feelings for Clint had gone far beyond friendship.

She never missed an opportunity to watch him, was attuned to every nuance of his voice, and she felt his presence almost before she saw him. Somehow, he filled a space that had long been empty in her soul. Somehow, she'd fallen in love with him.

What a terrible irony, she thought, as her eyes filled with tears and she looked away. She'd finally found a man she could love, but he loved someone else. She'd finally found children she could mother, but they'd never be part of her life. Within a few short months, Clint would be married and they'd all walk out of her life forever.

CHAPTER NINE

CLINT FOLLOWED Hal outside and lowered himself onto an old patio chair, grateful for the chance to slow down. If Hal hadn't wanted to talk to him, he'd have headed straight upstairs to bed after dinner. And he could probably have slept round the clock.

Hal struck a match on the railing and lit his cigarette. "How's that roof comin'?"

"We're half done."

"Good. Real good. We're damned lucky we ain't had any storms." He puffed for a few seconds. "What about the barn?"

Clint had to struggle not to groan aloud. Every muscle in his body ached, his eyes burned and his skin throbbed from overexposure to the sun. He felt ages older than Hal. Ancient. Decrepit. But he knew Hal would take over in a heartbeat if he showed any signs of weakness, so he asked, "You want us to do the barn roof before or after we thin the corn?"

"After. We'll work the crop first and use tarp to cover the danger spots if a storm hits." Hal studied him, and to Clint's surprise, he chuckled. "What's the matter? Work gettin' to ya?"

"No, I'm fine. A little tired tonight, that's all."

"Well, it's hard work, that's for sure. How's Justin holdin' up?"

"Tired. Sore. But I think he's actually starting to feel good about what we're doing."

"Figured he would. Not much that'll make you feel better than pitting yourself against Mother Nature and holdin' your own. She's a lot stronger than any man I ever knowed."

Clint tried to stretch out his legs, but his stiff muscles protested the movement and a groan escaped his lips.

Hal chuckled again. "Don't worry. You'll feel like a new man in a day or two."

This time, Clint allowed himself a smile. "God willing."

Hal inhaled deeply from his cigarette and scanned the yard. "Did Phyllis tell you that your gal-friend called this evening?"

"Leslie?"

"Yep."

"No, she didn't tell me. Am I supposed to call back?"

Hal shook his head. "Phyllis didn't say. She *did* say the young lady sounded upset."

Upset? Not again. The second that thought hit him, Clint tried to suppress it. But lately, Leslie seemed upset more often than not, and tonight he didn't have the energy to smooth anything over.

He stole a glance at his watch. "It's nearly eleven in Chicago. I'll wait and call her tomorrow."

Hal dragged on his cigarette again. "Probably just as well. She's probably asleep by now." He let a few seconds lapse before he spoke again. "How's Gail gettin' on?"

At the mention of her name, Gail's image formed in his mind so vividly he could almost feel her beside him. He closed his eyes for a second and tried to push her away, but failed miserably. "She's fine," he said at last. "Worried about Boone, of course. And Dorothy's anxious about the garden, so Gail spends most of her time canning."

Hal studied him for a moment then nodded and looked away. "I saw Dr. Lethbridge in town today. He don't seem too happy with Boone's progress."

"I don't think he is," Clint admitted.

"Damn. Looks like they're gonna have to sell, but I don't know who they'll find to buy," Hal said heavily.

"Don't you know anybody who'd be interested?"

"Nope. And I'll tell you what scares me." He gestured with his cigarette and left a trail of smoke. "I'm afraid Boone and Dorothy'll get shuffled into Billings, or down to California to be near Gail, and they'll wind up spendin' the rest of their days in some little three-room place—or worse. But they're farm folks and that kinda life'll kill 'em sure as anything." Emotion clogged his voice. Embarrassed, he paused to grind out his cigarette with the toe of his boot. "Whoever buys Boone's place'll probably break it up and sell to folks who want to build tract houses. Then, little by little, this whole area's gonna go. But this land wasn't meant to be broken into tiny pieces. It'll kill the land sure as it'll kill Boone."

A year ago, Clint might have doubted Hal's predictions. Now he not only believed them, he shared many of the older man's fears—especially about Boone. He'd seen the raw pride in the man's face and he'd talked with Dorothy often enough to know how she felt. Removing them from their home and their land would take the heart out of them, even if it didn't actually kill them.

"Well, there ain't no easy answers to this one, boy." Hal groaned loudly as he stood up, then cocked his head and listened to the telephone ringing inside the house. "Must be your gal-friend again."

It had to be. Nobody else would call this late. Clint made his stiff legs work quickly as he stepped inside and grabbed the receiver. "Hello?"

"Clint? Where in the hell have you been?" Leslie's voice sounded cold and brittle in the still summer night.

Though her immediate assault bothered him, he carefully screened the annoyance from his own voice before he answered. "I've been working."

"Didn't anybody tell you I called?"

"I just heard, but I figured it was too late to phone tonight. I was planning to do it in the morning."

She let a few seconds lapse, then said, "Didn't your aunt tell you it was important?"

"Actually, no. If I'd known it was urgent, I would have called. What's wrong?"

"I didn't say *wrong,* I said important. I need to talk to you about something. I have a wonderful idea."

He tried to work up a little enthusiasm. "What is it?"

"I know we've talked about your birthday to death, Clint, I really do. And I know you're convinced you have to stay there. But can't you give *me* a weekend? We need some time together—just you and me. Let me give you the airline ticket for your birthday. I'll get a room at the Hilton and we can spend the entire weekend there. Forget the birthday party. Forget a hundred friends. We'll have champagne and that caviar you like so much. I'll give you a birthday you'll never forget." Her voice dropped to the low, sultry tone that had sent chills of desire through him when they met. Her invitation was clear.

Maybe it *would* help their relationship if he could give her two days alone in bed at the Hilton. But with Dr. Lethbridge's latest prognosis and Boone's corn crop needing constant attention, he couldn't spare even a day. "I'm sorry, Les."

"You're *sorry?*" Her sultry tone vanished. "What in the hell is going on out there?"

"Just what I've told you. There's too much at stake for these people, and they can't fend for themselves."

"This isn't like you, Clint. You don't even sound the same when you talk to me. What's happening to us?"

"I was up on a roof for fourteen hours today, Les. I'm bushed. If I sound different, it's because I'm exhausted."

"Come home."

"I can't."

"Let what's-her-name find someone else to help."

He didn't bother to refuse again. But she obviously heard it in his silence.

"Will you tell me one thing?" she demanded. "What's she doing to keep you there?"

Unbidden, Gail's image filled his mind again. Eyes, hair, smile, laugh, energy, wit, intelligence. He shook his head slowly. "It's not that, Leslie."

"*That's* not what I meant."

He groaned silently and pulled in a deep breath. "Leslie, I know you're disappointed with me, and you can't even imagine how sorry I am. But there are half a dozen reasons I can't leave. Not even for a day."

Silence hummed between them for several seconds. "I see."

But he doubted she truly did. They'd been over the same ground so often, he'd almost started anticipating her telephone calls with the same kind of dread he'd once awaited Barbara's. Probably because he seemed unable to make Leslie any happier than he'd made Barbara.

"Then I guess there's nothing else to say." Her words fell between them like ice.

"I wish you could understand how bad things are right now," he said. "It's hail season out here, and the Knights' house doesn't even have a decent roof. I can't give my birthday—or even the chance at a weekend alone with you—priority over something this urgent." In the silence that followed, he willed her to understand.

"What I don't understand is how I—how *we've*—become such a low priority in your life."

"You're not a low priority, Leslie. And neither is our relationship."

She didn't respond. He knew she'd have supported his devotion to duty if a crisis arose at Garrity & Garr, but on this subject they'd reached an impasse.

His stomach tightened and burned, and a dull ache started in the base of his neck. He wanted to say something that would make everything right, but he couldn't find the words.

"Look, sweetheart," he said. "I'm tired. You're tired. Maybe we ought to drop this before one of us says something we'll regret."

"Maybe you're right." Her voice sounded tight and angry.

"I'll call you tomorrow after work."

"Don't. I won't be home. I'll call you Saturday. You can squeeze in a conversation on your birthday, can't you?"

"Leslie, please—"

But she went on as if she hadn't heard him. "Why don't you tell me what time to call. That way, I won't miss you."

"It'll have to be late. At least ten or ten-thirty your time."

"Fine." She didn't sound fine.

"I'll talk to you then. And Leslie—"

The dial tone cut him off. She'd hung up on him. Clint stared at the receiver for several seconds before he could make himself move. Then he slowly climbed the stairs to his bedroom and searched his dresser for the small brown prescription bottle that held the medication he took for his ulcers. He hadn't had to take it for months, but he knew tonight he wouldn't get to sleep without it.

CLINT DROVE as quickly as he dared over the rutted road from the fields back to Gail's house. He and Justin had stopped working on the roof earlier than usual this Saturday evening, and they'd spent over an hour checking the corn in Boone's south field.

For some reason Clint still didn't understand, Justin had shown a sudden interest in farming and expressed a desire to accompany his father to the cornfields. Though Clint had enjoyed every minute with his son, he'd have to hurry now to get home in time for Leslie's call.

Frankly, Justin's sudden about-face puzzled him. At first he'd wondered if Justin pretended an interest because it was Clint's birthday, but none of the kids had acknowledged it all day, so he didn't think that could be the reason.

No, something else had touched Justin, and Clint would give anything to know what. If Clint had accidentally done something right, he'd like to do it again. Confused, he stole another glance at Justin.

The boy leaned forward in his seat watching the road.

"Aren't you tired?" Clint asked.

Justin looked at him. "Yeah. A little, I guess."

"Well, I'm beat. And I'm going to sleep like a log tonight."

"Me, too."

"I kind of hoped we'd get through earlier than usual tonight."

"Why?"

"Well, I thought maybe we could drive in to Broken Bow for dinner. There's a nice little restaurant on the other side of town that serves great chicken."

"Oh." Justin looked baffled. "Why?"

Clint shrugged and tried not to feel disappointed. After all, the kids hadn't remembered his last two birthdays. Why should this one be any different? "No special reason," he lied. "But it *is* Saturday night—"

Justin stared back out the window. "Yeah. Sure. Sounds great."

Swerving to miss a deep rut, Clint cursed himself silently. If he were honest with himself, he'd admit it wasn't just the kids who'd disappointed him. *Nobody* had remembered his birthday. He'd seen Phyllis for a minute at breakfast, but she'd been too worked up about today's stampede-committee meeting to remember. Hal hadn't said a word, but then, he had his every-third-Saturday-night poker game with a bunch of friends and nothing ever got in the way of that.

Most of all, Gail hadn't even bothered to wish him a good day. But Gail couldn't possibly have known it was his birthday. He'd made a point of not mentioning it to her. He'd convinced himself he didn't want anyone to make a fuss. And they hadn't. So whose fault was that?

Well, he'd feel better once he talked to Leslie. At least he *hoped* he would.

Ahead, Gail's house loomed into view and Clint slowed to pull into the yard. But to his surprise, there was nobody in the yard, and the house looked almost deserted.

He glanced at Justin. "Did Gail say anything to you about leaving?"

Justin shook his head. "Nope."

"Where do you suppose they are?"

"I don't know. Maybe around back."

Justin didn't sound concerned, but something felt wrong to Clint. Every morning, Gail had a light on in the kitchen and coffee waiting for him. Every evening, she brought Megan to meet his truck at the end of a long, hard day. He counted on her welcome when he pulled into this yard. She'd become a part of his routine, and he missed her when she wasn't there.

He worked the truck into gear and killed the engine as Justin threw open his door and hopped out. The boy glanced over his shoulder and called, "Are you coming?"

With a nod, Clint got out and followed Justin to the house. "Maybe she and the kids went into town again."

"Yeah, maybe."

Clint studied the house once more, but it looked so deserted he stopped in his tracks. "Maybe we ought to wait in the truck. I'm sure they'll be back soon."

Justin jumped onto the porch and pulled open the back-door screen. "We can wait inside. Gail won't mind."

"Maybe not, but I don't want to get in Dorothy's way. We're underfoot enough, as it is."

Justin looked disappointed. "Let's go in and get a drink. I'm thirsty."

"We can get one from the hose. The water's good and cool, and we won't have to bother Dorothy." Clint pivoted away and took a few steps toward the truck.

"Maybe they didn't go to town," Justin called after him. "Maybe something's wrong. Don't you think we ought to check?"

Clint paused and looked back at his son. "You might be right. We ought to at least ask where Gail and the kids are. Knock on the door."

Justin knocked, and Clint closed the distance between them while they waited. But when a full two minutes crept by and Dorothy hadn't answered, he grew a little concerned.

He pounded on the door himself, making sure to knock loud enough for Dorothy to hear them from the back bedroom.

Still no answer.

Trying not to let alarm take over, Clint spoke softly. "Something's wrong."

"Yeah, maybe. Let's go in."

Under ordinary circumstances, Clint would never barge into someone's home uninvited. But with Boone's illness and his own children's safety a concern, he decided to follow Justin's suggestion.

Inside, the kitchen stood dark and silent. Between normal household activity and the garden produce Gail spent so much time preserving, he didn't think he'd ever seen it like this. And the silence disturbed him.

Fighting the cold fear that suddenly threatened to overwhelm him, Clint pushed open the door to the living room. Someone had pulled the curtains and the room was bathed in shadow. In the half light, something suddenly moved, lights blazed on and half a dozen voices shouted.

It took several beats to realize what they'd said, and before Clint could get his bearings, Megan threw herself at his legs. "Happy bir'fday, Daddy. We maked you a surprise party."

In confusion, he touched her shoulders and stared around the room. Near the window, Brad laughed aloud. Gail stood by the front door, grinning as if everything was all right. Justin pounded his shoulder and acted as if he'd engineered a grand joke. Even Dorothy looked pleased and happy. And Hal and Phyllis were as excited as the kids.

Slowly, Clint took it all in. Streamers trailed from every available fixture. Balloons floated in colorful clusters by the windows, rose on strings from the backs of chairs and drifted down on him from the ceiling.

A surprise party? They'd remembered. And somehow, every one of them had managed to act as if they didn't know.

Pulling in a deep breath, he tried to still the shaking of his knees while the kids clamored for his attention. He hugged Megan first, then Brad. As reality sank further into his consciousness, he felt even more pleased, even more foolish for pouting. And when

Justin submitted to a brief hug, the haze of confusion finally evaporated.

As he let Justin go, he found Gail before him. She grinned broadly and said something to Justin he couldn't quite make out over the kids' excited chatter. Without thinking, he pulled her into his arms.

She melted against him for a heartbeat, soft and yielding. His pulse raced and he had to fight the urge to tip her chin and lower his mouth to hers. She felt right in his arms, as if she'd been made to fit there.

Before he realized what she was doing, she pulled gently away and met his scrutiny with eyes so dark they looked like pools of liquid night. She averted her gaze almost immediately, and he wondered if he'd only imagined the flicker of desire he saw there.

Something tugged at his pant leg, and Megan's voice claimed his attention. "Daddy, can we play Pin the Tail on the Donkey first? Please?"

Reluctantly, he tore his gaze from Gail and smiled down at his daughter. "Sure. I guess." He laughed. "I'm so surprised, I don't know what to say."

Megan grinned at Gail. "I was a good girl. I didn't even tell."

"You're always a good girl," Gail said. "And I'm awfully proud of you for keeping our secret so well."

Justin laughed and leaned further into the circle they made. "Could you hear us out there? I almost didn't get him to come inside."

"I couldn't believe it," Brad said. "I thought the whole party was gonna be ruined."

Justin shook his head and looked so serious Clint had to fight the urge to laugh. "Well, if scaring him hadn't worked, I don't know what I would have done."

Hal grinned at Clint. "Got your head so far in the clouds, you couldn't see what was right in front of you."

Gail put an arm around Justin's shoulders. "It was a stroke of genius, Justin. It worked beautifully."

With a good-hearted hmmph, Dorothy crossed to the hallway. "I had no idea you thought I was such a terror, Clint." He opened his mouth to explain, but she laughed. "Happy birthday. And thank you for all you and your kids have done for Boone and me—*and* for Gail."

He didn't understand that last part, so he turned to Gail for an explanation. She looked almost embarrassed until Megan interrupted by grabbing a brightly colored paper hat from the coffee table and holding it out to him.

"We bought you a hat, Daddy." Megan waved the hat at him. "Put it on, okay?"

He grimaced. "You want me to wear *that?*" In answer, Megan only giggled, while Brad shot Justin an amused look.

Gail tried to look solemn as she nodded, but mischief tweaked the corners of her lips. "The hats were Justin's idea."

"He really wants you to wear it," Phyllis added.

"Yeah. Put it on." Justin said, and though his expression held a mild challenge, Clint couldn't hear animosity in his voice.

Pulling off his cowboy hat with a show of reluctance, Clint held out his hand. "All right. Give it to me."

"Let me put it on you," Megan pleaded.

Clint tried to look even more reluctant, but he couldn't deny he loved the smiles he earned from all three children.

Gail lifted Megan high enough to slip the hat on his head. Megan positioned the hat, then released the elastic chin strap too quickly and stung him. He winced, then managed a grin, which earned more giggles from Megan. "I can't even remember the last time I wore one of these," he said.

Justin laughed aloud, Brad looked pleased and Megan clapped her hands with delight.

Gail's eyes danced, but the other emotion he'd glimpsed earlier had vanished. "Well, you look wonderful. Okay, kids, what do we do first?"

"Pin the Tail on the Donkey," Megan cried. "And I go first."

"Well, that's out for me," Hal said as he pushed to his feet with a groan. "I'd stick around, but the boys're waitin' the poker game for me."

Phyllis hugged Clint quickly. "And I've got my committee meeting. Will you forgive us for leaving so soon?"

"Forgive you? You can't imagine how much it means to me that you even remembered."

Phyllis nodded toward Gail. "Don't give us the credit, son. Gail's the one who pulled this together." She stood on tiptoe to kiss his cheek, then took Hal's arm and walked with him to the barn where they'd apparently hidden Hal's truck.

"Pin the Tail on the Donkey," Megan cried a second time as Clint turned back from the door. And before he could even catch his breath, they swept him into the party.

For the first time in years, Clint played with his children. They shrieked with joy, groaned with disappointment and laughed almost constantly. After unsuccessfully trying to tail the donkey, they moved outside and took turns trying to smash the square purple *piñata* Gail and the kids had thrown together.

He played games he hadn't played since he was a boy. He and Brad lost their stride during a three-legged race and landed in a laughing heap on the lawn. He held Gail's ankles for the wheelbarrow race and tried like hell not to look at the way her hips and bottom swayed as she raced across the yard on her hands. He joined forces with Megan in a game of kick the can, and partnered with Justin for badminton. Their smiles and laughter fueled him and kept him going long after sheer exhaustion should have brought him to his knees.

He unwrapped a small box containing three packages of strawberry-flavored bubble gum from Megan, a pocketknife from Brad and a wide, silver-plated belt buckle from Justin. And he was touched and pleased by everything. But Gail's present—a surprise in itself—was the hit of the evening. She gave him a fishing pole and a cap sporting a picture of a minnow and the caption, The One That Got Away.

They sat around the picnic table under the still-light sky. Clint sipped Black Cherry Kool-Aid from a paper cup, wolfed down barbecued hot dogs, chips, three servings of Gail's potato salad and a double-scoop strawberry ice-cream cone for his birthday dinner. And for dessert, he had two pieces of milk-chocolate cake with milk-chocolate frosting.

When he pushed his plate away after the second piece, he glanced at his watch. Almost ten o'clock.

Because it stayed light so late up here, it was easy to lose track of time. And his body clock hadn't even warned him. It had been a full day, but he felt wonderful.

He stretched his legs and tried to find a comfortable position in which to let his last piece of cake settle. If anyone had told him even a month ago he'd have a birthday party like this one, he would have laughed. But things changed. *He'd* changed. And strangely, he thought this was the best party he'd ever had.

It took a split second for his thoughts to connect, and when they did he sat upright and checked his watch again as if he might have read it wrong. *Ten o'clock?* That made it eleven in Chicago. And that meant he'd missed Leslie's call.

Now what? He could bolt out of here, race home and call, but it would be at least half an hour before he could reach her. Besides, how would he explain his sudden departure to Gail and the kids? And what would he say to Leslie? She'd be hurt and angry, and he wouldn't blame her a bit. He'd have to work hard to dig himself out of this hole.

Gail sat across the picnic table, staring at him. "Are you all right?"

"Yes... No— I forgot about an important phone call. Would it be okay for me to use your phone? I'll use my calling card—"

She waved away his concern. "Of course."

Jumping to his feet, he tried to smile. "I'll be right back."

He jogged across the yard, took the porch steps two at a time and punched in Leslie's number on the kitchen phone as quickly as he could—as if that would

somehow make things better. He practiced his opening line while the call went through, and during the
first five rings. On six, he started to wonder. But after
eight, he realized she wasn't going to answer.

Gail gazed at the back door for several seconds after Clint disappeared inside. He'd obviously been in a
panic when he raced across the yard, and Gail could
guess why. He'd probably planned to speak to Leslie
tonight, but had lost track of time.

It was evident that the call was important to him.
He'd been frantic to get inside. And Gail tried not to
let his urgency hurt her.

On the lawn, Megan yawned and snuggled against
Justin's side. Brad had found a comfortable position,
and now he was clearly struggling to keep his eyes
open. She crossed the lawn and crouched in front of
the kids. Touching Megan's cheek, she let her dreams
take over for a second longer, imagining the little girl
and her brothers as her own family.

Brad grinned up at her, looking drowsy, contented,
happy. "The party was cool, wasn't it?"

"It was wonderful."

Justin looked over his shoulder at the house. "Do
you think *he* had fun?"

"I think he had a great time, don't you?"

He considered for a second, then nodded. "Yeah, I
guess so." He looked down at the top of Megan's
head. "Is she asleep?"

"Almost. Do you want to wait in the truck? I'm
sure your dad won't be long."

Brad nodded eagerly. "I do. The grass is getting
cold."

Justin looked reluctant, but he gave in without argument. "Okay. I guess we should."

Gail lifted Megan out of Justin's arms while he stood, then she walked with them to the truck. After Brad climbed into the cab and Justin settled by the door, she lifted Megan onto Justin's lap, letting her hand linger on the little girl's forehead.

Instinct urged her to kiss them all—the boys included. Common sense warned her not to. The boys seemed to like her so far, and she didn't want to push her luck. So she hopped from the running board to the ground and closed the door gently. "I'll tell your dad you're waiting as soon as he gets off the phone."

Justin grinned at her. "Okay. And, Gail? Thanks. It was a cool party."

Pleased, she patted his arm. "You're welcome. I enjoyed it, too."

"You still think I ought to talk to my dad?"

"More than ever."

He didn't look entirely convinced. "I'll think about it."

"Good."

Nearly asleep now, Megan stirred on his lap. Gail pressed a finger to her lips. "I'll see you in the morning."

Lost in pleasant thoughts, she rounded the corner of the house. To her surprise, Clint was already back outside. He stood in the shadows near the picnic table with his back to her. But as she grew closer, he whirled to face her. He looked miserable.

"The kids are waiting in the truck," she said.

He tried to smile. "Thanks. Let me help you clean up before I go."

"No, thanks. Just take them home and let them go to bed. They're tired. It's been a big day."

He grabbed his cowboy hat from the table, but stopped before he scooped up his gifts. "Thank you."

"You're welcome. Happy birthday."

But he made no further move to leave. Instead, he took a step toward her, holding her gaze with his, scorching her soul with the intensity in his eyes.

Her breath caught. Her skin tingled even before he touched her. And when he pulled her into his arms, her body cried out with longing. He held her too close for too long until finally, against her better judgment but unable to stop herself, she lifted her arms and ran her hands across his back. Suddenly afraid she'd drown in the emotions that overwhelmed her, she gripped his shoulders and held on.

He felt solid beneath her fingers. Warm and alive and masculine. But when his muscles shifted beneath her hands, she tried to force herself to release him.

He didn't move away. Instead, with a low growl deep in his throat, he pulled her closer and touched his lips to hers. For a heartbeat, his mouth hovered above hers as if waiting for her permission to go on. When she didn't push him away, he kissed her. When his tongue brushed her lips, she parted hers and his mouth claimed her.

Heat spiraled through her, and she lost herself in swirling sensation. Love and passion shot through her like fireworks and she wanted this kiss to last forever. She ached for him to hold her like this until the end of time. She clutched his shoulders and clung to him. She wanted *him*.

But he released her, and tears sprang into her eyes. She knew exactly why he'd kissed her. Caught up in the moment, unable to reach Leslie, he'd turned to her. In a few minutes, he'd realize what he'd done and apologize. And she would have to pretend the kiss had meant no more to her than it had to him. But she knew she'd never be the same.

Clint held Gail for several seconds until his breathing slowed and his heart stopped thudding. Until he could trust his legs to hold him up and his mouth not to say something he'd later regret. He knew he should apologize to her, but he couldn't form the words. He *wasn't* sorry.

He'd come back outside, worried about Leslie. Upset about not being able to reach her. And then he'd seen Gail walking toward him, her hair gleaming in the moonlight, her eyes looking deep and full of the promise he'd seen earlier. And he'd wanted her with an intensity he hadn't known he could feel.

Their kiss had been magic, a healing balm to his soul and more passionate than anything he'd ever felt. No woman had ever left him reeling like this.

He told himself not to let desire take control. He warned himself about the mess he could make of his life that way. He should probably feel guilty, but he didn't. He should turn around and walk away and head straight home to Leslie, but he couldn't. He wanted to stay here.

Honesty forced him to admit that while desire played a part in the way he felt about Gail, it was only a part. Until now, he'd only dreamed about loving a woman this way. About passion and friendship combining to form the deepest possible bond. With sudden clarity, he realized he'd been looking for her all his life.

He studied her face, wanting to memorize every detail. But when he saw the tears in her eyes, he froze. "Gail? What's wrong?"

She shook her head as if she couldn't speak. "Nothing."

"You're crying."

She didn't answer.

"Gail?"

"I'm all right," she said. "But would you please go now?"

"Go?"

She pulled away and turned from him. "Please."

"Gail, I—"

"No," she cried. "Please, don't say anything."

He stared at her for one long moment. Surely he hadn't imagined her response to his kiss or misread the passion in her eyes.

When she faced him again, her softness had vanished. "Your kids are waiting in the truck," she said. Pivoting away, she left him staring after her, unable to believe what had just happened.

He'd finally found her. But she didn't want him.

CHAPTER TEN

HOLDING HIS BOOTS in one hand, Clint crept down the stairs long before daylight the next morning. He'd spent most of the night lying awake and thinking about Gail. And all those hours alone had given him time to clarify his thoughts and reach a decision.

Colonel Mustard stretched his way from under the table into the middle of the room and wound his furry body around Clint's ankles. They'd become fast friends in the early-morning hours. Megan had lost interest in toilet-bowl swims and strolls along the highway since Gail became a part of their lives.

"Poor fella," Clint whispered. "You lost your best friend, didn't you? Or maybe you're a little relieved."

As if he understood, the Colonel flopped to his side. Clint scratched the cat's ears and the base of his tail and thought about the changes Gail had brought about in all their lives. And he thought about Leslie.

He'd met her at the lowest point in his life. He'd been anxious to find someone to fill the void left by the divorce, and Leslie had done that. And for that, she'd always hold a special place in his heart.

But he loved Gail as he'd never loved any other woman. She touched him deep in his soul. She answered questions he hadn't thought to ask and filled places he hadn't known were empty. He couldn't imagine spending the rest of his life without her, but

he couldn't reconcile himself to the idea of coldheart-
edly jilting Leslie because he'd fallen in love with
someone else. He might love Gail, but he still had a
commitment to Leslie.

He rubbed the cat's stomach and smiled. "Come
on, old boy. I'll let you out. See what mischief you can
stir up. Go find a female cat somewhere—I highly
recommend it."

Clint tiptoed across the kitchen floor and pushed
open the back door for the cat, then bent to pull on his
boots. When he imagined Gail waiting for him the way
she did every morning, he smiled. He'd relived their
kiss a thousand times during the night, remembered
her eager response, and he'd seen again the passion in
her eyes. Maybe she didn't love him, but she wasn't
totally immune to him, either. And this morning he
intended to find out how she felt about him.

When he reached for his second boot, his smile
faded. He knew it wouldn't be easy to end his relationship with Leslie, but even if Gail didn't want him,
he had to do it. Leslie deserved a man who adored her.
He just wasn't that man.

Before he could open the back door, the telephone
jangled in the predawn stillness. He answered as it
rang a second time.

"Happy birthday a day late." Leslie's voice sounded
warm, friendly and fully awake.

"Thanks, Les. I'm sorry about last night. I tried to
call as soon as I realized what time it was."

"I waited until eleven, but you still weren't home.
Your aunt said you were at a birthday party. Is that
true?"

"It's true."

"I see." The warmth evaporated. "I guess I misunderstood what you told me, Clint. I thought you couldn't come home because you were in the middle of a crisis out there."

"It was a surprise party. I didn't know anything about it."

She laughed without humor. "Maybe *I* should have planned a surprise party. Remind me about this next year."

"Look, I had no idea the kids were planning a party for me. It's the first time they've even remembered my birthday since the divorce."

"The kids?" She sounded surprised. "But your aunt said...You mean, what's-her-name didn't throw the party for you?"

"Gail? No, but she helped the kids put it together."

"Really?" She added a little more ice to her tone. "How sweet. So, what did you do?"

"We played games and ran races and barbecued hot dogs—"

Leslie groaned aloud. "Ugh. It sounds awful. I don't know why I was worried." She let another small silence grow, then gave an embarrassed laugh. "Look, believe it or not, I didn't call to argue with you. In fact, I have a surprise."

Clint welcomed the chance to change to any other subject. "What is it?"

"I've decided to take a week off work."

"You're kidding?"

This time when she laughed, she sounded delighted. "I really surprised you?"

"I'll say. You haven't taken a single day off since we met. Now you're taking a *week?*"

"I've been doing a lot of thinking lately, sweetheart. Our relationship needs attention—from both of us. I've been nagging you to do things, make changes and sacrifices, but *I* haven't been willing to do the same. Well, I've decided to turn over a new leaf. I've finally accepted that you can't come here, so I'm coming out there to spend time with you."

"Coming *here?* I don't know what to say."

"I bought my ticket last night. I've got a late meeting Tuesday, so I can't come until Wednesday, but I should arrive in Billings a little after noon. Will you be able to meet me or should I rent a car?"

How could he let her come, knowing what he had to tell her? On the other hand, breaking it to her in person wouldn't be as cowardly as hiding behind the phone.

"Don't rent a car," he said. "I'll come and get you. What airline?"

"Delta with a stopover in Salt Lake. But really, sweetheart, if you're too busy—"

"No. I'll be there." He wrote down her flight information and made a note to check the ticket price with the airline so he could reimburse her.

"I can't wait to see you again," she said. "Will your aunt mind if we share a room?"

"She wouldn't like it," Clint admitted. "Besides, I don't think it would be a good idea. The kids are here, you know."

She sighed deeply. "Of course, you're right. Well, I won't pretend I'm happy about it, but maybe we can still manage to find some time alone."

"Maybe," he said softly. But he knew they wouldn't. He couldn't continue that part of their relationship and ever face Gail again. Or look Leslie in the eye when he told her he didn't love her. Or face himself in the mirror.

"I love you," Leslie said.

He couldn't respond for a long time. Finally, he managed to say, "I'm looking forward to seeing you."

"I can't wait." A brief pause. "Listen, I hate to go, but I'm going to have to. I'll probably be too busy to call again, so if you run into a problem picking me up, let me know."

"I'll be there no matter what happens."

"I'm counting on you," she said.

Clint rubbed his forehead and stared at the floor beneath his feet. She could have gone a lifetime without saying *that*.

By the time he disconnected a minute later, he realized no matter how anxious he was to find out how Gail felt about him, he couldn't do anything until he'd ended his relationship with Leslie. Leslie deserved his respect. She deserved a clean break and Gail deserved a fresh start. For him to do anything else would be unfair to both women. And to himself.

WHEN GAIL HEARD Clint's truck start down the lane, she poured two cups of coffee and stepped outside to wait on the porch the way she did every morning. It wouldn't be easy to act as if nothing had changed between them, but she had to try. If he guessed she loved him, he'd blame himself for leading her on. And while she'd welcome his love, she didn't want his pity or guilt.

She managed to smile when the truck's lights hit her, but the minute he climbed out of the cab, her smile faded. He looked drained and unhappy.

She waited for him to draw closer before she asked, "What's wrong?"

"Nothing. I'm just tired." His voice came out clipped and harsh, but he smiled an apology. "I'm sorry. I just got off the phone with Leslie."

Gail forced her face to hold its smile as she handed him a cup.

He let his gaze travel over the yard, and his jaw worked as if he had to struggle to form his next words. "She's coming for a visit."

For a second, Gail wondered if she'd heard him right. "Leslie is?"

"She'll be here Wednesday."

Gail pulled in a deep breath and tried to keep her voice level. "Well, at least the kids'll finally get to meet her."

He nodded without looking up. "Yeah. That'll be good."

She sipped coffee and tried to keep her hand from trembling. "You'll pick her up from the airport, won't you?"

He nodded again. "Her flight gets in about noon, so we won't get much done around here that day. The kids can go with me, we'll show her around Billings and stop somewhere for dinner—"

"But you haven't seen her in months," Gail said quickly, then drew in a deep breath so she could make herself say what came next. "She's going to want some time alone with you. Why don't you leave the kids here with me?"

"I couldn't ask you to do that."

"You're not asking, I'm offering. You can pick them up after dinner." It took all her effort not to show how much the offer cost her.

Clint drained his cup and finally looked at her. "You're sure you don't mind?"

"Of course not," she lied.

Even with that assurance, he stewed on the offer for a few more seconds. "Well, all right, then. Thanks. I appreciate it." He stepped off the porch and took a step away before he asked, "Talk to you later?"

"Sure," she whispered. But she knew she'd have to avoid him whenever possible. It would be too difficult to be near him—she couldn't deny her feelings any longer.

She watched him cross the yard, and forced herself not to run after him and tell him she loved him. No matter how much she loved him, she couldn't tell him as long as he was committed to Leslie.

GAIL GAVE the kitchen table one last swipe with a clean cloth and surveyed the boxes of peas that represented her day's work. Not bad for an amateur. She was getting better at harvesting every day. There'd be something else to pick tomorrow, but right now she wanted to spend time with her father and let her mother get some much-needed rest.

She hurried down the hall and into her father's room. Late-afternoon sunlight spilled across his pale face and made him look more fragile than usual. Her mother, weary and worn, sat in a chair by the bed with her eyes closed.

Gail crossed to the window and pulled the curtain, then touched her mother's shoulders gently. "Mom, why don't you go lie down? I'll stay with Daddy for a while."

Dorothy opened her eyes and managed a thin smile. "No thanks, sweetheart. I'm fine right here."

"How's he feeling this afternoon?"

"He's all right. He's been sleeping most of the day."

Gail examined her father's face, hoping for some sign of improvement, but she found none. Even with the curtain drawn, he looked weaker than he had yesterday. "Has he eaten anything?"

"Nothing to speak of."

"Have you talked to Dr. Lethbridge today?"

Dorothy shook her head and her smile faded. "Not yet."

"Maybe you ought to phone him. If Daddy's not eating—"

With a weary shrug, Dorothy turned to Boone and concern creased her features. "I mentioned it to Arnold yesterday, but he doesn't want to start feeding your dad intravenously unless he gets worse."

Gail perched on the arm of her mother's chair and studied her father's face again, praying he'd show improvement soon, fearing he wouldn't.

As if she couldn't bear to talk about it any longer, her mother patted her hand and put on a matter-of-fact expression. "So, did you finish the peas?"

Gail nodded. "And it looks like there'll be more spinach in the morning."

"I haven't heard Clint moving around on the roof today. What's he working on?"

Gail lowered her eyes. "I'm not sure."

"And the kids? They haven't been inside all day."

"Megan and Brad are with Phyllis today, and Justin stayed home after lunch."

"Really? Why?"

She managed a casual shrug. "Clint's girlfriend is coming for a visit. I guess they're getting ready for it."

Dorothy's eyes narrowed. "Oh? I see." She smoothed her hands across her lap. "And how do you feel about that?"

Gail flushed. "How *should* I feel?"

"That's not what I asked you. I know what's going on with you two."

"There isn't anything going on," Gail insisted.

"Nothing a blind man couldn't see," Dorothy said with a tiny laugh. "Clint's a fine man, Gail, and he cares deeply for you."

Gail plucked at the curtains with numb fingers and battled the tears that sprang into her eyes. "Maybe. But he *loves* someone else."

"Nonsense."

"Mom, please don't. He's committed to someone else. I can't do anything to come between them."

Her mother nodded reluctantly. "I suppose you're right. But he's going to end up breaking your heart because he's too stubborn to admit how he really feels."

Gail shook her head. "I don't think so. He doesn't feel that way about me."

Dorothy made a noise of disbelief but, thankfully, she didn't argue.

Silence fell between them while Gail tried to find a subject they could discuss that wouldn't rub their emotions raw. After several long minutes, she abandoned the effort and kissed her mother's cheek. "I'll check back in an hour and see if you're ready for a break."

She tiptoed from the room, but her father's pale face continued to haunt her and her mother's prediction about Clint echoed in her mind with every step she took. Anxious to escape her troubled thoughts, she crossed the living room and stepped onto the front porch.

She stood for a minute soaking in the sunlight. It felt warm on her face and shoulders, soothing to her troubled heart, and she wished she could stay there for hours absorbing its magic. But with Clint somewhere nearby, she didn't want to risk running into him. Then she remembered that the last time she'd registered movement in the yard, she'd heard him entering the barn. If she followed the lane to the highway, she could stay outside a little longer and still avoid him.

Walking slowly, she listened to the meadowlarks and twisted a sunflower from its stalk. She held its prickly stem in her fingers and brushed its petals across her cheek the way she'd done as a child. Life was so simple then. No decisions to make, no heartaches to heal, no disappointments to forget.

She gazed out over the fields, then closed her eyes and turned her face to the sun. Only when she heard footsteps on the road ahead did she open her eyes.

Clint stood at the edge of the field, watching her and smiling. Her heart leaped with anticipation, and her step faltered, but she recovered quickly and returned his smile until she thought of losing him to Leslie. Then, a lump grew in her throat and she wondered how she'd ever manage to speak around it.

Clint pushed back his hat and wiped his forehead, then watched Gail's approach without moving. She looked so beautiful it took all his self-control not to pull her into his arms and cover her mouth with his.

She forced another smile when she drew closer. "I thought you were in the barn." She said no more, but he knew she'd intended to avoid him.

"I needed to check the crop." It almost sounded like an apology. He pulled in a steadying breath and tried not to notice her eyes, her lips, the curve of her hips beneath her jeans and the swell of her breasts under her soft cotton shirt. "How's your father?" he asked at last.

"Not good. I think he's weaker. Even my mother notices—she hasn't left his side all day."

Every instinct demanded that he take her into his arms and hold her there, but he had no right to follow his instincts. Not yet. "I'm sorry. What can I do?"

She turned from him with a brittle laugh. "More than what you're *already* doing?"

"It's not enough." When she didn't respond, he touched her shoulders and pulled her around to face him. "Quit trying to be so independent. You need help. Let me do what I can."

"You're already doing too much. Your kids need you, and Leslie will be here in a few days. There's no way you can take on something new."

He wanted to dispute her argument, but his mind refused to provide him with the right words to say. When he didn't speak, her eyes darkened as if his silence answered a question she hadn't asked. She met his gaze, and he could see her closing the channels between them.

"I need to get back," she said softly.

But he couldn't make himself release her shoulders; instead, he drew her to him and wrapped his arms around her. She melted against him and he could feel her heart racing to match the rhythm of his own. He whispered her name a second before he touched her lips.

His resolve weakened, and he crushed her against him. Her mouth opened to him and her kiss ignited a passion such as he'd never felt before. He gave himself to her without restraint and let his love forge a silent bond between them.

Hungry to feel her beneath him, he loosened his arms and let his hands trail up her sides and down to her hips. She didn't pull away; if anything, she moved closer until he was no longer certain where he ended and she began. Doubt faded and hope for the future together replaced it.

When her fingers ran up his back, he shuddered with desire. When her arm encircled his neck, he deepened the kiss further. When she moaned with pleasure, he trailed kisses down her neck and into the hollow of her throat.

She tilted her head back in a posture of abandon, opened her mouth slightly and closed her eyes. She looked more beautiful than any woman he'd ever known, and he wanted her with such intensity he didn't know whether he could refrain from making love with her on this gravel driveway.

He drew strength from the soft touch of her fingers on his shoulders, his back and his face, and finally managed to pull himself under control long enough to recognize the danger in his actions.

As if she'd read his thoughts, Gail pressed him away. "No, Clint."

Dragging in a shaky breath, he released her reluctantly and tried to keep his voice steady. "I'm sorry. I shouldn't have done that. Not while Leslie—"

Gail stiffened and turned away. "I need to get back," she whispered once more.

"Gail, wait. Let me explain—"

She faced him again and held his gaze for a long moment, but the look on her face chilled him. He watched, suddenly unable to speak, as her desire faded before his eyes and she pivoted from him and hurried toward the house.

He ached to follow and tell her everything in his heart, but he forced himself to stand his ground and let her walk away. And he prayed she'd understand when he finally set things right with Leslie and came to her again.

CLINT HURRIED down the airport concourse toward Gate B-1 and scanned the small crowd for Leslie's face. Considering everything else that had gone wrong between them, he didn't want to add tardiness to his long list of sins.

He tugged at his tie and shifted his arms and shoulders uncomfortably as he walked. This suit used to fit like a second skin; now it gave him claustrophobia. The shoulders were too snug, the sleeves too tight. And this damned tie—

He pressed through the flow of disembarking passengers, stepped around families who met midstream and stopped traffic while they greeted one another. He dodged anxious business travelers and moved around a few lost-looking souls who scanned video-display terminals for flight information.

Just as he avoided yet another loving family, Leslie came into view near the gate. She searched the terminal for him once, didn't see him, checked her watch, then cast another anxious glance around. This time she spotted him, and a smile replaced her weary frown as she started toward him.

He sidestepped a rolling suitcase and its oblivious owner, and closed the distance between them. But Leslie's delight at seeing him increased his guilt by a hundred percent.

When she was only a step or two away, she dropped her carry-on bag and launched herself into his embrace. She wrapped her arms around his neck and pressed her lips to his with the passion born of ten months' separation.

Clint held her, tried to return the kiss with equal fervor, and almost wished he could find something there that would remove Gail from his mind. But when Leslie parted her lips to invite him to deepen the kiss, he thought of Gail. When she snuggled further into his embrace, he imagined Gail in her place. And when at last she pulled away, he felt more of a heel than ever.

If he'd imagined he'd find the right way to tell Leslie how he felt once he saw her again, he'd been wrong. Seeing her only made it harder.

With a throaty laugh, she ran her fingers through his hair. "You look wonderful. Different, but wonderful."

"You look beautiful, Leslie." He meant it. She did look beautiful. Even if she couldn't eclipse the image he held of Gail.

She tucked her hand under his arm in a gesture she'd used on him a thousand times. Her touch felt warm in its familiarity but didn't stir the passion Gail's did. "I am *so* glad to be here," she said. "What a week I've had. I had a thousand things to take care of before I could leave the office last night, and Katie called me half a dozen times this morning. There isn't a soul at the firm who understands how urgent it is to wrap up the Baxter account. I swear, if I didn't follow through on everything I assigned to Katie, nothing would ever get done.''

He felt a momentary flush of sympathy for Katie. "Not everyone likes the advertising game as much as you do.''

Leslie scowled up at him. "Not everyone *cares* the way I do. But let's not talk about that. Tell me everything. Have you talked to A. J. Garrity lately? Is he holding the vice presidency for you?''

The vice presidency and Garrity & Garr were the furthest things from his mind. "I haven't talked to him for a few weeks,'' he confessed.

"What? Oh, Clint, you can't lose contact with him now. For heaven's sake, sweetheart. You're coming home in a couple of months. You've got to make sure you're in the front of his mind all the time.''

He picked up her carry-on case and led her down the concourse. "I know. And once I get everything under control at the Knights' place, I'll call him.''

Leslie pulled up short and stared at him. "The Knights' place? Clint, what's happening to you? Why are you letting those people take priority over everything else?''

"They need me.''

"Well, so do *I*. And so does Garrity & Garr—''

"We'll be picking up the kids there after dinner tonight. Once you meet them, once you see what shape Boone's in—''

She pulled her arm away and stared at him. "You want me to meet them *tonight?* For heaven's sake, why?''

"The kids are waiting there for us.''

"You could have brought them with you.''

"Gail offered to let them stay so we could have some time alone."

"Really?" She sent him a provocative smile and brushed her breasts against his arm. "How much time do we have?"

Not long enough for what she had in mind. He tried to steer her gently away from the direction she obviously wanted to take. "How many bags did you check?"

"Bags?" She smiled wickedly. "As far as I'm concerned, we can come back for my bags in the morning. Why don't we just find a room at the nearest hotel—"

"Unfortunately, we can't do that. The kids are waiting."

She looked irritated for a second, then sighed and straightened her jacket. "Well, we can't keep them waiting, can we? I have two bags, and I hope I brought the right clothing."

"All you'll need are jeans and T-shirts."

She nodded. "I actually bought two pair of Girbauds."

He glanced at her feet. She was wearing her favorite high-heeled sandals with thin straps of black leather crisscrossing her feet. "Did you bring any other shoes?"

"Yes, I brought my Adidas. I don't plan to wear these to muck around on the farm." When he chuckled, she held his arm tighter and beamed up at him. "I love you."

His smile threatened to slip, but he tried desperately to keep it in place. Pulling her into his arms, he leaned his cheek on the top of her head. He held her there for a long moment, remembering how she felt in his arms, breathing in her perfume, feeling her silky hair against his cheek. But he didn't speak. Even when he held her like this, he couldn't put Gail out of his mind.

He'd have to tell Leslie the truth—soon. But not tonight. It would be heartless to hit her with it the minute she arrived. So he'd wait until he could find the right time and place. He just hoped he could find a way to explain what had happened to him without breaking her heart.

CHAPTER ELEVEN

GAIL LIFTED the kitchen curtain and looked outside. For the past three hours, she'd done her best not to watch for Clint's return. She'd fed the kids dinner and scoured the kitchen afterward until it gleamed.

She'd showered, lotioned and perfumed herself, then slipped into her nicest pair of jeans and a freshly ironed blouse so she could look her casual best without it appearing that she'd gone to any trouble. Now she had nothing to do but wait. But the waiting was driving her crazy.

She lifted the curtain again, this time to check on the kids. For an instant, she considered waiting outside with them, but quickly decided against it. She didn't want to seem too anxious. She thought about piecing together more quilt squares, but she didn't want to clutter the house with that project just before Leslie arrived.

Though she'd been anticipating it for hours, when she finally heard the sound of tires turning into the yard, her heart raced. Dashing to the bathroom, she checked her makeup and hair. She added another coat of lipstick for good measure, wiped half of it off again, and decided she looked too dowdy with her hair pulled back, so she yanked out the clip and threw it on the counter.

Finally, somewhat satisfied with the results, she started for the front door to greet her guests. She could hear Megan shouting as she raced to her daddy, doors slamming, and muted voices as Clint made introductions.

She waited with bated breath, trying to calm her nerves. But she was about to lose her entire world, and decency demanded that she be gracious to the person who was taking it.

A voice she knew must be Leslie's floated on the summer breeze through the open windows. Gail found herself analyzing it and immediately forced herself to stop. She'd already formed a mental picture of Leslie as a stunning beauty. Tall. Willowy. Flawless features. Successful, ambitious, intelligent. Witty, loving and gentle. The perfect woman for Clint. The perfect stepmother for the children. And that image haunted her. She didn't need to add to it.

When a knock sounded on the door, Gail turned toward it slowly. As she reached for it, Justin threw it open, and she found herself face-to-face with the woman of her nightmares. Tall and willowy, with short, blond hair and close-enough-to-perfect features to make Gail's heart drop. Ice blue eyes, a tiny nose, a figure most women would die to have and a level of sophistication Gail could never hope to match.

Clint stood beside Leslie, but he might as well have been a stranger. Instead of his usual jeans and Stetson, he was wearing a dark gray pinstriped business suit. He looked like someone from Richard's world.

Through the open door, Gail could see a sleek late-model Mercedes where he usually parked the pickup. Both this Clint and that car were exactly right for

Leslie. He obviously cared for her a great deal to go to all this trouble.

"They're *finally* here," Justin said.

Taking Leslie's elbow, Clint stepped forward. "Gail, this is Leslie Hampton. Leslie, I'd like you to meet Gail Wheeler."

He even *sounded* different. And Gail could scarcely breathe. Seeing him this way suddenly made her realize what a fantasy she'd been living. With effort, she forced a thin smile and tried to make her voice sound natural. "Please, come in."

While Leslie took her measure, Gail tried not to look as uncomfortable as she felt. When Leslie darted a glance at Clint, Gail quickly moistened her lips. And when Leslie looked back at her, a smile firmly fixed in place, Gail reset her own.

Leslie stepped inside and gave the living room the once-over with an attitude so like Richard's, Gail couldn't help resenting it. "So you're Gail?"

"I am. And you're Leslie."

From behind Clint's back, Justin shot her a guarded look, and in his eyes Gail could see he'd been equally affected by Clint's altered appearance. This was the father Justin knew best, and she could feel the boy's hostility taking on new life.

She forced herself to meet Leslie's ice blue stare. "I hope you had a good flight."

"It was fine, but too long." As if Gail had personally set the flight schedule.

Gail turned to Clint, but words suddenly failed her, so she pivoted toward Justin. "Do you kids want to come inside for your dessert now?"

"No, thanks."

Clint scowled at his son. "I'd like you to."

But Justin glared back. "We're not hungry." And he slammed the door behind him on his way out.

Nobody spoke until Clint finally broke the strained silence. "They'll stay outside just as long as we let them."

Gail nodded. "I was lucky to get them inside for dinner."

Leslie didn't even crack a smile.

Gail's smile faded. Anxious to break the tension, she guided Leslie to the couch, but left Clint to decide where he wanted to sit. "Can I get you anything to drink?"

Leslie perched on the edge of her seat and shook her head as she adjusted her skirt above her perfectly shaped knees. "No, thank you. We just had the most marvelous champagne with dinner, didn't we?"

Clint didn't respond to Leslie's question, but took his place at the other end of the couch. "Nothing for me, either. Thanks."

With a little frown, Leslie moved closer to Clint and dropped one hand to his thigh in a possessive gesture that wasn't lost on Gail. "Clint tells me your father's quite ill."

"Yes, he is. He had a massive stroke several weeks ago."

Leslie's forehead puckered. "How sad for you. Will you be here with him long?"

Gail shook her head. "I'm due home in another week. My leave of absence is about over."

"Really?" Leslie looked pleased as she adjusted her skirt again. "What is it you do?"

That was always one of the first questions Richard asked a new acquaintance. He'd habitually measured a person's worth by the title on their job description, and his doing so had always annoyed her. She didn't like it any better in this woman. "I work in a law office in San Mateo, California."

"Corporate law? Or domestic?" Leslie managed to inject a faint note of aversion into the last word.

"Corporate."

Leslie's smile thinned. "It must be fascinating."

"It isn't, really. But it's a paycheck."

Leslie readjusted her smile again. "Clint's mentioned you several times. He speaks highly of you."

"And of you."

Leslie leaned a little closer to Clint and gazed up at him. "He's a wonderful man. You don't find what we've got every day."

Clint didn't move a muscle, his expression didn't waver, but Gail sensed him tightening up. Tensing. And she searched for an excuse to leave the room. "Could I interest you in some pie à la mode? I made strawberry-rhubarb. And the kids haven't had their dessert yet."

"*Homemade* pie?" Leslie spoke to Gail, but she leaned a little closer to Clint. "What a treat! I haven't had *homemade* pie in ages. Have you?"

He didn't confirm or deny, he just said, "I'd love some. Gail's a great cook."

Almost imperceptibly, Leslie's jaw tightened. "Then I can't wait." She sent Gail a frigid look. "I'm afraid cooking isn't one of my strong points. I'd do more of it, but I do so much business over meals, I really never get the chance. And when I'm *not* working, Clint and I are out together. He loves Greek food—did he tell you that?"

Even if he had, Gail didn't think she would have admitted it. "No, I don't think he did."

As if she'd won a minor victory, Leslie relaxed a little. But in doing so, she leaned still closer to Clint. "Did I tell you, sweetheart, that Glenn Johnson approached me with a job offer last week?"

"You didn't mention it. Is it a good one?"

"It's wonderful. A significant salary increase and a guaranteed partnership within three years. It would mean longer hours at first, but I'm seriously considering it. What do you think?"

An expression Gail couldn't read flashed across Clint's face. "It's up to you, Les. Do whatever you think is best."

She snuggled a little closer. "Well, of course I will. But it's going to affect you, too. And now that we'll have the kids for the next few months, we'll have to discuss what arrangements to make for them. You'll be so much busier once you get Duncan's job, and I don't want to leave the kids unattended."

Again Clint's expression left Gail bewildered. Was he holding something back? "Really, Les. It's up to you," he repeated. "I don't want you to make a career decision based on what I want."

Leslie laughed softly and traced her finger along his chin. "That's what I love about you, do you know that? So many men would be threatened by their woman's success." She leaned up and kissed his lips gently.

Suddenly sick to her stomach, Gail averted her eyes. How could Clint expect her to sit here and watch this? When she looked back and saw him watching her, she recognized the anguish in his expression and her heart softened a little.

She reminded herself that Leslie had initiated the kiss, Clint hadn't. Even so, she couldn't stay in the same room with them. "I'll go get the pie," she muttered, and escaped into the kitchen. Once there, she gripped the edge of the counter and struggled to pull herself together.

A soft touch on her shoulder brought her around sharply. Clint stood behind her, his eyes still dark with emotion. "I'm sorry."

She tried to keep her chin up when she faced him, to look as if she didn't hurt as badly as she did. "For what?"

"We need to talk, Gail. I want to explain."

Her heart leaped with anticipation, which she immediately pushed away. "You don't have to explain anything to me, Clint. We're friends."

He took her by the shoulders and scoured her face with his eyes. "We're more than that, and you know it. I want to stop playing these games—" But at the sound of someone moving outside the kitchen door, he released her suddenly and took a step away.

Leslie was wearing a smile when she opened the door, but her eyes looked knowing and cold as she took in their proximity and their expressions. "I changed my mind, sweetheart. I think I'll have gin and tonic—if you have it, Gail."

Flustered and confused, Gail nodded. "I'm sure we do. I'll get it." She took a step away from the counter, but Clint stopped her.

"Let me do it. Just tell me where your dad keeps the bar."

"Look in the bottom cupboard under the silverware," Gail said softly.

Leslie's laugh cut through the tension like a knife. "You mean, you and Gail haven't had one drink together? After all these weeks?"

"I haven't been drinking much lately," he said.

"Really? Dr. Anderson will be so pleased." Leslie didn't sound at all pleased. She forced a smile and turned to Gail again. "You will let me help you with the pie, won't you? It will give us a chance to get to know each other."

Gail nodded, though the last thing she wanted was to get to know Leslie. "There's not much left to do, but I guess you could get the ice cream out of the freezer."

"I'd love to."

In silence, Clint fixed Leslie's drink, then held up an empty glass in a silent question to Gail. She shook her head, but immediately wished she'd said yes. She hadn't faced someone so openly hostile toward her since the day she'd first met Shelly. She just hoped Clint would be more aware of the undercurrents than Richard had been.

She couldn't blame Leslie; she was just protecting what she considered hers. But understanding didn't make Leslie's hostility easier to face. Especially when Gail *was* guilty of what the other woman suspected.

Pasting on the most pleasant expression she could muster, Gail pulled the pie off the warming tray and plunged a knife into it.

She had the distinct impression this was going to be a very long evening.

CLINT SAT on the steps of Hal and Phyllis's porch and watched the sun slip low in the western horizon. It hadn't taken him long to change out of his designer suit and loafers and into his soft old jeans and well-worn cowboy boots, but Leslie was taking a little longer to dress.

The drive home from Gail's had been excruciating. Justin didn't bother to conceal his animosity, and Leslie's silence had felt like a wall of ice. But Clint knew she had plenty to say. And that she'd say it as soon as they were alone.

In spite of his best efforts to hide the way he felt about Gail, he'd seen the growing realization in Leslie's eyes throughout the evening. If he'd been smart, he would have kept the two women apart until he could resolve his relationship with Leslie. But, unable to bear the separation from Gail, he'd put both women and himself through an emotional wringer. He acknowledged silently that he'd acted selfishly.

Leaning back against a post, he listened to Leslie's footsteps moving slowly through the kitchen. Perhaps she was as reluctant as he to have this conversation. The back door creaked open and she stepped out onto the porch. Dressed in jeans, a T-shirt and running shoes, she looked like a different woman. He'd never seen her attired so casually, and he knew for certain he never would again.

After crossing to stand beside him, she stared out over the dusty yard. "All right, I'm ready. Where shall we go?"

He got to his feet, brushing against her arm as he did, but she still didn't look at him. "It's about half a mile to the highway. We could walk down there."

She pushed past him and started toward the gate. With her arms folded high on her chest and her shoulders rigid, she was making if perfectly clear she didn't want him to touch her.

Matching her stride, he stuffed his hands into his pockets and they walked in silence for several minutes. Their shadows stretched across the lane and danced along the tops of the cornstalks. Dust puffed from their feet and swirled away in the light breeze. Soft clouds overhead caught the last rays of summer sunlight and reflected deep-hued pastels across the horizon.

Clint tried several times to speak, but he couldn't find the words to explain how sorry he was for hurting her.

Leslie kept her chin jutted forward, a sure sign of agitation. She studied their surroundings the way she studied anything new—as if by analyzing she could understand and make everything all right again.

Finally, she sighed heavily and looked at him from the corner of her eye. "You like it here, don't you?"

"Surprisingly, yes."

She kicked several pebbles across the dirt road before she spoke again. "Are you planning to stay?"

The question took him by surprise. He'd never really considered staying even though some part of him often wanted to. He gave it a moment's thought before he shook his head. "No. My life's in Chicago. I still plan to go home in the fall."

Her posture softened a little, but she didn't look at him again. "Good. I was worried."

"That I might stay here?"

She nodded. "You seem so comfortable. So at home. So content being a farmer. I've been worried that I'm losing you."

He hesitated a split second as he tried to choose the right way to respond.

But she rushed on before he could say anything. "Look, Clint, I know I haven't been very understanding the past few weeks, but you've been so distant—and the more remote you sounded on the phone, the more frightened I grew." She turned to face him and her eyes glittered with unshed tears. "I just want you to know I'm sorry."

He couldn't stand to hear her apologize. "Leslie—"

But she touched his lips with her fingertips and cut him off. "I know I tend to get caught up in my career. I know I can be hard to live with. I'm demanding, and I've been pushing you away by asking too much. Obviously, that's why you and Gail have become such good friends. But I love you, Clint. With all my heart."

He couldn't look at her, so he watched the sunset for several long seconds. "You haven't done anything wrong," he insisted.

With a self-mocking laugh, Leslie looked away again. "I watched you two tonight, and I saw the way she looks at you. I suppose you realize she's in love with you."

His heart filled with hope, but he tried to keep his face blank so she wouldn't see it.

She smiled gently. "And you think you love her, don't you?"

It sounded childish and meaningless when she said it that way. He wasn't a small boy with a crush on a cute girl. "It's not like that, Leslie—"

She stopped him by tracing her fingers up his arm and caressing his cheek. "I'm here now, sweetheart. You don't need her anymore. I'm not going to pretend I'm happy about this little infatuation—"

He couldn't let her go on, it was time to tell her the truth. "Look, I should have told you this before you flew all the way out here, but I thought it would be easier to tell you in person."

"Have you been sleeping with her?"

"No." He pulled her hand from his cheek and held it in both of his. "You're a wonderful woman, Leslie, and I'll always love you for what we've had together. But what I feel for Gail is different than anything I've felt before. I don't know how to explain it."

"You can't honestly think of throwing away what we have for some woman you've only known a few weeks." When he didn't respond, her eyes narrowed for a fraction of a second, then softened again. "I know you've been lonely, Clint. But so have I. If you'd stayed in Chicago, we would have been married by now."

She was right about that. They would have been married. Settled. And probably reasonably happy— for a while. He never would have met Gail, and he'd probably never have known how it felt to come alive inside again. But the narrow trail of chance had led him to his future. He might easily have missed it, but now that he'd found it, he couldn't turn away. "Yes, we probably would have been. But that wouldn't have made it right."

"I can't believe you're saying this to me." Her eyes filled with tears, and when he lifted his hand to brush them away, she jerked back as if he'd tried to strike her. "So, is this it? You've decided we're through, and that's that?"

"I love her, Les."

She shook her head emphatically. "Don't say that. You don't even know her. You can't *possibly* love her."

"Leslie—"

"What's so wonderful about her? What's she got that I haven't?"

"Don't do this to yourself. You're a wonderful woman."

She glared at him. "And you're a son of a bitch. *I'm* not doing this, *you* are."

"I don't want to hurt you."

She laughed harshly. "I feel *so* much better knowing that." She took three angry steps away, then whirled to face him. "When I think of the hours I spent listening to you talk about Barbara, how badly she hurt you when she fell in love with Dave, how it felt for you to lose everything— She threw away thirteen years of marriage without a second thought, and now here *you* are, doing the same thing to *me*."

Her words hit hard. She was right. He'd longed for another chance to make things right with Barbara. He'd pleaded for the opportunity to prove himself capable of loving her the way she needed him to. And she'd denied it to him. How could he, in good conscience, do the same to Leslie? Didn't he owe her more?

Deeply shaken, he stared at her in silence. He couldn't tear his eyes from her face, couldn't speak, couldn't move. Without warning, Gail's image formed in his mind and he knew in that moment that he couldn't leave Leslie for Gail. He couldn't ask Gail to start a relationship or Leslie to end one this way.

With tears stinging his eyes, he forced Gail's image away and took Leslie's hand. "You're right," he said, but his throat felt thick and tight and the words had to work their way past the lump there.

Relief played across her face and the tears she'd been holding back finally spilled onto her cheeks. "You'll try again?"

He could only nod, but he felt dishonest. Loving Gail as he did, how could he turn his back on her and give his all to Leslie?

"Thank God." Leslie met his gaze and held it. "Promise me you won't see her anymore?"

"I can't promise that, Leslie. I still have to work her dad's place."

"All right. See her when you have to. But no social visits. No lunches. No dinners. No more early-morning coffee."

He could feel a headache low in the base of his neck and his stomach twisted. "How did you know about that?"

She laughed bitterly. "Megan asked if I was going with you in the morning. You have no idea how it felt to hear about *that*. All those times you hung up from talking to me so you could rush over there to be with her—"

"It wasn't like that."

Her face darkened. "Do us both a favor, Clint. Don't try to minimize this. You were falling for her. And when you imagine yourself in love, you do it all the way. *I* know how deeply you feel things."

If that were true, she'd know how badly he hurt right now and she wouldn't ask him to give up Gail completely.

With a bright smile, she took his arm. "Now, tell me what we're going to do while I'm here."

"I have to work most of the time. We've got to finish that roof."

No emotion crossed her face, but her fingers stiffened on his sleeve. "I know that. What about the kids?"

"Phyllis has been so busy with the stampede, Gail's been watching them most of the time."

"Well, *that's* got to stop. Why don't I watch them? After all, I am going to be their stepmother. It's about time we got to know one another."

He knew this would hurt Gail and the kids, but he also knew it was important for Leslie and the children to get used to each other. "All right. I'll let Gail know in the morning."

"I have a better idea," she said. "Why don't *I* phone her? Maybe it would help her understand where things stand."

He shook his head. This news had to come from him. "I'll tell her. I owe her that much."

Leslie sighed again, and he knew he was trying her patience to the very end, but she managed to smile at him. "Yes, I suppose you think you do. All right, tell her yourself. I'd just as soon not talk to her, anyway." She dragged in a deep breath and tried to look as if the entire conversation had never taken place. "So, tell me what there is to do around here."

"Work. Fish. Drive into Broken Bow on Friday nights and dance."

She looked suspicious. "You go dancing?"

"No. But I've thought about it." Clint managed a weak smile. "Actually, I promised the kids I'd take them to the stampede this weekend. I thought maybe we could go Friday."

She didn't look thrilled, but she tried to look interested. "What's the stampede?" When he explained, she curled her nose. "A *rodeo?* Are you kidding? Bulls and horses and cowboys?"

He nodded. "I guess so. This will be my first one—"

"And your last."

"And my last," he repeated slowly.

"Well, if you've promised the kids, I suppose we'll have to go. I just hope it's not as bad as it sounds." She gave an exaggerated shudder and studied him thoughtfully. "You know, I'm glad this year's almost over. I can't wait to get you home to Chicago and back into a suit full-time."

"It'll come soon enough."

"No. It won't be soon enough. But I'm glad it's going to happen, even if I do have to wait a while longer." Without warning, she threw her arms around his neck and kissed him. "I love you. And everything will be wonderful now that we're together again, you'll see."

Clint held her against him and strained to find something warm and tender in the embrace. But he couldn't help wondering if he'd just made the biggest mistake of his life.

IN THE DIM LIGHT of her bedside lamp, Gail dressed quickly. She stopped to listen for Clint's truck to turn into the lane and shivered with cold in spite of the warmth of the morning. Maybe she was being foolish to get up early this morning. Now that Leslie was here, she really didn't expect Clint to come for coffee. But if he *did,* she wanted to be ready.

She zipped her jeans and looked out her window at the moonlit lane. Still empty, but she had a few minutes before the time he usually arrived.

Dropping to the edge of her bed, she pulled on her shoes and told herself she was being ridiculous. But she remembered Clint's face just before Leslie had joined them in the kitchen last night and wondered what he'd been about to say. She pulled open a dresser drawer to look for a T-shirt, then stopped herself. She ought to go back to bed, turn out the lights and sleep through his arrival. Or at least pretend to.

But she couldn't. She longed to see him. Yanking the T-shirt from her dresser, she pulled it over her head and thought about Leslie again.

No doubt she was a fine woman—just as Clint said. Under other circumstances, Gail might have liked her. But even she could see Leslie was the wrong woman for Clint. Using every effort to push jealousy aside, Gail had watched them last night. To Gail's ears, their conversation had sounded like dialogue between two people who speak different dialects of the same language, and in some ways they'd reminded her of herself and Richard.

But would Clint and Leslie run into the same kinds of problems as she and Richard? Would Clint's hard-won progress with the kids go down the drain because he needed all his energy to maintain his relationship with Leslie?

Maybe he'd be smarter than Gail had been. Maybe he'd recognize the problem before it got out of hand. She just hoped one of them would figure it out soon— *before* they got married.

She abandoned her hairbrush and tiptoed downstairs, lost in thought. Almost automatically, she made coffee and filled two mugs, then took them outside to the porch swing, just as she did every morning. But five-fifteen came and went without any sign of Clint. And his coffee grew cold as the minutes crept past.

At last, Gail had to acknowledge that he wasn't coming. Blinking back tears of disappointment, she wondered how he'd become such a huge part of her days. How she'd allowed him to work his way into her life so completely in such a short time. But most of all, she asked herself how she'd ever manage without him.

When the rising sun painted streaks of lavender and peach across the sky and the birds broke the stillness with their early-morning chatter, she told herself to go inside. She had to face the truth, accept reality and let him go. But she couldn't make herself move until she finally saw his truck turn off the highway and start toward her.

Ditching both mugs of coffee, she pasted on a brave smile and stood to greet him. If Leslie had come with him, she needed to appear unruffled. For the kids' sake, she needed to look calm.

But Clint had come alone. Without Leslie. Without Justin and Brad. Without Megan.

He climbed out of the truck and hurried in her direction. His face betrayed everything. She knew what he'd come to say even before he spoke.

She waited until he reached the porch, then beat him to the punch. "Where are the kids?"

His step faltered and his face darkened. "With Leslie. She wants to take care of them while she's here."

"Well, I guess I won't need to get up so early anymore." She tried to sound casual and unaffected by the news, but her voice cracked and she felt tears burning her eyes.

He studied her, as if he suspected the emotions that churned within her.

Turning from him, she stiffened her resolve and brought herself under control before she faced him again. "Leslie seems very nice. The kids will like her."

He sent her another look she couldn't read. "They've grown very close to you. I'm not sure how they'll take this. Megan was in tears when I left this morning, and Justin was back to his surly self."

Her heart dropped. "And Brad?"

"He was searching for a radio station on his Walkman." He smiled, but he looked so sad it broke Gail's heart. "I'm going to try to finish early today so I can get back and see how things are going."

"Yes, of course. They'll need you to help smooth the transition." She managed to keep her voice steady, and she didn't think she betrayed her anxiety. "Did you want a cup of coffee before you start work?"

He shook his head, still without looking at her. "I had some at home."

Funny how such a little thing could hurt so much. She forced another smile. "Good. Well, then, I'd better get back to my strawberries."

For a heartbeat, she thought he was going to say something, but he clamped his lips together and nodded. "And I'd better get out to the fields."

Though it cost her a great effort, she managed to keep her shoulders back and her chin up as she turned away and walked into the house. She didn't let herself look at him again, even though she felt his eyes on her all the way. Even when she opened the back door, she allowed herself no more than a glance from the corner of her eye.

She stepped inside the house and closed the door firmly between them. And only then did she allow herself to cry.

GAIL STRUGGLED all morning to ignore the sound of Clint moving around in the yard. She forced herself not to look out the window, not to watch him stride from the house to the barn, but she could map every step in her mind.

Freezing spinach was mindless work, which left her plenty of time to think. And her thoughts were anything but pleasant. So when the telephone rang midmorning, she swiped sand and water from her arms with a damp cloth and snagged the receiver, anxious to talk to anyone.

"Hello?"

"Is this Gail Knight?" The voice on the other end sounded so familiar, she would have recognized it anywhere—even after fifteen years.

"Bette Heywood? Is it really you?"

"Well, I *think* so, but this week your guess is as good as mine." Bette's familiar laugh rang through the wire, then faded. "I heard you were back in town, but I haven't seen you around anywhere. Where've you been?"

"Where did you look?"

"Jay's Drive-In. The Chicken Inn. Pappas's Drugstore."

All places they'd frequented as teenagers. A lifetime ago. "No wonder you haven't found me. I've been right here in the kitchen making strawberry jam and freezing vegetables."

"*You?* I never would have believed it. Wait until I tell Tom."

Her shocked tone teased a laugh from Gail. "You're not the only one who doesn't believe it. I think my mother's in seventh heaven now that she's finally got me in the kitchen."

"You held out longer than I did. I had Tom convinced I couldn't cook for the first five years we were married, but he finally figured me out. And now he's developed some foolish notion that running a mere forty miles into Billings for take-out every night is extravagant."

Gail dropped into her chair and kicked her feet onto the chair across from her. "He always was demanding, even in high school. I never could figure out why you married him."

"Sex."

This time Gail laughed aloud. As if the invisible cords that had always linked them still existed, Bette had called just when Gail needed her most, and it felt good to laugh again.

"I'm not kidding," Bette insisted. "He's great in bed."

"I don't want to hear about it."

"I have to say that whenever he's listening," Bette whispered. "He thinks he's got a reputation to protect."

"As a great lover?"

"Delusions of grandeur," Bette said. "They keep him happy."

"So how is he when you're not in bed?"

Bette sighed extravagantly. "I think he's going through a mid-life crisis or something. He went out last month and bought himself a motorcycle."

"Tom? I don't believe it."

"You can believe it, all right. He came home with a great big Harley, and now he thinks he's king of the hill."

"Well, that makes two of you. So, how is it?"

Bette's voice changed pitch. "It's great. To be honest with you, it makes me feel sixteen again."

Gail grinned and envied her friend the relationship she'd always enjoyed with her husband. Bette and

Tom had been friends since childhood, and neither had looked at any member of the opposite sex since they were old enough to date.

Obviously, they were as much in love as ever. And he still made her laugh. It must be wonderful to be so comfortable with the man you loved. The way she'd felt around Clint until Leslie arrived.

Gail pushed away that thought immediately. A one-sided love couldn't compare to Bette's relationship with Tom. Besides, she didn't want to think about Clint anymore today. "It's good to hear from you, Bette. I've thought about calling you a hundred times since I've been home."

"That's all right. I know how things are over there with your dad sick and everything. You know Tom's mom died last year, and she stayed with us at the end. It was horrible to watch her go, and neither of us could see straight for months afterward."

"I thought of you both the day of the funeral. I wished I could have been there. Did you get the flowers I sent?"

"Yes. They meant a lot. But I never did send you a thank-you note, did I? See what I mean? We were basket cases." Bette paused for a second, then drew in a breath as a prelude to a subject change. "To be honest with you, I wouldn't have bothered you today if I didn't have a crisis on my hands."

"What kind of crisis?"

Bette gave an uneasy laugh. "This is so embarrassing... I just realized your mom's scheduled to work the ticket booth at the stampede tomorrow night. We were supposed to find a replacement, but everybody thought somebody else was taking care of it. You know how it goes—"

"You'd better find somebody else. She won't leave my dad for that."

"I *know.* But there isn't anybody else except Jonelle Davis—*that's* the crisis."

"I don't think I know her."

"Jonelle *Heiner* Davis." Bette's voice climbed a notch and took on a pleading tone.

Gail rolled her eyes and leaned her head against the chair. "The one who tried to get Tom drunk that night at the drive-in?"

"That's the one."

"Is she still around? I thought she married some big shot and moved to Portland."

"He dumped her for a younger woman, so she came home again. And she's still exactly the same. She stopped into the hardware store just last week and asked Tom all sorts of questions about plumbing and electrical wiring. I know what kind of wiring *she's* interested in. Gail, I *can't* get stuck in the ticket booth with her. I'll be forced to kill her. You've got to help me."

"So what do you want me to do?"

"Take her place."

Gail groaned. "At the ticket booth? You've got to be kidding? That's the worst job there is."

"No, it's not. Cleaning under the bleachers is the worst job there is."

"It's hot and stuffy in the booth—"

"It's hotter if you're stuck frying French fries in the snack bar. And a *lot* dirtier. Besides, this way, you'll be through when the rodeo starts. And you can watch it with me and Tom. Valerie's decided the world will end if she doesn't sit with her friends, so we have an extra ticket."

"I don't want to go to the rodeo," Gail insisted.

"Randy Russell's going to be there." Bette clearly intended the announcement as an inducement.

"Along with his wife and four kids," Gail reminded her.

"He got divorced last year, and he's dying to see you again."

"Randy Russell and I dated for six months during our senior year, and no matter what you think, we were *never* in love the way you and Tom were."

"He's still interested—"

"But I'm not."

"All right, forget Randy. It was a long shot, anyway. But I really do need your help."

Gail hesitated. Maybe this was what she needed to get her out of the house and take her mind off Clint and the kids.

"Okay, Bette. What time do you want me there?"

"Five o'clock."

"I'll be there."

"Great," Bette chirped. "No wonder you're still my best friend." Her voice changed pitch again. "Look, I've got to run now. I'm supposed to cashier for Tom at eleven. See you tomorrow at five."

"You owe me one for this."

"I offered Randy Russell—"

"Forget it. This one's free." Gail replaced the receiver and smiled at it for a few seconds before she turned back to the spinach.

Like a summer storm, Bette had cleared away Gail's stagnant thoughts and brought a breath of fresh air to her mind. She couldn't have planned anything more perfect if she'd tried.

CHAPTER TWELVE

CLINT SHIFTED Megan in his arms and moved another half step when the line into the rodeo arena crept forward. Just ahead, Justin and Brad craned to see everything, but Leslie stood at his side with barely concealed impatience. The set of her jaw, the hard light in her eyes and the tilt of her head all told him she'd had better times.

It had already been a hard day. Leslie had endured the parade and endured wandering through the street carnival behind Clint's excited children. But they still had the entire rodeo to sit through, and her tolerance level looked low.

Megan touched his face with baby-soft hands and put her face directly in front of his. "Can we sit in front, Daddy?"

"No, sweetie. Our seats are about halfway up, I think. So you can see everything."

"But I want to pet the horsies."

"Even if we sat in the front row, you wouldn't be able to do that. They're working horses, not petting horses."

But she didn't seem to hear him. Something new had already caught her eye. With a sudden lurch forward, she nearly toppled out of his arms. "Oooh. Sno-Kones. Can I have one, Daddy? Please?"

Clint reached into his pocket for some change and searched the crowd for the Sno-Kone vendor.

But Leslie shook her head and touched his arm to stop him. "They're nothing but sugar and ice, Clint. They'll rot her teeth."

Brad pivoted toward them, eyes wide with excitement, hand extended. "They've got *blue* ones. Give me the money, Dad. I'll take Megan to buy them. Want one, Justin?"

Justin shrugged. "I guess. I can go with them if you want me to."

Again Leslie shook her head. "Don't let them waste your money, Clint. Those things are toxic."

Clint didn't see Sno-Kones as quite the danger Leslie did, but he didn't want to contradict her in front of the kids.

When he hesitated, Justin rolled his eyes and sent him a hostile look. "Great. *This* is a lot of fun."

Megan stuck out her lower lip and used her wide eyes to their best advantage. "You should have bringed Gail. *She'd* let me have a Sno-Kone."

Clint didn't have to look at Leslie to know the impact of that statement. He could see her tension level rise a dozen notches as animosity radiated from her.

"Just let me get this day over with," she muttered almost too low for Clint to hear.

He looked at the kids, almost pleading with them to understand his dilemma. "No Sno-Kones, kids."

"But I'm firsty." Megan started to sob.

"I know. Maybe we can find a soda or something."

Leslie looked exasperated. "If you're going to do that, just let them have the Sno-Kones. There's not much difference."

Justin reached for Megan and pulled her from Clint's arms. "Come on, you guys. Let's just forget it."

Brad stared at Leslie with a dark frown, but turned away a second later without saying a word.

"They hate me," she said when the children moved out of earshot.

Clint put an arm around her, but watched the kids to make sure they didn't wander too far. "They don't hate you. They're still confused."

"They *hate* me."

Though he thought *hate* was too strong a word, he knew the kids weren't overly fond of her yet. By the time he'd gotten home last night, Leslie's mood and the kids' faces had given him a clear indication how their day had gone. He'd done his best to smooth things over, but the decision to take the kids away from Gail wasn't winning Leslie any points with them. Still, he suspected if she'd tried a little harder to get along, they'd have gone halfway to meet her. "They don't hate you," he repeated, then cut off her next argument with, "Let's just worry about getting through this line and finding our seats."

"Fine." She mopped at the hollow of her throat with a handkerchief and sent an accusing look at the sky. "I can't believe how hot it is. And dirty. I'll be covered in mud by the time we're through here."

"The sun's going down. It'll start to cool off soon."

"Wonderful. That means the bugs will come out."

Had she always been such a negative person? Would he run into this kind of attitude any time he asked her to do something she didn't particularly like? Or was today the exception?

He couldn't help thinking that if Gail had been here, she'd be making the most of the situation—even if she were hot and tired and thirsty and perspiring. She was probably the most adaptable woman he'd ever met. She'd be equally at home at the symphony or the stampede, and she'd look as comfortable in an evening gown as she did in cutoffs and a T-shirt. He'd never known how important flexibility was to him—until he'd begun to realize Leslie didn't have any.

Just then, a tall cowboy holding a plastic cup jostled past them. Beer sloshed out of the cup and onto Leslie's arm. Apologizing profusely, the cowboy mopped at her arm.

Leslie waved him away with a look of disgust, and snapped, "I certainly hope the kids are enjoying this more than I am."

Clint didn't answer, but he couldn't imagine anyone enjoying it less.

When they reached the entrance gate several minutes later, he flagged the kids back, handed over their tickets and received cursory directions to their seats. Leading the way to the red seating section, he glanced over his shoulder every few seconds to check Leslie's progress. She followed resolutely, her face set in a deep frown, her eyes squinting into the late-afternoon sunlight.

To his dismay, their seats faced into the sunset. And by the expression on Leslie's face, he could tell the seating arrangement didn't thrill her. It would be at least another hour before the glare disappeared.

Megan leaned forward on the bleachers and whined, "Daddy, I'm *firsty*." Beside her, Brad clutched his throat in a silent signal that he was about to expire, and Justin glared out over the dusty stadium.

This time, Clint didn't let Leslie's opinion sway him. Laced with sugar or not, he was going to find something for his kids to drink. And for himself, while he was at it. "I'm going after refreshments," he told Leslie. "Do you want anything?"

She could have cut metal with the look she sent him. "I need *something* to get me through the rest of this day, but I suppose my only choice is beer?"

"I'd imagine you're right. Will you keep an eye on the kids? I'll be right back." Swimming against the traffic stream, he pushed his way down the stairs and toward a small white shack with a huge sign advertising refreshments.

Four attendants staffed positions inside, and the line stretched across the dirt about twenty wide and a dozen deep. Realizing he had a long wait, he made himself as comfortable as possible in the afternoon heat.

Within minutes, he began to feel better. Smiling faces surrounded him. Laughter rang out from every corner. Couples with arms entwined walked slowly past. Children ran and laughed and played. Women hugged. Men slapped backs. And everywhere, people smiled. After the long day he'd had, the smiles looked good. He'd almost forgotten today was supposed to be fun.

When his turn finally came, the woman inside the refreshment stand beamed at him. "What'll it be, cowboy?"

He grinned back. "Two draft beers and three colas, please."

"Hot dogs? French fries?"

"No, just the drinks." Not even in his wildest dreams could he imagine Leslie eating a hot dog.

The woman didn't look convinced. "Well, you can't watch the rodeo without a little popcorn. How about a jumbo? Buttered. It's just about right for five people."

The woman was so affable, Clint couldn't help smiling again. "All right, I'm sold." And on impulse, he added, "Where can I find Sno-Kones?"

The woman shoved a tub of popcorn at him and worked five cups into a cardboard tray. "The vendors have those out in the stadium."

He handed her the money, gathered his change and tucked the popcorn under his arm. Clutching the drink tray in both hands, he worked his way through the crowd toward his seat.

Leslie would have something to say about his choice of treats, but he'd let the day go on too long without seeing his kids happy—and he wanted to find their smiles again. If it took junk food to do the trick, so be it.

Holding the drink tray close to his chest, he climbed the bleacher stairs and began the trek toward his seat. Halfway there, he saw Leslie standing, scouring the crowd below. Justin ran up the stairs to the section above, holding his hands to his mouth as if he was shouting something. White-faced and obviously upset, Brad stood beside Leslie. But Clint couldn't see Megan anywhere.

He pushed through the crowd, spilling popcorn and drinks as he jostled elbows and backs, and reached Leslie within seconds. "What's wrong?"

"Megan's gone. I don't know where she is." She started away from him, calling frantically.

Shoving the refreshments onto the empty bleacher seats, Clint gripped Leslie's shoulders and brought her back around to face him. "Tell me what happened."

"I just took my eyes off of her for a second, Clint, and she wandered away. How could she do this? She's old enough to know better, isn't she?"

"Justin didn't see her leave?"

"No. He was mad at me and pouting—you know how he does. I thought Brad was helping keep an eye on her, but he didn't see where she went, either."

Blame and accusations wouldn't find Megan. Clint wanted facts. "What happened just before she disappeared? Was there anything that caught her attention?"

She looked over his shoulder at the arena. "The horses."

He released her as suddenly as he'd gripped her and pointed behind her. "You go that way. I'm going down to the gates. If I can't find her, I'll round up some help. If you see her, bring her straight back here and wait."

Racing through the crowd, he prayed for Megan's safety. Faces still smiled, people still laughed, but this time their happiness seemed to mock his mounting terror.

He plowed past a small group of people and shouted for Megan, but he knew she'd never hear him above the noise in the arena. He cursed himself for his stupidity. He'd worked for weeks to gain his sons' respect, his daughter's trust and Gail's friendship, and in a matter of days he'd managed to lose them all.

Well, he *wouldn't* let himself screw up his life again. He'd find Megan safe and sound. He'd win back his sons if it killed him. And somehow, he'd settle things once and for all with Leslie.

GAIL MADE CHANGE for a red-faced man she thought looked vaguely familiar and handed him his tickets. "Third row from the top in the blue section."

He turned away and a young boy pushed his way to the window. "Will-call for Horrocks?"

Gail pulled out the will-call box and flipped through the *H*'s. Hart. Hempstead. Hill. Hunter. No Horrocks. She started from the top and worked her way through again, more carefully this time. "Are you sure that's the name your tickets are under?"

The boy nodded. "H-O-R-R-O-C-K-S." He spelled the name slowly, as if her failure to know who he was signaled a distinct lack of mental agility.

But even with his help, she couldn't find his tickets. With a heavy sigh, she turned to Bette. "I'm missing a will-call. There's supposed to be a Horrocks here."

Stretching to see Gail's customer from her own window, Bette waved a hand at the boy. "Hey there, Cody Ray." She turned back to Gail. "Look under W for Western Automaster."

"*Western Automaster?* How am I supposed to know that from Horrocks?"

Bette flashed her a grin. "That's why I'm helping you out. Check the *W*'s. I'll bet you money that's where they are."

This time, Gail found the tickets immediately, and exchanged them for Cody Ray's handful of cash.

Bette finished her transaction and leaned on the counter. "Are there many left?"

"A few. But most are for tomorrow night."

"Good. We're almost out of here." Bette checked her watch. "Another three minutes and I'm locking up."

"What if somebody's late?"

"What about it? Cyril Douglas is working the entrance gate, and he has a key if anybody gets upset." She stuffed an errant part of her shirttail into her jeans and tossed her shoulder-length hair that looked blonder than Gail remembered. "And *I* intend to watch the rodeo. Tom's going to have cold drinks and hot popcorn waiting for us."

"This is like a case of *déjà vu*," Gail said with a laugh. "I feel like we're back in high school."

Bette nudged her with an elbow and laughed. "Yeah, isn't it great? Wait until you see Randy Russell, though. That'll make you realize how many years have passed." She wiggled her eyebrows comically and leaned up to look out her window for stragglers. Apparently satisfied that she and Gail had left no business unattended, she closed the shutters over her window and locked them into place. "Come on, let's go."

Gail closed her own window, stuffed her keys and wallet into her pockets and followed Bette outside the sweltering shack into the welcome evening breeze. "So, tell me about Randy's divorce. What happened?"

Simple curiosity prompted her question, but Bette must have misread it as interest because she gripped Gail's arm and widened her eyes. "Well, what *I* heard, was that his wife—you remember Kathleen Gable, don't you? That's who he ended up marrying— Anyway, Kathleen always thought she wanted to be a country-western singer, you know. So one day, after a dozen years of marriage and four kids, she leaves. But the weird part is that she took the kids with her. I'd have thought she'd leave the kids and make a clean break." She shrugged and grinned as she dragged Gail toward the entrance gate. "Anyway, last I heard, she was in Nashville waiting tables and trying to break into the record business. And poor Randy's up here nursing a broken heart."

"Don't look at *me* to mend it. I've got troubles enough of my own."

"What's his name?" Bette asked.

For a split second, Gail wondered how she'd given herself away. But Bette's teasing grin put her fears to rest and she managed a smile. "That's a secret."

"Well, don't marry him unless he makes you laugh. Money's important, and sex is great. But a man who makes you laugh will get you through the bad times in one piece. Believe me." Bette released Gail's arm and started up the bleacher stairs.

Gail followed closely, trying to match Bette's sure step and determined progress. She pushed her way through a group of grinning teenagers and tried to ease around an aging cowboy and his white-haired wife. Forced to wait while a Sno-Kone vendor worked her box of treats through the crowd, Gail stopped dead in her tracks when a small blond girl in bright red overalls scampered after the treats.

"Megan?"

Megan whirled and squealed with delight when she saw Gail. Throwing her arms around Gail's knees, she cried. "You'll buy us a Sno-Kone, won't you?" She looked over her shoulder, then back at Gail with a frown. "I think my brother's lost."

Taking the girl's hand in hers, she crouched to face her. "Does your daddy know where you are?"

Wide-eyed, Megan shook her head slowly. "I don't think so. I just wanted to ask the lady for a Sno-Kone."

"Did your daddy say you could have one?"

The girl's frown deepened and she put on a pitiful expression. "No."

"Do you know where your seats are?"

Megan studied the stadium for a few seconds. "No."

Standing, Gail kept Megan's hand tight in her own. "I think we'd better find your daddy."

"But he's not there. He went to get Leslie something."

"Oh. I see. Does Leslie know where you are?"

A solemn shake of the head. "She said I couldn't have a Sno-Kone because it would make my teeth fall out. But they have *blue* ones and they turn your tongue blue, too, and they taste like bubble gum sometimes, and Brad likes 'em because they're nummy, and I'm really firsty, and I wanted to see if the lady would give me one for free so we wouldn't waste my daddy's money."

"I see." Gail lifted Megan and propped her on one hip. Several yards ahead, she could see Bette still working her way through the crowd. She'd have to let her know what was going on, then try to find Clint—who'd obviously been paying more attention to Leslie than Megan.

Moving quickly now, she shouldered her way through the crowd and caught Bette just as she prepared to step over one set of seats to her own. Tom Heywood stood at the edge of one row and Gail knew she would have recognized him anywhere. He wore his dark hair a little longer than Gail remembered and gray streaked it lightly, but other than that—and a few smile lines around his eyes—he looked exactly the same.

He beamed when he saw Bette, grinned at Gail and tweaked Megan under the chin. "Who's this? Bette didn't tell me you had kids."

Bette looked from Gail to Megan in confusion. "She didn't have any a few minutes ago."

"This is the daughter of a friend," Gail said. "I'm afraid she's lost, so I'm going to help her find her daddy."

Bette looked concerned. "Do you want us to help?"

"No, that's okay. You stay here and enjoy yourselves. I'm sure I can find him in a minute. I'll be back soon."

Tom chucked Megan's chin again. "You'd better be careful, little one. Stay with Gail until you find your daddy, okay? He must be worried."

Megan nodded solemnly. "I will. I *like* Gail."

"And I like you, too," Gail told the little girl. Then she took a few seconds to plan her best course of action. Once Clint realized Megan was missing, she reasoned, he'd probably try to find someone in authority to start an organized search, so Gail headed toward the entrance gates.

The crowds had thinned considerably, allowing them to move fairly rapidly. When a loudspeaker cranked to life, the crowd sent up a cheer. Someone launched into a speech, welcoming the crowd, acknowledging local dignitaries and honoring visiting celebrities. Gail tried to follow it, but the words echoed off the bleachers. Though most of the speech was lost to background noise, she didn't think the person had mentioned a lost child.

Megan leaned against her shoulder, warm and soft, obviously content to stay there, and oblivious to Gail's mounting anger.

She'd believed in Clint's devotion to his children. She'd accepted at face value the apparent shift of his priorities. Evidently, she'd been wrong. Well, she'd kept her mouth shut long enough. She'd watched him toy with his children's affections, only to toss them aside the minute Leslie reappeared on the scene. But *this—*

As if she'd conjured him up in her head, she suddenly saw Clint straight ahead of her and her temper snapped. He looked panicked, worried and anxious, but she'd worked herself up too far to hold her tongue now.

Squaring her shoulders, she bulldozed through a group of teenage girls.

Clint saw her almost immediately, and his relief was so evident she might have backed down if she'd been any less irate. He reached them in two strides, stroked Megan's hair and whispered, "Thank God. Where did you find her?" as he pulled Gail into a grateful embrace.

Gail pushed him away. "Following the Sno-Kone lady. Why weren't you watching her?"

He flushed a deeper shade of red than Gail had ever seen him. "I wasn't there. When I got back—"

Running footsteps and a relieved-looking Justin cut off the rest of his comment. "Meggie, where did you go?"

"I wanted a Sno-Kone."

Justin held out his arms and Megan fell into them with an unconcerned giggle. "I'm going to find Brad," he announced.

Clint nodded. "Go straight back to the seats. And keep her with you."

"Yeah. Right." Justin sent him a look that said everything Gail wanted to say, before he carried Megan away.

She waited to speak until the children moved out of earshot. "This is inexcusable, Clint. Maybe you ought to rethink your kids staying with you."

"What?"

"It seems to me, you've gone right back to where you were before they got here—too busy with everything else to worry about them. If you and Leslie want to be wrapped up in each other, that's fine. But let the kids stay somewhere else. Let them stay with somebody who'll give them a little attention, who'll put them *somewhere* on their list of priorities."

"What in the hell are you talking about?"

"You don't even know how lucky you are to have those kids. You certainly don't appreciate how much they love you. And I can't believe you're willing to throw it all away for things that don't even matter. Do you have any idea what might have happened to Megan, left to wander around alone in a place like this? She could have fallen through the bleachers. She could have been kidnapped. She could have crawled through the gate and gotten in with the animals. She could have been seriously hurt, Clint—or killed. And I don't know how any career—any *woman*—could ever compensate for that."

His eyes darkened and a muscle in his jaw tightened. "You don't know what you're talking about."

"Don't I?"

Gripping her shoulders, he drew her closer and for one brief moment she thought he intended to kiss her. Instead, he seemed to gradually gain control over his temper, and he released her suddenly. "No, you don't. You have no idea how I feel about my kids or about Leslie."

His words cut like a knife. "I know what I see. I know what *they* see. Did you pay attention to Justin's face just now? And where's Brad? You're losing them again, Clint. Is that what you want?"

"You know it's not."

She shook her head. "I don't know anything anymore. Megan's a wonderful child who just wants to see and feel everything. She's easily distracted. You *know* that about her. If you're going to bring her to an event like this, you have to be prepared to watch her every second."

"Stop it, Gail—"

It sounded like a warning, but she'd gone too far to let him intimidate her now. "Dammit, Clint. Don't do this to them. Don't do this to *yourself*."

He stared at her for a long time. The muscle in his jaw jerked as he stared at her. He looked as if he had a thousand things to say but wouldn't let himself say any of them. Well, he could get angry if he wanted. Maybe it would do some good.

With her hands clenched into tight fists, she pivoted away and ran back to her seat. Wedging herself into a spot beside Bette, she tried to fix her attention on the barrel racing.

But Bette nudged her with an elbow and looked back at where she'd left Clint standing. "Who's that?"

"Who?"

"The guy over there you were yelling at. The tall, good-looking cowboy. Is that your friend?"

"I wasn't yelling at him," she insisted, but she could still hear the anger in her voice betraying her.

"He's still watching you."

"What?" She glanced back to where she'd left Clint, shocked to see him still there. She looked away quickly. "Don't stare at him."

"Why not? He's a stud."

"For heaven's sake, Bette. Don't look at him."

But Bette studied him for several seconds before she turned her eyes to the rodeo again. "I think he likes you."

"You couldn't be more wrong. He has a girlfriend already. They're getting married soon."

"Whatever you say. But I still think he likes you."

Gail scowled at her. "Will you stop that?"

Laughing, Bette snuggled into the crook of Tom's arm. "If you insist. But denying it doesn't make it true."

"Be quiet."

Bette laughed again, then jumped to her feet to applaud one of the riders.

Gail stared straight ahead for several minutes. Her anger faded gradually and left her exhausted. Maybe she'd made a big mistake telling Clint what she thought of him and Leslie. But it was only a drop in the bucket compared to what she could have said. Giving in to the impulse to see if Clint had gone, she shot a quick peek over her shoulder. He'd disappeared.

She tried not to be disappointed. In fact, she told herself to be glad. Maybe he'd be angry enough to write her off completely, and maybe that was the best thing for everyone. He'd made his choice. Now let him live with it. Gail had no intention of letting him walk down the middle of the road with Leslie on one side and herself on the other.

CHAPTER THIRTEEN

GAIL ROLLED DOWN her window and cranked up the radio, hoping she could find something to get her out of this foul mood. But when Reba McEntire started singing "Till You Love Me," she glared at the radio and switched if off. She didn't need to hear a love song right now. Especially one like that.

This had probably been the most frustrating night of her life. No matter how hard she'd tried, she hadn't been able to put Clint or his kids out of her mind all evening. Watching the rodeo hadn't helped. She'd spent the whole time fending off questions from Bette and Tom. Meeting old friends and their families hadn't helped—they'd only made her long for a future she'd never have with Clint. And seeing Randy Russell again *certainly* hadn't helped. He'd paled by comparison to the man she loved now.

The minute the rodeo ended, she'd made her excuses and broken away. And now she followed a steady stream of traffic out of Broken Bow and tried to clear her mind.

It had been an exhausting day—and she wanted it to be over. She wanted to get home, crawl into bed and fall asleep immediately. Tomorrow she'd sleep late and avoid Clint completely. She didn't want to hear his voice. Didn't want to see him. Didn't want to even *think* about him.

With a sigh, she steered around another car as it turned off the road. Who was she kidding? She might be able to pull the wool over Clint's eyes, but she couldn't lie to herself. She longed to see him, ached to feel his arms around her, needed to feel his lips on hers again. No matter how hard she tried to put him out of her mind, she saw his face in every shadow, heard his voice in the whisper of the wind and felt his touch in the warm night air.

She drove until most of the traffic had turned off the highway and only an occasional vehicle passed her on its way to town. Undiluted by the lights from the arena or passing traffic, the night looked deep and black and the stars glittered like diamonds overhead. Silence rang around her, interrupted only by the sound of the car rushing along the highway.

With a pang, she realized how quickly her time here was passing; how soon she'd have to go home. Back to a job she didn't like, back to live in a place that still didn't feel like home even after all these years. Richard had chosen that life for her and she'd lost herself in that world, but she belonged here. And she wanted to find herself again.

The idea unnerved her. *Could* she come home? It would be easy to quit her job and pack her things, but not so easy to carve out a new life. She wanted the life she'd been living the past few weeks, but that included Clint and his children. Once they went back to Chicago, would she still want this?

In a quandary, she drove the rest of the way home. After waiting for a pickup to pass the turnoff, she swung the car onto the lane that led to her parents' house. But as she made the turn, her heart froze.

Red and blue lights beat a steady rhythm and streaked the night sky like a strobe. Gripping the wheel, Gail pressed down on the accelerator. She turned into the gate in a rush of dust, chilled by the way the lights played their eerie shadows across the front of the house.

Jamming the transmission into park, she leaped from the car almost before it came to a full stop. Panic slammed her heart in her chest and fear roared in her ears as she raced toward the house.

Before she reached the porch, the front door opened and a paramedic backed out pulling a gurney. Gail took the porch steps two at a time and reached the gurney just as its front end and the second paramedic came through the door.

Her father's face looked so still, so white and lifeless, that for one heart-stopping moment she feared he was dead. But a breath rattled in his chest and the paramedics pushed past her with such solemn faces, she knew he was still alive.

Whipping open the screen door, Gail raced through the living room and down the hall. "Mom? Where are you?" She ran into her mother and Dr. Lethbridge coming out of her father's bedroom.

The instant Dorothy saw her, she sobbed and threw herself into Gail's arms. "Oh, sweetheart, did you see your father?"

"What happened?"

Touching a gentle hand to Gail's shoulder, Dr. Lethbridge steered both women into the living room. "Your dad's had another stroke, Gail, and it's a massive one. I'm not going to lie to you, he's in bad shape. And we don't know yet what his chances are or what kind of damage this one's done. We're taking him to

Deaconess Hospital in Billings and we ought to know more soon." He wiped his face with his palm and patted her shoulder. "I'm sure glad you're here. I didn't know how we were going to get your mother into Billings without taking her in the ambulance."

"We'll follow in the car."

Dr. Lethbridge stared into her eyes. "Can you drive all right?"

Gail nodded. "Yes. I'm—I'm fine."

"I'm glad you're here," he said again. "Your mother needs you."

Wrapping her arm around Dorothy's fragile shoulders, Gail led her mother out the door behind the doctor and watched as he climbed into the back of the ambulance.

Like a rag doll, Dorothy followed her lead down the stairs and to the car. She looked as if she'd aged twenty years in the space of one evening. Inside the car, Gail fastened Dorothy's seat belt and snapped her own in place before backing the car around in the yard.

A thousand thoughts raced through her mind as she chased the ambulance down the highway. In the seat beside her, Dorothy alternated between sobbing quietly and watching the road. Tears burned Gail's eyes, but she couldn't allow herself to cry. Not yet.

She gripped the wheel and glared out the windshield, almost daring herself to show weakness now. She cursed herself silently for going to the stampede. She should have been home—that's why she'd come back in the first place.

She stole another glance at Dorothy's pale face and haunted eyes. How would she ever forgive herself for leaving her parents alone tonight? With a heavy heart, she promised herself that no matter what happened now, she wouldn't make that mistake again. All her earlier misgivings evaporated as she understood with blinding clarity what she had to do. She was coming home. Her parents needed her.

With white knuckles and clenched teeth, she maneuvered the car over a series of potholes and prayed silently for one more chance to show her father how much she loved him.

CLINT GUIDED the Mercedes through traffic and onto the highway. In the back seat, Megan yawned widely and battled sleep, while Brad chattered about the rodeo and Justin stared out the window in surly silence.

In the front seat beside him, Leslie sighed and leaned her head against the seat back. She looked infinitely weary and put upon. "I'm so glad that's over with. I thought this day would never end."

Clint had no intention of letting her lead them into a discussion of the day's disasters, so he grunted a noncommittal response and kept his eyes focused on the road. *Nobody* had enjoyed the day less than he had. He could only hope tomorrow would be better.

Leslie touched his hand with her fingertips. "What are we doing tomorrow?"

"I'm going to have to spend most of the day at the Knights' place."

"Of course. But you'll make that call to Garrity & Garr, won't you?"

"I don't know. If I get time."

"Clint—" She pulled her hand away and he heard exasperation in her voice. "They're not going to keep you in mind for the vice presidency indefinitely, and you know as well as I do that Steve Michels will leap at the chance to steal it from you. You'd better get your priorities straight or you'll lose the opportunity of a lifetime.''

For the first time in his life, Clint knew he had priorities straight, but he didn't want the kids to hear them arguing, so he cranked up the radio a notch and spoke softly. ''This has nothing to do with priorities, Les. It's simply a matter of timing, and I think we'd better discuss this later.''

''When? Next month? *After* Steve's already got the job in the bag?''

''When the kids aren't listening.''

She clicked her tongue against her teeth and looked annoyed. ''If I let you use that excuse to avoid the issue now, you'll just find some other reason to avoid it later.''

''That's not fair.''

''All I'm saying is that you could find the time to make one phone call if you wanted to.''

''When?'' he whispered. ''At midnight or six in the morning?''

''A few months ago, *nothing* could have kept you from making that call.''

''A few months ago, I didn't have the obligations I have now.''

''Obligations you're willing to give up the rest of your life for? Is what's-her-name's farm so important, you're willing to lose your chance to advance yourself? Dammit, Clint. You've worked so long to get where you are, and now you're going to let some *woman* throw you off track?''

Clint rubbed the bridge of his nose and clenched his jaw to keep from saying something he'd regret. ''This has nothing to do with Gail.''

''I wish I could believe you.''

"And I wish you wouldn't try to blame her for every disagreement we have."

"I wish she *wasn't* at the center of every disagreement we have."

He glanced into the rearview mirror and caught Justin watching them. Obviously, some of their conversation had carried into the back seat. "We're going to have to finish this later, Leslie. The kids can hear us."

He could feel her glaring at him for a long moment before she sighed heavily and turned away to stare out the window.

He'd upset her again, but it was too bad. The kids had heard far too much fighting during his last years with Barbara. More than once he'd gone to tuck them into bed after a brutal argument and discovered the silvery tracks of dried tears on their cheeks. Hostility and anger had torn his children apart, and he wouldn't put them through it again. Not for anyone.

Several minutes passed before Leslie spoke again, but time hadn't dulled her anger. "This isn't working, Clint. Come home with me."

"I can't do that."

"Why?" She shifted in her seat so she could better face him.

"Dr. Anderson ordered a full year away from work—"

"Why do you need to stay here? You could come home and still take your full year's leave of absence—"

"I can't leave."

"At least be honest with me. You *could* leave, but you *won't.*"

"Not for another couple of months," he admitted.

"I don't think you're ever coming home. You like it here too much."

"Yes, I like it. I get a surprising sense of accomplishment out of what I do here. And I have a commitment to these people."

"You have a commitment to *me*."

He stole a glance at her face and the heartache there twisted his insides. "I've already told you, I'm not staying here permanently. My life's in Chicago. My career—everything I've worked for all these years is there."

"And?"

He knew what she wanted him to say, but he couldn't.

She looked away and pulled in a deep breath. "So, tell me how you felt when you saw *her* today."

With the kids in the car, he couldn't tell her how he'd really felt. "Gail? I was relieved. She had Megan, remember?"

"That's not what I mean."

He stole another glance at her. "Don't you think this discussion is counterproductive?"

"Do you?"

"If we're trying to keep our relationship together, it is."

Leslie crossed her legs and leaned back against the seat again. "*Are* we? I know I am, but sometimes I wonder about you."

Clint couldn't offer any defense without hurting her. He hated living with each foot in a different world. He couldn't go on this way any longer.

She sighed softly. "I need to know about her, Clint. Maybe it's morbid curiosity. Maybe it's the instinct for self-preservation. I don't know what it is, but I can't seem to help myself."

Clint understood that. He'd been consumed by the need to know everything about Barbara and Dave after he'd first learned of their affair—as if understanding what had pulled them together would help him comprehend what had driven his marriage apart.

But for the first time in his life, he saw true love as a sort of magic that defied explanation, and any answer he gave would sound meaningless to Leslie. "What do you say we change the subject?"

She seemed to make an effort to smile at him. "Maybe you're right. I'm only making it harder on myself."

A sudden awkwardness kept them both silent for several minutes. Clint checked the rearview mirror again and smiled at the sight of Megan asleep, leaning against Justin's arm. Brad snored softly, and even Justin had finally succumbed.

When he turned his attention back to the road, flashing red and blue lights somewhere ahead caught his attention. At first, he wondered if someone had been speeding or driving under the influence. But he soon realized the lights were rapidly moving closer, and within seconds he could see the outline of an emergency vehicle tearing toward them.

He swerved onto the shoulder of the road and waited while an ambulance flashed past. Before he could pull back onto the highway, the lights from another vehicle hit the windshield—someone obviously following the ambulance to the hospital in Billings.

The car shot past in a blur, but even at such a high speed Clint recognized it as Dorothy's. Boone must have taken a turn for the worse.

With his heart drumming against his rib cage, Clint pulled onto the highway. He kept one eye on his rearview mirror and watched as the taillights of both vehicles disappeared. Clutching the steering wheel, he forced himself to drive toward home, but he ached with frustration and burned with the need to help. And as if Gail were beside him, he could feel her fear and grief.

Leslie shot a glance at him. "What's wrong?"

"That was Gail and her mother following the ambulance."

Genuine concern flashed across Leslie's face. "Her dad again?"

"It must be."

"I'm sure she'll call from the hospital and let you know how he is."

"I suppose so," he said, but he didn't share Leslie's certainty. Gail had been so angry with him earlier, he couldn't imagine her turning to him for anything now.

If he thought for one minute she'd welcome him, he'd turn the car around and follow her. He'd offer his support, give her a shoulder to lean on. But he had no right to go to her unless he could offer a permanent relationship.

He looked into the rearview mirror once more, but only the night stared back at him. Empty, black and cold. He silently argued logic against emotion all the way home, but none of his reasoning sounded convincing, even to himself.

He couldn't stop thinking of what Gail must be going through. He couldn't stop wondering how ill Boone was this time. He needed to know. He needed to do something. He needed to help.

He glanced at Leslie. Illuminated by the moonlight, her face looked tired and unhappy. And he realized this was as hard on her as it was on him. No—
probably harder. Pretending to work on their relationship while his heart belonged somewhere else
wasn't fair to her. Unless he was ready to give up Gail
completely, this would never work. And he couldn't
even think of turning his back on Gail.

By the time he drove into the yard at Hal and Phyllis's, he knew what he had to do. He also knew it
wouldn't be easy. He pulled close to the back door,
roused the kids and sent them upstairs to bed. Leslie
held open the door for them, but instead of following
them into the house, she let the door close and crossed
the porch to stand beside him. "Should I wait while
you put away the car? Maybe we can take a walk or
something."

Holding her gaze with his own, he shook his head.
"I'm going to the hospital."

Her face froze. "*No, Clint.*"

"I have to go."

"*Why?*"

"I'm not being honest with either one of us, Les. I
could stay here and try to get through the night. I
could try to pretend my thoughts weren't with Gail.
But even these past two days, I haven't given our relationship an honest chance. It's not fair to you for me
to pretend I have."

"Who gave you the idea I wanted you to be so
damned honest?" Her words carried a note of resignation.

"I can't let Gail and Dorothy go through this alone.
I need to be there for them."

Her eyes glittered with unshed tears. "I don't believe this is happening."

"I'm sorry, Leslie," he said softly. "I did love you."

Her lips trembled when she tried to force them into a sad smile. "You know, I'd feel so much better if I could claim you had no idea how much this hurts." When he didn't say anything, she took a step or two away and spoke over her shoulder. "I'll be going home tomorrow."

She dashed away tears with the back of her hand. "The minute I saw you with her, I was afraid it would end up this way."

"You're a wonderful woman, Leslie. You deserve someone who adores you."

She dropped to the steps and laughed softly. "I thought *you* did."

Clint sat beside her and studied her face. "So did I. I *wanted* to."

"I'll be honest with you, Clint. I want to blame Gail for this, but even I know it's not just her. You've changed since you've been here and I can't live the kind of life you want now. Unfortunately, she can."

He touched her hand. "I need my kids with me—at least part of the time every year."

"I know."

"I've decided to pursue a joint-custody arrangement. I don't know whether Barbara will fight me or not—"

"Then you've known all along how this had to end."

"We might have been able to work it out."

She laughed. "I guess. But the limited amount of time I'm willing to devote to motherhood wouldn't be fair to the kids." Her smile softened. "They're nice kids, Clint. But I can't give up my life for them."

"I know."

She met his gaze finally, and looked deep into his eyes for a long moment. "I'm going upstairs to bed." She stood and looked down at him, then turned and walked to the back door.

Clint waited until she'd gone inside and switched off the kitchen light before he climbed back in the car. Knowing Leslie was probably watching him drive away, he maintained a steady speed all the way down the lane and turned onto the highway cautiously. But the minute he left her line of vision, he punched the accelerator and felt the gratifying leap as the car's powerful engine kicked in.

He only hoped he could make it in time.

CLINT FOUND Gail and Dorothy sitting in the corner of a tiny waiting room on the hospital's second floor. Gail looked up when he entered and watched him approach uncertainly, as if he were an apparition walking out of a mist.

He crossed the room and touched her shoulder lightly, but she pulled away. "How's your dad?" he asked. "Is there any word yet?"

She shook her head and looked away. "They're not telling us anything," she said softly.

He hunkered down to face her. "What can I do to help?"

"Nothing. I don't think anyone can help right now." She rubbed Dorothy's back absently and managed to avoid looking at him. "All we can do is wait."

"Do you mind if I stay with you for a while?"

Gail seemed to consider, then shook her head again. "I don't mind. But where are the kids?"

"They're at home."

She nodded her approval and looked toward the door as if she expected to see someone else there. "Is Leslie with you?"

"No." He hesitated, uncertain how much to tell her. He knew this wasn't the time or place to discuss their future, but he didn't want to leave her in the dark. "She's decided to go back to Chicago in the morning. We won't be getting married, after all."

He didn't know what he'd expected—maybe a small sign of pleasure in spite of her pain and fear—but her expression didn't waver. The only sign that she'd heard him was the way her hand stilled on her mother's back and the way she pushed to her feet and paced to the window.

He followed her and touched her shoulders gently. "You look exhausted."

"I'll be fine." She stared out over the parking lot. He could see her reflection in the window. "Why did Leslie leave?"

"We finally realized we weren't right for each other." When Gail didn't respond right away, Clint went on, "I'm sorry for everything that's happened between us, Gail, and I want you to know I'm here for you now."

She turned to face him, and the steel he'd seen the first night showed clearly in her face. "I can't talk about it now, Clint. I don't know how I feel about you, about Leslie. My father's lying in the other room so ill they won't even let me see him. And I wasn't there with him when it happened. I didn't even spare him a thought while he was suffering."

"You didn't know."

"I came home to be with him, but I didn't follow through very well." She laughed bitterly. "I let myself be distracted by other things. I can't let that happen again. My mother needs me, and I pray to God my father will need me, too. I can't even think about anything else."

"I'm not asking you to. I just want you to know I'm here if you need me."

She turned back to the window. "Thank you."

Clint ached to take her into his arms and comfort her, but she'd erected an invisible barrier that kept his hands glued to his sides. "Can I get you anything? There must be a cafeteria somewhere—"

She shook her head but didn't bother to look at him. "No, thank you."

Across the room, Dorothy shot to her feet and strode to the door. "I want to know what's going on in there."

Gail glanced over her shoulder. Everything about her mother looked weary. "Dr. Lethbridge will talk to us as soon as he can, Mom."

"I want to see Boone. They can't keep me out. They *have* to let me in."

"There's nothing you can do right now," Gail said softly, but her voice carried a weary note, as if she'd said the same thing several times before. "We just have to wait."

Dorothy caught back a sob and cast a longing glance at a door across the hall. For one split second, Clint thought she intended to ignore Gail's counsel. "I can't wait. I can't stand knowing he's in that room alone, sick and helpless..."

Gail crossed to Dorothy's side and wrapped her arms around her shoulders. Tenderly, she guided the older woman back to her seat and sat beside her. "They're doing everything they can for him, Mom. The best thing we can do for him right now is stay out of the doctor's way."

Clint sat in a chair near the window and watched them, powerless in the face of their misery. Every word he thought of saying sounded trite. Every action he imagined taking seemed superficial. Yet he couldn't walk away. Gail might need him, and he had to be here if she did.

Resting his elbows on his knees, he linked his fingers together and dropped his forehead onto the bridge they made. He closed his eyes and listened to Gail comforting Dorothy, to the subdued activity of the hospital staff, to the sharp click of footsteps in the corridor outside. When he realized the footsteps had stopped in the doorway, he opened his eyes and focused on the figure standing there.

"We're going to let you in to see him now," Dr. Lethbridge said, and in his hushed tone Clint heard a soft warning.

Gail and Dorothy left the waiting room without a backward glance and followed the doctor into Boone's room. The door swung shut behind them and Clint felt as if fate had slammed the door in his face once more.

But this time he wouldn't take no for an answer. He wouldn't leave.

He didn't know how long he waited, how long he watched the door without taking his eyes from it. He only knew he had to be here when it opened again. Maybe self-delusion allowed him to hope she'd turn to him for comfort. Maybe she really didn't want him here. All he knew for sure was that he couldn't leave her here alone.

After what felt like hours, the door to Boone's room opened again and Gail emerged, but the grief on her face spoke clearly of what had happened inside. With a slow, steady step, she led a sobbing Dorothy into the corridor. The older woman leaned heavily on Gail and lifted a trembling hand to touch her face, her arm, her shoulder, as if she expected Gail to evaporate.

He moved to the doorway, ready to go to her if she gave him even the slightest sign. She held her mother and let her cry, but Clint could see she wasn't crying herself. His arms ached to hold her. His eyes burned with unshed tears. His throat constricted around the grief he felt for her. But she didn't look at him.

When Dr. Lethbridge stepped into the corridor several minutes later, he spoke briefly to Gail and Dorothy, then crossed to Clint. "You're Hal Taylor's nephew, aren't you?"

Clint nodded. "Clint Andrews. I think we've met before."

The doctor nodded toward Gail and Dorothy. "Are you with them?"

"If they need me."

Dr. Lethbridge stared up at him with watery blue eyes and smiled feebly. "They're going to need you. We lost Boone. Did everything we could, but the poor old guy—" He made a visible effort to pull himself together. "I don't know what Dorothy's going to do now. That man was her whole life. I told Gail it's a good thing Dorothy's got her here." He paused and shook his head, then muttered, "Poor woman."

As if she felt Clint watching her, Gail lifted her eyes and met his. But she immediately looked away again.

Clint was ready, willing and able to help, but Gail didn't want him. Not now.

So he'd wait. And hope. He couldn't do anything else.

WIPING TEARS from her cloudy brown eyes, Mary Parker pulled Gail into an embrace and patted her cheek. "It was a lovely service, dear. Your father would have loved it."

Gail managed a tired smile for her mother's friend. With the funeral behind her, the adrenaline rush she'd been living on the past few days had already begun to evaporate, and exhaustion threatened to overtake her.

Bette materialized out of the crowd, took Mary by the arm and steered her away. "It's wonderful to see you again, Mary. I was afraid your arthritis would keep you home today... Yes, it was a *lovely* service..."

Gail's smile drooped. Friends and neighbors milled around the living room and spilled onto the front porch. The women's auxiliary group from her mother's church had taken over the kitchen to serve the luncheon, and more children than she could count swarmed over the front yard while their parents visited and reminisced.

This show of affection for her father and support for her mother warmed and comforted her. She wouldn't offend any of these kindhearted souls for the world, but more than almost anything she could think of, she wanted to lie down somewhere for a few minutes.

She could hear someone retelling the story of her dad's first encounter with Tommy Derringer's bull, a tale that never failed to draw a laugh, even today.

Someone else sobbed quietly. Outside, children laughed and played, and the smell of ham and freshly baked rolls filled the air.

Scanning the crowded living room, she pushed away a rising disappointment. She'd seen Clint only once all day, for a minute before the funeral. The sorrow and caring in his eyes had threatened to release the tears she'd been battling all morning, so she'd turned away before he said anything too kind or asked something she couldn't answer. To her dismay, he hadn't come by the house yet, and now she had to admit he probably wasn't coming at all.

She forced her attention back to more immediate concerns and told herself it was just as well. She was confused already, seeing him would only make it worse.

She drew a steadying breath and searched the crowd for her mother. Dorothy sat on the couch with Floyd Peterson on one side and his wife, Edith, on the other. Dorothy nodded at something Floyd said, managed a warm smile in his direction, and patted Edith's hand as if Dorothy were the one offering comfort.

Unshed tears burned Gail's eyes, her feet ached and her head pounded. She stood in a corner and watched her mother for a few minutes, marveling at Dorothy's newfound strength.

Bette deposited Mary Parker with a group of friends, then made a beeline back to Gail's side. "How are you holding up?"

Gail shrugged and smiled weakly. "I'm all right, I guess. A few more hours and it'll be over ... Right?"

"Right. But I'll be honest with you, it won't get any easier for a while. The hardest part comes when everyone leaves." Bette took Gail's arm and started toward the kitchen. "Let's go find you something to eat."

Gail stopped moving. "I don't want anything."

"It might help. You look worn-out."

"I'll have something later," Gail said, and tempered her response with the best smile she could offer. "Thank God you're here, Bette. I don't know what I'd do without you."

Bette squeezed her arm. "Tom and I went through this last year when his mom died." She leaned a little closer and lowered her voice. "They all mean well, but it can be a bit overwhelming when the entire county's in your living room at once."

Another of Dorothy's friends swept past Bette and threw her arms around Gail. "It was *such* a lovely service, honey. Your dad would have been so pleased."

Gail dredged up another smile. "It was nice, wasn't it?"

"Absolutely beautiful. And the flowers— Didn't you think the flowers were lovely, Bette?"

"That daughter of yours outdid herself this time, Lorna," Bette said.

Beaming, the older woman scurried on to another cluster of people, leaving Gail with a clear view of the front door as she moved away.

Clint stood there, framed in the doorway, obviously looking for her.

Torn between joy and confusion, Gail turned away.

But Bette pulled her around and pointed. "Isn't that the guy from the rodeo?"

"Yes." Gail managed to slide into the hallway where Clint couldn't see her.

Bette followed, allowing herself one last glance at Clint. "Well, well, well. So, who is he?"

"Clint Andrews. He's been helping with the farm since Dad got sick."

"Really? *He's* the one?" She peeked around the corner again. "Lucky you." Gail glared at her, but Bette didn't seem to notice. "I'm glad he's here. You need all the friends you can get at a time like this."

Gail shook her head. "I don't want to see him."

"Why not?"

"I can't explain. It's too complicated."

"Do you like him?"

"I don't know how I feel anymore."

Bette's expression softened. "Well, that's natural enough considering everything that's happened lately. Maybe it'll help if you talk to him."

Gail shook her head more firmly and tried to pull away. "I can't."

As tenacious as ever, Bette refused to relinquish Gail's arm. "Look, I know this probably isn't the best time to think about getting involved, but even I can see how that guy feels about you—it's written all over his face. At least talk to him."

"I can't."

"Why?"

The tears she'd been battling all day finally came to the surface. "I came home to be with my dad during his illness, but from the minute I met Clint, I forgot about everything else. I wasn't even here when Dad had the second stroke—"

"You were at the rodeo," Bette said. "Helping me."

"I could have come home before the rodeo. Instead, I stayed there. I was thinking about Clint and his kids—*not* about Dad. Now Mom's alone and she needs me, and I'm not going to let myself get pulled off course again."

"I understand all that, Gail. But falling in love is the natural order of things. Do you really think your dad would want you to turn your back on a chance at happiness because of him?"

"Of course not."

"I *know* your mom wouldn't."

"You don't understand," Gail said. "It's more than just that."

"His kids?"

In spite of herself, Gail smiled. "No. His kids are wonderful."

"Then what?" Bette demanded.

Gail leaned her back against the wall and met Bette's gaze squarely. "When I met Richard, I knew he'd never belong here. But I married him, anyway. I spent over nine years of my life living somewhere I didn't want to live, doing something I didn't want to do—" She broke off and wiped her eyes with her fingertips. "At first, I thought Clint would be different, but it's the same story all over again. I saw him the way he really is just before Daddy died. He doesn't want to live here, and I don't want to live in Chicago. I'd be miserable. I'd make him miserable. Montana's my home. I belong here, and I'm not leaving again."

Bette touched Gail's cheek with the palm of her hand. "Have you talked to him about it? Asked him how he feels?"

"No."

"Don't you think you ought to? You could be making the biggest mistake of your life..."

Gail tried to blink tears away, but they still blurred her vision. "I don't want to argue about this today, okay? Can we just drop it for now?"

Bette opened her mouth as if to protest, but clamped it shut on whatever she'd been about to say.

Gail smiled her thanks. "I really need to lie down for a minute. Would you mind keeping an eye on Mom? If she needs anything, come and get me."

Bette nodded. "Of course. I'm sorry, Gail. I didn't mean to be pushy."

"That's what I like about you. You can be pushy without even meaning to."

Bette chuckled softly. "You can thank your lucky stars I was taking it easy on you, or you wouldn't have gotten off so lightly."

"I thank my lucky stars that I have a good friend like you to help me over the rough spots. Even if you do tend to push." Gail hugged Bette quickly, then turned toward the stairs.

She hadn't made it up two steps before she heard Tom's voice in the hallway. "Hey, Bette. Have you seen Gail? This guy's been looking all over for her."

She heard Clint introduce himself, and the deep, familiar sound of his voice almost made her turn around and go back. But she gripped the handrail and forced herself to climb to the top. Below, she could hear Bette leading Clint and Tom away.

Fresh tears filled her eyes, and she leaned her head against the wall and let them flow. Great gulping sobs shuddered through her body, and she cried until her stomach muscles hurt, her eyes stung and her throat burned. All the grief she'd been storing for her father came to the surface and overflowed. Love and longing for a life with Clint and his children soon followed.

She sank to her knees and buried her face in her hands. She wanted to do what Bette suggested. She wanted to believe she could make a relationship with Clint work in spite of their differences. But the facts spoke for themselves.

CHAPTER FOURTEEN

HAL SPOONED a heap of steaming mashed potatoes onto his plate and passed the serving dish to Clint. "So, did those folks stop by the Knights' place today?"

Clint nodded and dropped a spoonful of potatoes on his own plate. "They stopped by, but Dorothy refused to discuss their offer, so Gail showed them around a bit and then they left."

"Were they interested in buyin'?"

"I honestly don't know." Clint poured gravy and put a small serving of peas on Megan's plate. "Gail didn't say a word to me. She's still avoiding me."

After placing a basket of rolls in front of Hal, Phyllis sat in her place and adjusted her apron across her lap. "She's upset about losing her dad. Give her time. It's only been two weeks."

"I know." But those two weeks felt like two years to Clint. "There's so much I'd like to do to help, but she doesn't seem to want me to do anything. I feel helpless."

Phyllis smiled gently. "She'll come around."

Hal chewed and used his fork to indicate he wanted to speak as soon as he swallowed. "You know what'd be good is if *you* was to buy Boone's place. You could stay here and see to things, and between us, we'd make sure Dorothy was taken care of."

Brad nodded his agreement. "Yeah, Dad. Do it. We could come here to visit you in the summers—"

Megan clapped her hands and bounced in her chair. "Oh, please, Daddy."

Clint shook his head slowly, although part of him liked the idea for a number of reasons. But his life waited for him in Chicago. Every day brought him closer to his destiny. And every day left him more determined to ask Gail to share it with him—just as soon as a decent time passed after her father's death. "I can't stay."

Frowning, Hal stabbed a mound of salad and lifted it to his lips, but he stopped short of popping it into his mouth. "Least you could do is think on it. You've done real good. You've come a long way." He used the fork to add emphasis to his words. "You could handle that place easy."

"Maybe. But I can't just throw away everything I've worked for on a whim."

Hal grunted his disapproval. "Don't sound like no whim to me. Sounds like common sense. Things have been going good for you here." He sent a meaningful look toward Justin and Brad.

Clint wouldn't even think of arguing that point. Things had gone well with the boys for the most part, although he and Justin still had a way to go. He'd learned a lot, and because of his stay here he'd be a better parent from now on.

When it became apparent he wasn't going to change his mind, Hal jutted his chin out and scowled at him. "How long've we got before Gail goes back to California?"

She'd been so elusive, Clint didn't know the answer to that.

But to his surprise, Justin spoke up. "She's not."

Clint stared at him. "She's *not?*"

Justin shot him a look of pity mixed with triumph as he reached for the potatoes. "Nope. She decided to stay here. She's even quit her job and she's having some friend pack up her stuff and send it out here."

Hal and Phyllis stared at Clint, obviously as confused by this news as he was. Phyllis said, "I talked to Dorothy just yesterday. She didn't mention it to me."

"Are you sure that's what she's doing, son?" Clint asked. "I thought she was planning to leave soon."

Megan frowned. "I don't want Gail to leave."

"Well, she's not." Justin downed half a glass of milk and wiped his mouth. "She told me all about it today."

"When did you see her?" Brad demanded.

"When she came outside to check the mailbox."

Brad threw down his fork and pouted. "Well, I didn't see her."

Megan's mouth puckered. "*I* want to see Gail."

Sympathizing, Clint patted her shoulder. "I know, sweetie. So do I."

Phyllis chewed thoughtfully. "Well, this is certainly a surprise. Wonder why she's moving back here."

"Must be worried about her mother," Hal said and filled his mouth with roast beef.

"Yes, but that's no reason to quit her job..." Phyllis looked puzzled. "And I don't know why she didn't tell you, Clint."

Clint tried not to look hurt by Justin's revelation or by Phyllis's observation. He worked up a stiff smile and concentrated on buttering a roll. "She hasn't told me much of anything the past couple of weeks."

"Maybe she doesn't want to talk to you," Brad suggested.

Much as it hurt to admit it, Clint had to agree. "It looks like you're right about that."

"I don't think she trusts you," Justin said.

Lowering his roll slowly, Clint held Justin's gaze with his own. "Why wouldn't she trust me?"

Justin shrugged with mock innocence. "I don't know."

Phyllis's face darkened and she frowned at Justin. "Well, of course she trusts your dad. What's not to trust?"

Justin shrugged again and studied his plate intently.

"Do you know something I don't?" Clint asked.

"Like what?"

"Like why Gail wouldn't trust me."

Justin tried looking innocent for another second or two, but he finally abandoned the effort, pushed away his plate and glared at Clint. "Why *should* she trust you? Why should *anybody* trust you?" He shot to his feet. "First you dumped Mom. Then you dumped Leslie. What do you expect Gail to do, sit around and wait for you to dump her, too?"

A stunned silence followed the boy's outburst. Tension radiated from every corner of the room until Megan's tiny wail shattered it. "Don't yell at Daddy. Don't be so mean."

"Just leave me alone, Megan. You're too little to know what you're talking about," Justin shouted.

Phyllis made a choking noise and shot to her feet. "Now, listen here, young man—"

But Clint waved her back to her seat without taking his eyes from Justin's red face. "It's okay, Phyllis. Justin's obviously got a few things he wants to say to me." He stood and tossed down his napkin. "But maybe we ought to take this someplace besides the dinner table. Why don't you and I step outside, son."

Justin hesitated only a fraction of a second before he shrugged. "Okay. Sure. Whatever."

Clint pushed open the screen door and led Justin outside. They moved away from the house without speaking, but Justin's anger fairly crackled in the cool night air. Clint hooked his thumbs in his pockets and broke the silence. "So, is that why you're so angry with me? You think I abandoned your mother?"

"It's one reason."

"What else?"

Justin snorted his answer, but he didn't speak.

"Be honest with me, son. Get it out. We can't fix what's wrong until we do that."

Justin shot him a mocking look. "You want me to be honest? Okay. You got it. I think you're a jerk."

Though the accusation hurt, Clint tried not to react badly. He wanted to clear the channel of communication between them—no matter what it took. So he let the words settle over him and nodded. "You might be right. Maybe I am a jerk. And maybe I did abandon your mother, but not in the way you think."

That earned him a curious glance.

And Clint pressed his advantage. "Look, I've learned a lot this past year, son. I've learned to accept my share of the blame for the divorce. I've learned to readjust my priorities. And I've learned just how much you kids mean to me." He kicked at a couple of loose pebbles and tried to smile. "When I was married to your mother, I worked too much. I left home early, came home late, went to the office on weekends and brought work home with me. If I abandoned your mom, that's how I did it. But I honestly believed I was doing it for her—and for you. I thought that by giving you things, by providing a big house and lots of money I was doing everything I needed to."

Justin sent him another look from under furrowed brows. "Yeah, I know."

"Your mother tried to get me to understand for years. I should have come to your Little League games. I should have gone to the Halloween parade at school and Back-To-School Night." He broke off with an embarrassed laugh. "I made too many mistakes, and she finally got tired of waiting for me to figure it out."

Justin's step slowed. "You're trying to claim the divorce was Mom's idea?"

Clint nodded.

"But *you* left *her*."

"Only because she asked me to. And only under protest."

Justin turned away from him sharply. "You're a liar."

"It's the truth, son. I'll take the blame for every mistake I made, but leaving wasn't my idea. *That* I'll swear to you."

Justin didn't speak again for several seconds, but Clint could see the emotions flitting across his face in the bright summer moonlight. "If it is true, why didn't Mom tell us?"

"I don't know. I do know we were both hurt and angry. Maybe she wanted to hurt me by letting you guys believe I'd deserted you." Clint stuffed his hands into his pockets and drew a deep breath. "But I've learned a lot about that, too, and I think I understand more about what your mother felt, and why she made the decisions she did.''

Justin digested that in silence. "Then what about Leslie? What happened with her?"

Clint smiled sadly. "Leslie and I grew apart."

"I didn't like her," Justin admitted, and his honesty gave Clint's hopes a boost.

"When we met, there was nothing more important to me than my work. But circumstances forced me to pull back and gave me another chance to set things right with you kids. Leslie's a wonderful woman, Justin, but she doesn't want children. Our lives are on different tracks."

"Are you going to have more kids someday?"

"I don't know. Maybe. But it's kind of a moot point right now, isn't it?" He chuckled, then sobered almost instantly. "Look, losing you finally made me see that you're more important than anything. I've made a lot of decisions the last couple of months. I want to have you guys around more. I want to *be* around more. I want to talk to your mother about some changes in our arrangements when she comes home."

Justin didn't scorn the idea, and Clint's hopes climbed another notch. But the boy's face grew solemn and he stared at Clint through narrowed eyes. "Okay. What about Gail?"

Clint barked a laugh. "I don't remember you being so direct when you were younger. Where'd you learn that?"

In spite of himself, Justin grinned. "It was a hidden talent. So, what about Gail?"

"I love her," Clint said truthfully. "And I hope she feels the same about me. I have to give her time to get over losing her father and to put her life in order, then I'll ask her to marry me.''

Justin almost looked pleased. "Do you think she'll say yes?"

"I *hope* so. I'm not sure what I'll do if she says no. But she's obviously talked to you more than she has to me lately. What do you think?"

This time, Justin laughed. "She'd be getting a great bargain—four for the price of one. How could she resist?"

Clint dropped his hand across Justin's shoulders. "You've given me new hope."

"When do you think you'll ask her?"

Clint sobered. "When the time's right. I don't want to rush her."

"Yeah. Well, you're probably smart." Justin grinned over at him. "Just for the record, I hope she says yes."

"That makes two of us."

The back door opened and soft golden light spilled across the porch. Phyllis stepped out and called, "Clint? You've got a phone call from a Larry or Harry something-or-other in Chicago. I wouldn't have interrupted, except he said it's urgent."

Clint stepped out of the shadows and hurried toward her. "Larry? What does he want?" he muttered.

Phyllis held open the screen while Clint ducked inside. "He says it's important, that's all I know."

He hurried into the living room where he could take the call in relative privacy. Snagging the receiver, he demanded, "Larry? What's up?"

"Clint? I was hoping I'd catch you. Big news, buddy. Duncan Morris announced his retirement today—effective the first of October. If you want his position, you'd better get back here pronto."

The news left Clint reeling as if someone had landed a swift punch to his midsection, and he clutched the receiver a little tighter. "Are you sure?"

"I kid you not. And I'm here to tell you, Steve Michels has already started moving on it. How soon can you get back?"

Back? Now? So soon? He couldn't leave now, but he couldn't risk staying. This was what he'd been waiting for. "How about the first of next week?"

"Not good enough. How about tomorrow?"

Clint managed a laugh. "Monday's the soonest I can make it, Larry. And I can only do that if you'll help me out."

"You name it."

Clint gave him a list of phone calls to make and things to do, then added, "I'll call A.J. myself in the morning."

"Good idea. Do that and the position's as good as yours. You're still his favorite."

"I've been gone a long time."

"But not forgotten."

Clint smiled. "I guess we're about to find out, aren't we? Can you give me a call tomorrow after you have a chance to check on those accounts?"

"Sure. No problem."

When they disconnected a minute later, Clint stared around the now-familiar living room and battled an unexpected pang of homesickness. In less than three days, this part of his life would be over forever.

For half a beat, he considered Hal's idea. He could stay here, buy the Knights' place, work the land and let Dorothy live in the house she loved so much. But in Chicago, he had a chance to accomplish everything he'd ever dreamed of, everything he'd spent his life working for. His time here had been a nice hiatus, nothing more. He couldn't stay.

He felt fit and healthy and more than ready to tackle his career again. It would mean long hours, but he was used to that. And this time, he'd keep his kids a priority. He wouldn't let them suffer. But there would be something—or more accurately, *someone*—missing.

Gail.

With her by his side, he'd have been a truly happy man. With her in his life, he could accomplish anything. But getting called home so soon threw all his plans out of whack. He couldn't talk to her yet. She hadn't had long enough to grieve. He might lose her forever if he approached her too soon.

On the other hand, he'd lose her for sure if he waited too long. He caught sight of his reflection in the mirror over Phyllis's piano as he turned to leave the room and walked toward it slowly, arguing both sides of the question with himself.

Speak now or wait? Push or hold back? Would she even want him? If he timed the question right, would she accept? Or would she push him away again?

He stared at his reflection as if it might know something he didn't. But there were no answers in the mirror. With an embarrassed laugh, he started to turn away. How ironic, he thought. Here he was, a successful, capable, respected professional, heading into one of the most challenging positions of his career. A man who'd proved he could hold his own on a farm in Montana as well as in the big city. But the thought of losing the woman he loved reduced him to a bundle of nerves.

Well, he had to stop letting his fears dictate his actions. He could worry about losing Gail forever, but worry wouldn't get him anywhere. It never had.

This time, he'd put his fears aside. This time, he'd meet the situation head-on. He'd talk to her honestly. No more hiding behind the guise of friendship. No more pretending. He'd tell her he loved her and ask her to build a life with him.

And in the meantime, he'd try not to worry about what would happen to his heart if she turned him down.

GAIL POURED her second cup of coffee and sat at the kitchen table with the morning newspaper and the Yellow Pages. She didn't feel ready to look for a job, but she had to. She might like to indulge her grief a little longer, but reality insisted that she take steps to increase the income she and her mother depended on. That meant finding a job nearby.

Somehow, she could tell this would be one of her better days. Enjoying the bright summer sunshine streaming through the kitchen windows and the roses in bloom by the back porch, her spirits felt higher than they had in two weeks. Maybe longer.

She could hear her mother moving around in the living room. Probably dusting again. Dorothy had already polished every knickknack in the house a dozen times or more, and she'd used so much lemon oil on the furniture, the place fairly reeked of it. But if the process helped her heal, Gail wouldn't argue with it.

She wished she could convince her mother to sell the house. If they moved to Billings, Dorothy would still be close enough to see old friends often, and Gail would stand a better chance of finding a decent-paying job. But so far, Dorothy refused to even discuss the idea. And the only set of prospective buyers Gail had rounded up hadn't been interested in a piece of property with someone else's house and yard in the middle.

So she'd just have to find a way to make ends meet from here. Turning to the classified ads, Gail scanned the Help-Wanted notices. She found one advertisement for a law firm in Billings looking for a legal secretary, but it was a long commute. Broken Bow had an opening for counter help at the Tastee-Freez and a cashier at Western Automaster. Nothing promising, but they might bring in a few dollars while she looked for something better.

She jotted down the telephone numbers, including the law firm in Billings, just in case. If she had to, she could make the commute until winter. After that, she'd have to find a house in Billings or another job.

She'd read half the listings, when the sound of an approaching vehicle caught her attention. Curious, she peeked out the window. But when she recognized Clint's truck, she let the curtain drop back into place.

He still came by to work every day, still brought Justin and sometimes Brad. But he'd been coming later in the day—probably so he wouldn't disturb them too early. And he hadn't brought Megan since Boone's death.

She peeked out of a narrow slit between the curtains, expecting him to head straight to the barn, but he pulled into the yard, hopped out of the cab and strode toward the back door like a man with a mission. As always, the sight of him took her breath away and sent her pulse racing.

Drawing a steadying breath, Gail waited for his knock then opened the door. If watching him cross the yard had left her weak, facing him through the screen door sucked every bit of air from her lungs. And she wondered whether she could find the strength to speak.

But she didn't need to worry for the first few seconds, because he studied her silently, his eyes intent and almost hungry. "Hello, Gail," he said at last.

"Clint. What are you doing here?" Her voice sounded harsh, so she tried to temper it with a smile.

"I need to talk to you."

She hesitated only a split second, then stepped away from the door. "Come in."

He stepped inside without surrendering her gaze. "This is important."

"Have a seat."

But he didn't. He stood right in front of her, so near she could almost feel his breath on her cheek. "You've been avoiding me since your dad's funeral."

Her face flamed. "I've been busy."

"You've been avoiding me."

In all the time she'd known him, she'd never seen him like this—direct, determined, decisive. And suddenly she understood how he'd reached such a successful position with his firm in Chicago. But she knew she could meet him head on and hold her own. "All right. Yes, I've been avoiding you."

"Why?"

She managed a tiny laugh. "Do you want the whole list? Or just the top ten reasons?"

"The whole list."

"Because I can't play this game anymore, Clint. I've been attracted to you since the day we met, and I've had to control the way I feel, hide it, push it away..."

"Why? Because of Leslie?"

"Yes."

"She's gone."

"I know. But now *my* life's different. And I can't go on seeing you, laughing with you, playing the part of your friend when I feel the way I do."

"I love you," he whispered.

Her voice faltered. Gulping for a breath of air, she managed to say, "Don't."

But he didn't listen to her. Taking her by the shoulders, he pulled her closer. "I love you, Gail. I think I've loved you from the minute we met. Even if I did try to prove myself wrong for a while." He smiled sadly. "I know it's too soon after your dad's death to come to you like this, but I've been called back to Chicago right away and I can't leave without you. I want to marry you. Please say you'll come with me."

Tears filled her eyes and she blinked furiously, trying to keep control. She wanted to be with him so desperately her head drummed with need, but she couldn't leave her mother alone. She couldn't desert her now. "I can't."

His lips tightened into a frown and he held her even closer. "I love you. Gail."

"I love you," She did little more than breathe the words, but the expression in his eyes told her he'd heard.

"Then marry me."

"Oh, Clint, I wish I could. I love you more than I've ever loved anyone, but I can't leave my mother. She needs me."

"Bring her with us. The kids think she's great, and I wouldn't mind—"

"You don't understand. She won't leave here."

"I'll talk to her."

"No. She'd think I put you up to it, or she'd think she was standing in my way, and that would only make everything worse."

He touched his lips to her forehead. "I can't leave you here. I can't go back there without you."

This time, she couldn't respond, the lump in her throat had grown too thick. She couldn't look at him any longer. The pain of wanting to be with him but not being able to was too sharp to bear.

With infinite tenderness, he touched his lips to hers but almost immediately gentleness gave way to passion. Closing her eyes, Gail felt tears slip down her cheeks as desire swept through her. His arms tightened around her and she clutched him to her with all the strength she possessed. His tongue touched her lips and she opened to him, giving everything she had and taking all he offered at the same time. His chest pressed against her breasts, his hips crushed hers against the table, and even through her tears and pain she wanted him.

He loosened his grip and let his hands roam up her sides. She clutched his shoulders and gasped as heat spiraled through her. Lost in sensation, drowning in desire, Gail abandoned herself to him. But she couldn't prolong such a kiss in her heightened state of desire without carrying it a step further. And she knew Clint couldn't, either.

With her mother in the next room grieving over the loss of her husband, taking that step was impossible. And Gail knew that Clint was as aware of that as she was. The instant Gail thought of her father, cold reality replaced hot desire and she pulled away from Clint's embrace.

But he didn't release her. Instead, he pressed delicate kisses to the hollow of her neck, trailed his lips up her chin and captured her lips in a kiss so sweet and tender it melted her heart.

"I love you," he said again. "Come with me to Chicago. Marry me."

"And I love you. But I can't."

This time he pulled back a little and studied her face. "You *can't?*"

"Clint, please understand—"

"You're serious."

"Did you think I wasn't?"

He released her and his eyes darkened. "I don't know. I guess I did. At least, I hoped you were."

"Please understand," she said again.

"Understand that you don't love me enough to go with me? I think I'm beginning to."

"No—"

He held up both hands to stop her from saying anything more and laughed harshly. "I can't believe this. It's like a nightmare. I've lived my whole life looking for you. And I've finally found you. But I can't have you."

"I feel exactly the same way."

Stiffening, he looked away and tightened his jaw. "I don't think so."

"Well, I do. I left here once, and it was a disaster. I *can't* live in Chicago." She touched one hand to his shoulder. "I will marry you, Clint, if you'll stay here in Broken Bow with me."

Silence rang between them for what felt like hours before his posture relaxed and he met her gaze again. He swallowed convulsively several times and closed his eyes. She hadn't expected him to agree, but the look of anguish on his face hit her like a bolt of lightning. "Dammit," he whispered.

Pulling her into his arms again, he kissed her once more, gently, sweetly, lingeringly. But the passion was gone. The hunger had died. And in this kiss, Gail could feel him telling her goodbye.

CHAPTER FIFTEEN

FOR THE THIRD TIME in half an hour, Clint interrupted Larry Gardner's analysis of the Winsom portfolio to call home. And for the third time in a row, he reached the answering machine, which could only mean Mrs. Olson and the kids were glued to the television as they'd been every night for the past two months, while he'd been glued here in his new corner office.

Instead of hanging up again, he decided to leave a message in case someone happened by and checked the machine. "Hey, guys, it's Dad. I'm afraid I'm going to be late again tonight. But tell Mrs. Olson not to worry about dinner—I'll pick up pizza on the way home. Call me if you get this message, I'll be here a while longer."

Before he could hang up, someone lifted the receiver on the other end. "Dad? Don't hang up."

"Brad? Good. I'm glad I caught you. Where's Mrs. Olson?"

"Watching that new show she likes. Where are you? We're starving."

"I'm still at work, buddy. It looks like it's going to be a long night."

"Oh. So you're not coming home again?"

From across the desk, Larry pointed to a column of figures and shoved a file folder toward Clint.

Clint held up a finger to signal he needed another minute and swiveled around in his chair. "I'll be home, son, but it'll be late."

"Same thing," Brad groused. "So what did you call for?"

"To let you know I'm still here and to ask Mrs. Olson if she can stay a while longer."

Brad groaned. "I don't want her to stay."

"Why not?"

"I don't like her. I wish we were back in Montana—with Gail."

As it always did, the mention of Gail's name stabbed at Clint's heart. Since he'd come home, he'd had to struggle to keep her out of his mind and to focus on what had once seemed so important. Before Gail, nothing had come between him and his work. Now it seemed nothing came between him and her memory.

He pulled in a deep breath and said, "That's not an option, Brad."

"Yeah, that's what you always say."

"That's because it's true."

"It's *not* true," Brad argued. "We *could* go back."

They'd had this argument a dozen times before, and Clint suspected they'd have it a dozen more. Nothing he could say would help. "Where's your brother?"

"Standing right here. We're trying to figure out how to find Gail's phone number."

Clint bolted upright in his chair. "*What? Why?*"

"'Cause we want to talk to her."

"Put Justin on," he snapped.

"Whatever," Brad said in a tone that sounded too close to Justin's surly one and handed the phone to his brother.

"What?" Justin demanded.

"Brad says you're trying to find Gail's number. Why?"

"We want to call her. You haven't been around and Megan's been whining for her the past two days. I thought if we called, Megan might feel better."

"I don't think that's a good idea."

"Why not?"

For half a dozen reasons, but Clint couldn't elaborate. "You know things didn't work out. I don't think Gail's going to want you kids bothering her, that's all."

"Things didn't work out with *you,* not us. She might not want you to bother her, but she wants us to keep in touch. She said so before we left."

Clint shot a glance over his shoulder at Larry's pinched face. "Just don't do anything until I get there, all right? Promise me that. We'll talk about this when I get home."

"Sure." He could almost hear the hostility curling Justin's lip. "Any idea what century that'll be in?"

"Knock it off, Justin," Clint growled. But he immediately forced his temper under control and tried again. "I'm sorry, son. I'm tired and cranky and my stomach's in knots—"

"Just like old times, huh? I should have known all that stuff you told me at Uncle Hal's was a bunch of crap."

Before Clint could answer, Justin slammed down the receiver and the dial tone hummed in his ear.

"Dammit." He jammed his own receiver back into place and swiveled toward Larry.

The other man raised his eyebrows and tried to look sympathetic. "Trouble at home?"

Clint managed a terse laugh. "That's an understatement. Now, show me the Winsom portfolio again—did you find the problem?"

Larry shoved the file folder toward him and Clint stared at the column of figures for several long seconds, but he couldn't seem to make sense of the numbers. Instead, he replayed Brad's and Justin's words and tried not to think about Gail and Montana.

With a dark scowl, Larry pulled the file back across the desk. "Come on, Clint. Get your mind back on what's important. We've got an eight o'clock meeting with A.J. tomorrow morning."

"I'm aware of that. Let's just hurry and finish so I can get home."

Clint unscrewed the lid on his bottle of Zantac and popped a pill, washing it down with tepid coffee. His stomach burned, he couldn't remember his last decent meal and his eyelids felt as if they were lined with sandpaper. He hadn't felt this bad in months.

He checked his watch and grimaced. It was already after eight. Pushing his chair away from the desk, he picked up his jacket and slung it over his shoulder. "On second thought, I'm going home now. I'll take the MacAfee portfolio with me and finish it up tonight. Why don't we get together a few minutes before the meeting in the morning?"

Larry leaned back in his chair and stared at him, openmouthed. "You're kidding. You're leaving? *Now?* What the hell's up with you?"

"I've got kids, Larry." Clint stacked the files he needed in his briefcase.

"Yeah? Well, so do I."

"But the difference is, I lost mine once." He snapped the case shut and flipped off the banker's light on his desk. "Go home, Larry. Kiss your daughter. Tuck her into bed and read her a story."

Larry checked his watch and shook his head. "Ashlee's already in bed, Trish never lets her stay up past eight. Saturday afternoon's when I spend quality time with her."

"You'd better watch out. Someday, she may tell you how she feels about it. For that matter, Trish might tell you how *she* feels."

Larry waved his hand with the arrogance of one who believes life will always give him what he expects. "Trish knows what I've got to do to make it in this business. She's behind me all the way."

Clint paused by the door and smiled sadly. "I hope so, Larry. For your sake. I just hope you're not as blind as I was. Go home. I'll see you in the morning."

But he knew as he hurried toward the elevators that by leaving now he was making a decision that would seal his fate. He'd never climb any farther up the corporate ladder at Garrity & Garr.

But he'd been given one more chance to put his life in order, and he wasn't about to let it slip between his fingers.

"I SUPPOSE WE CAN FIND room for a few more cases of peaches down there." Dorothy pointed to the bottom shelves of her pantry and rearranged a line of jars on the upper shelves. "And some pears if we can still find some."

Gail nodded and tried to make herself pay attention to the inventory. Her father had been gone nearly two months now, and her mother had finally started taking an interest in something. But Gail hadn't been able to shake this strange lethargy that had plagued her for weeks.

Work helped a little, but cashiering at Western Automaster didn't demand a great deal of mental energy, and she still had plenty of time to think—or more appropriately, to avoid thinking. It took all her energy not to daydream about Clint and his kids every waking moment. All her concentration not to fantasize about the life she would have had if she'd accepted his proposal.

"What do you think?" Dorothy asked. "Will we want to put up applesauce this year?"

"That's fine."

With concern evident in every line of her face, Dorothy turned to confront her. "Do you still *like* applesauce?"

"Yes. It's fine."

Shoving her hands on her hips, Dorothy studied her for a few seconds. "What's wrong, honey? I can't seem to find anything to interest you these days."

"It's nothing. Still just getting over Daddy's death, I guess."

"Well, *I* don't guess. I believe this mood of yours has more to do with Clint than with your dad."

Gail frowned. "That's not true."

Dorothy shook her head and wagged a finger at her. "It *is* true. I've seen plenty of women in love in my day. Plenty of women who've been jilted by a man. My advice is to just forget him."

"Clint didn't jilt me."

"Okay, if you say so. But he's gone back to Chicago, hasn't he? And he's probably married to that woman by now. Agonizing over him isn't going to do a bit of good."

"He's not married to Leslie."

"How do you know that?"

"They broke up before he left here."

Dorothy's eyebrows knit as she looked directly at her daughter. "Why didn't you tell me that?"

"It all happened right when Daddy died."

"So where did you hear that Clint broke up with her?"

"He told me."

"Really? Right when Daddy died? Why?"

Gail turned away and studied a row of bottled cherries. "How do I know why he told me? I guess because we were friends."

To Gail's surprise, Dorothy barked a laugh. "You've never been a very good liar, Gail. What did he do? Ask you to go out with him?"

"No." At least she could answer that truthfully. A marriage proposal didn't fall in the same category as a dinner date.

"Then what *did* he do?"

Gail put on her most innocent expression and faced her mother squarely. "He didn't *do* anything."

Dorothy didn't buy it. "What is it you're trying to hide from me?"

"Nothing."

She raised her eyebrows and managed to look even less convinced. "You're not going to tell me, are you?"

"There's nothing to tell."

"Gail, sweetheart, you've never been good at keeping secrets. But I won't insist." Dorothy stepped around Gail, touched her daughter tenderly on the shoulder and began to climb the stairs.

As soon as Dorothy disappeared, Gail yanked on the chain to turn off the light. Instead of following her mother into the kitchen, she climbed the second flight of stairs to her bedroom. All this talk about Clint left her edgy and nervous. Full of restless energy. Unable to keep thoughts of him at bay any longer.

She wondered if he'd been made vice president at Garrity & Garr. If he'd settled into his old life again. If he'd found a reliable sitter for Megan. She wondered how the boys were doing in school and whether they ever thought about her. Whether Clint had talked to his lawyers about a joint-custody arrangement with Barbara.

And she wondered whether he ever regretted leaving Montana. And her. Because no matter how often she told herself she'd made the right decision—no matter how strongly she believed that—she regretted letting him go.

She straightened the few things on her dresser and rearranged the throw pillows on her bed. But that chore took only a few minutes and didn't leave her feeling any better. She needed something stronger to work out her frustrations. Something physical, like rearranging the furniture in her bedroom.

With hands on hips, she surveyed the room and tried to picture the dresser near the window and the bed against the far wall. No, that would make the room feel too crowded. She tried another arrangement in her mind, decided she liked it and tugged at the foot of her bed to pull it out of place. But the bed's heavy poster frame moved sluggishly.

Leaning her bottom against it, she pushed, using her legs for leverage. This time, the bed shifted about six inches. She readjusted her position against the bed and shoved again. The bed slid several more inches across the floor and coughed up a handful of dust bunnies and a cardboard box.

Gail didn't recognize it, and she wondered why it wasn't in the attic with everything else. Kneeling beside the bed, she pulled the box toward her and lifted the lid to expose a row of leather-bound journals.

When she realized they must be her father's, tears burned her eyes. She pulled one from the box and turned the pages carefully. Every so often, she found a page into which he'd tucked an old black-and-white photograph.

The sweet words he'd written tugged a smile from Gail's lips. How in love he'd been with Dorothy—and she with him. Lowering the journal to her lap, Gail silently amended that thought. How in love they were always. Until the day Boone died, and even beyond that. He still held a large portion of her mother's heart. She hadn't relinquished him to death yet. She probably never would.

With a sigh, Gail turned several more pages. She read the account of her birth written in her father's hand. She sobbed at his words of joy, smiled at his obvious elation and laughed aloud at his scorn when he'd recorded someone asking whether he was disappointed she hadn't been a boy. What a marvellous man he'd been. How much she'd loved him.

When she reached the back of the book, she uncovered a photograph in which she stood with both parents. In the picture, a wide grin split her small face. She reached up to find safety in the hands of her parents and her eyes glowed with excitement for whatever lay before them. But it wasn't her appearance that caught Gail's attention now, it was the expression on her parents' faces.

Over the top of her head, they held each other's gaze and smiled. Their smile hadn't been for the camera or for anyone else in the world. Love and longing stretched between them. Trust and devotion connected them. And Gail knew every good and solid thing in her life had been built on the foundation of that love.

Unbidden, she heard Clint's voice echoing through her memory, and for a split second she felt again the heart-stopping joy his presence always brought. Maybe with him she could have had a love like the one her parents had had. But circumstances had conspired to keep her and Clint apart, and she'd lost her chance at that kind of happiness.

She battled tears of regret and turned toward a sound in her doorway. Dorothy stood there, watching her.

"You found Daddy's journals."

"They're wonderful, Mom. Just wonderful."

Crossing the room, Dorothy sat at the foot of the bed and held out her hand for the picture Gail had been studying. A soft smile touched her lips.

"Who took this picture, Mom?"

"Grandma Casey. It was the day we left her house after my dad died. Remember?"

Gail clearly remembered Grandpa Casey's funeral. She remembered the long, cold train ride to South Dakota and the trip back. But she didn't remember having that picture taken.

"I don't know how I would have gotten through that time without your dad," Dorothy said softly. "For that matter, how I'd have gotten through any of the rough times in my life." She caressed the cover of one of his journals and tried to smile, but her lips quivered and tears filled her eyes. "I miss him, Gail. I never knew I could hurt this badly and still be alive."

"Oh, Mom . . ."

Dorothy shook her head. "Don't feel sorry for me. That's the last thing I want. Don't you see what a lucky woman I was? I had the love of a good man, and I loved him with all my heart. A chance like that doesn't come along every day, and I wouldn't trade a minute of it just to avoid hurting now."

"I know you wouldn't."

"He wasn't perfect," Dorothy said with a tight smile. "He made his mistakes. And I made mine. But we had forty great years together."

"I envy you that."

Dorothy reached down and tilted Gail's chin up until their eyes met. "Life gives us all chances, honey. The trick is to take the right ones."

"How do you know which are the right ones?"

Dorothy patted her cheek. "Nobody knows for sure how anything will turn out until they try it. Look at me now—I've certainly got an adventure ahead of me, and I don't have any idea what I'll do with myself."

Gail tried to smile. "An *adventure?*"

"Well, not one I'd have chosen for myself, that's for sure. But sometimes we don't get to choose. Sometimes we just have to make the best of things that come along." Dorothy pulled her hand away slowly and stood. "Guess I'll go check on the green beans. There might be a few I can pick and get into the freezer."

Gail watched her mother walk away and her heart filled with admiration for the courage Dorothy was showing. Looking down at the photograph, Gail suddenly saw her own situation with blinding clarity.

The circumstances that had left her mother alone were beyond anyone's control, but Gail had chosen her own fate. She'd turned down the love of a good and honest man, turned her back on three terrific children, and thrown away her chance for happiness. And why? Duty? Guilt? Fear?

Was she afraid to leave Broken Bow again? Afraid to try again? Afraid to fail? But what if she didn't fail? What if she succeeded this time?

Jumping up, she followed her mother downstairs. She found Dorothy in the kitchen, pulling a pan from one of the cupboards.

"Mom? What would you say if I told you I was thinking of moving to Chicago?"

Without batting an eye, Dorothy smiled up at her. "I'd say it's about time you got your head on straight."

"Will you come with me?"

Dorothy shook her head. "No, honey. I'll stay here. But stop worrying about me. I'll be fine."

"How? What will you do?"

"I'll take life one step at a time, just the way I always have. Who knows? I might even change my mind about selling this old place once I've had a chance to think about it. That's my worry. *Your* place is with Clint and his kids. You know that as well as I do."

"What if he doesn't want me? What if he's changed his mind?"

Dorothy opened the back door and stepped through. "If it was me, I wouldn't waste time what-ifing. I'd call the man and find out." She let the screen door slam shut between them.

Gail didn't waste another second. She ran to the telephone and dialed Phyllis's number as quickly as she could make her fingers work. Phyllis answered as if she'd been waiting for Gail's call and rattled off both Clint's office number and the one for home.

Gail tried the home number first. She waited through two rings before a recording intercepted her call and announced the number was no longer in service. Certain she'd misdialed, she tried a second time, but again the recording intercepted.

Sick dread curled in the pit of her stomach. Had he gone back to Leslie? Had they married and moved somewhere together?

Trying to convince herself it couldn't be true, Gail tried Garrity & Garr. A receptionist answered on the first ring. "Good afternoon, Garrity & Garr. How may I help you?"

"Could I speak with Clint Andrews, please?"

"Clint Andrews?" The woman paused. "I'm sorry, I'm unable to connect you with Mr. Andrews. His calls are being taken by Lawrence Gardner. Should I put you through?"

"No, I really need to speak with Mr. Andrews. It's very important."

"I'm sorry. I'm unable to connect you with Mr. Andrews. Maybe Mr. Gardner can help you."

"When will Mr. Andrews be available?" Gail demanded.

"If you're one of Mr. Andrews's clients, I'll be glad to put you through to Mr. Gardner..."

Gail disconnected quickly and stared at the telephone. Should she call Phyllis again? Maybe get Clint's address? No. If he'd disconnected his phone, he'd obviously moved. And Phyllis didn't have the new number or address.

Gail knew she'd waited too long. She'd lost him. She leaned her head against the wall as her eyes filled with tears.

GAIL LAY IN BED staring into the early-morning darkness. She hadn't slept well for the past week—ever since she'd tried unsuccessfully to reach Clint. Ever since she'd had to acknowledge that she'd lost him.

She flopped onto her back and gazed at the shadows on the ceiling for several long minutes, but she already knew she wouldn't go back to sleep. She might as well get up and put on the coffee. She could mope as easily on the porch swing as she could here in bed.

Tugging on a pair of jeans, she yanked a light sweater over her head and slipped on her running shoes. She tiptoed past her mother's bedroom and

down the stairs, then crept into the kitchen without a
sound. She'd gotten good at this when Clint was here.

The thought of him brought a lump to her throat,
but she pushed it down and jutted out her chin and
promised herself that today she wouldn't cry. It was
time to get on with life. Time to put him behind her.
Time to give up on her dreams of summers with the
boys and Megan. It would never happen.

She pulled two mugs from the cupboard from force
of habit, and left one on the table for her mother.
While the coffee perked, she flipped idly through a
gardening magazine and scanned an article on the war
against aphids.

"Gail?"

She jerked up at the sound of her mother's voice,
surprised to see her framed in the kitchen doorway.
"Mom . . . Did I wake you?"

"No. I was already up." Dorothy padded into the
kitchen on bare feet and brought the coffeepot to the
table. She filled both mugs, put the pot back on the
burner and sat across from Gail. "I thought maybe we
should talk before you go to work this morning."

"About what?"

"About the farm. I've decided to sell it."

Gail blinked rapidly, as if somehow it would help
her comprehend what her mother had just said. "Sell?
Why? What made you change your mind?"

"Bailey White called me with an offer from a buyer
the other day. It was too good to pass up."

"Who?"

"They're not from around here." Dorothy sipped
from her mug and held it between both hands as if she

wanted the warmth from the cup. "But it's a real good offer. And they're good people."

Though Gail had wanted her mother to eventually reach this decision, she'd imagined they'd discuss it first. "Have you signed anything yet? Did you get an attorney to look at the contract?"

Dorothy shook her head.

"How much are they offering? And what about the house?"

Dorothy lowered her cup to the table and covered one of Gail's hands with hers. "Sweetheart, it's okay. Nobody's taking advantage of me. They're coming by this morning to look the place over and negotiate the rest of the deal. Can you arrange to take the morning off?"

"Well, I don't know." Gail shot to her feet and paced toward the window. "It's awfully short notice. Maybe we ought to do it tomorrow."

Dorothy smiled. "They're probably already on their way."

"All right, then, I want you to give me the details. What are they offering for the land?"

"Oh, sweetheart. Let's not get into all that until they get here."

Frustrated by her mother's lack of concern, Gail paced back to the table. "What does Bailey say about their offer?"

"Obviously, he thinks it's a good one or he wouldn't have approached me with it. Relax, sweetheart. Bailey's been a friend of your dad's since before time. He isn't going to let anyone pull the wool over my eyes."

Gail certainly hoped not. But if Bailey didn't protect her mother, she would. "When are they coming?"

Dorothy glanced at the wall clock. "It won't be long. They're in the process of relocating, and they want to get the final arrangements taken care of early."

"Are they going to farm the place? Or will they subdivide it?" Gail couldn't keep a bitter edge from lining her voice.

"I imagine they're going to farm it—Bailey didn't tell me anything different."

"But you don't know." Gail came back to her chair and dropped into it. "Mom, you can't just sell this place without *some* idea what these people intend to do."

"What they do with it after I sell it isn't any of my concern," Dorothy insisted.

Gail opened her mouth to protest, but clamped it shut again when the sound of a car's engine cut through the silence of the early morning. "When they said early, they really meant it, didn't they?"

"I told them we're early risers. Maybe I'd better make sure we have enough coffee."

Gail sighed with exasperation. "We don't have to give them coffee, Mother. I'm not worried about social amenities. All I want to know is what they're offering."

"Well, you go find out, honey. I'll make another pot."

Gail jerked open the back door and hurried outside toward the approaching car. Considering how unconcerned her mother seemed, maybe it *would* be best if she talked with them alone first.

Even from a distance, the car looked sleek and expensive, and Gail's heart plummeted. It couldn't belong to someone who intended to farm the land.

The driver stopped the car on the lane in the shadow of the old cottonwood tree, and Gail strained to see the occupants as the doors flew open and heads emerged. A second later, her heart started hammering almost before she realized why.

The sun peeked over the horizon just as Megan came around the tree. "Gail. It's me. I comed back."

With tears in her eyes, Gail sprinted toward the child and scooped her into an embrace. A second later, Brad raced through the gate with Justin only a step behind. They tackled her from both sides and hugged her with such exuberance, she wondered if she'd ever catch her breath.

Their eyes danced with excitement. Their faces stretched wide with smiles of joy. Their mouths moved and words tumbled over her, but she couldn't understand a thing. She'd missed them too much, and now her pulse roared in her ears and tears blurred her eyes.

Megan took Gail's face in both hands and pulled it around until they were eye to eye. "I cried for you every day."

"And I cried for you," Gail said honestly.

"I *hated* our sitter," Brad groaned. "She was old and boring. And all she ever wanted to do was watch TV."

"What about you, Justin?"

"It was all right," he said with a shrug. "But Dad wasn't ever home."

Gail's heart went out to him. If Clint continued putting work first, he'd lose the kids again. Couldn't he see that?

Just then, movement at the edge of her peripheral vision pulled her back around to look at the car. This time, Clint stood beside it. He held his hat in his hands and his blond hair glistened in the new morning sun. And he studied her with an intensity she'd thought she'd never see again.

Lowering Megan to the ground, Gail started walking toward him. But she managed only a step or two before desire broke through her restraint and she started to run.

Clint met her halfway, wrapping his arms around her, lifting her off her feet and spinning her around just before his lips met hers. His kiss held everything. Passion and desire. Friendship and trust. Devotion and promise. Love.

He released her reluctantly and smiled into her eyes. "I love you."

"Where have you been? I've been trying to reach you."

He pulled back and studied her with that quizzical look of his. "You have? Why?"

"To tell you I'd changed my mind. I was ready to pack up and move to Chicago."

"We've been closing up the condo in Chicago, picking up more of the kids' stuff in St. Louis and driving every second we weren't at some gas-station bathroom." He grinned and kissed her again lightly. "I spent a couple of days with Barbara's attorney. She's more amenable to the idea of joint custody than I ever dared hope."

"Oh, Clint. I'm so glad." She ran her fingers along his shoulders and touched his face, almost afraid he was a dream. "Are you really going to buy this place?"

He nodded and squinted into the sun as he looked out over the property. "Had to."

"Why?"

He smiled down at her with that teasing smile she'd grown to love so much. "You've ruined me, woman. I can't think of anything else but you." His eyes grew serious and he pulled her closer. "From the moment we met, you've made me come alive again. I don't ever want to lose that. Besides, you still owe us a fishing lesson."

Laughing with joy, she threw her arms around his neck. "Oh, Clint. I love you. I'm so glad you came back."

"I'm here to stay," he promised. "I like the man I become when I'm with you."

"I like him, too. Very much."

He slipped an arm around her waist and led her back into the yard. The kids had joined Dorothy on the porch, but Gail could see they were having to struggle to keep Megan from rushing over to join them.

Clint stopped on the lawn and drew his fingers down her cheek almost reverently. "I'm going to ask you this once more, Gail, this time in front of witnesses." He tried to smile, but his lip trembled. "I know I'm not perfect. I make mistakes, but I try hard. I'll be honest and faithful. I'm devoted. And you can trust me."

"I already know that."

He released her and dropped to one knee on the dew-covered lawn. Taking one hand in his, he looked deep into her eyes. "I'll love you forever. And believe me, I won't ever leave you again. Will you marry me?"

Somehow, she managed to speak around the lump in her throat. "Yes," she whispered. "Yes, yes, yes."

"And me?" Megan shouted.

Through the rush of emotion, Gail managed a shaky laugh. "Yes. And you, Megan."

With a cry of delight, Megan squirmed out of Justin's arms. But instead of joining Clint and Gail, she raced across the porch in the opposite direction. "Where's your kitty?"

Dorothy hurried after her. "Megan, sweetheart, you can't play with the cat right now, she just had kittens. Do you want to see the babies?"

Megan nodded.

"Then hold my hand, and I'll take you out to the barn." Dorothy extended her hand, and Megan slipped hers into it.

"I'm going with the grandma, Daddy."

"Come on, Justin. Let's go with them." Brad jumped off the porch and landed on his knees in a cloud of dust. Without missing a beat, he picked himself up and tore across the yard.

Rolling his eyes in one of his now-familiar expressions of indifference, Justin followed. But Gail could see by the set of his shoulders and the curve of his lips that he was interested.

Clint pulled Gail to him again and looked out over the yard. "I can't believe how much I missed all this. You know, I really feel as if I belong here."

"You do." When he laughed and rubbed her shoulders, waves of desire coiled through her.

"Who would have thought it?" He sobered and looked into her eyes. "I still don't know that much about farming."

"I know."

"Leaving Garrity & Garr might be the biggest mistake I've ever made."

"It isn't."

"What if I'm no good at this? What if we lose everything?"

"We'll start over."

He smiled. "You're not scared?"

She touched his cheek and caressed his lips with her thumb. "Of course I am. I'm terrified. What if I'm a lousy stepmother?"

He kissed her fingers. "You won't be."

"What if I'm no good at being a wife?"

"Impossible." He lowered his lips to hers again and kissed her, and she answered him with more passion than she'd ever known she could feel.

"When do you want to get married?" His voice, deep and rich, worked magic on her. His eyes held hers captive.

"Immediately."

He smiled. "I suppose with your mother and my kids around, we'd better wait until after we're married to start the honeymoon."

She raised her eyebrows suggestively. "That's why I want to get married immediately."

"You know something, Gail?"

"What?"

"I like the way you think."

From inside the barn, Megan shrieked with delight at something. Justin's laughter rang out and Brad suddenly appeared high overhead in the open door of the hayloft.

Wrapped in love, surrounded by joy, weak with desire, Gail smiled. "You know something? I have the feeling we're headed for a grand adventure."